Return to the Belt
Cosmic Ark Book Three

Scott Boss

Published by Rogue Phoenix Press, LLP
Copyright © 2022

ISBN: 978-1-62420-704-4

Editor: Amanda Armstrong

Dedication
To Iris and Knox

Part I

Prelude

47 years ago, March 2044.
Expedition Shuttle launch site
Cape Canaveral, Florida

The Expedition Shuttle stood tall against the morning sun. Robin Visser watched his father as they walked. Phillip Visser continued to give him reassuring looks and head nods, but when Robin eyed his mother, she quickly looked away, remarking how beautiful a day it was.

"I-I don't know about this," said Robin.

"You'll be fine." Phillip gave a dismissive wave.

"I want to go back home."

"They're going to take you home," said his mother, Deborah. "Your new home."

"But I don't want—"

Phillip turned and put a strong hand on each of Robin's shoulders. "You are going to a place with a future. Just as Dr. Ramirez promised." He gave a firm nod as he met Robin's eyes. "Now, you're going to scope it out for us, then one day, your mother and I can join you out there."

Before Robin could reply with more doubts, they were moving again.

Rows of people streamed toward the shuttle while crowds stood behind metal fencing set around the launch pad. Phillip pushed through the crowd with Deborah behind, clutching the back of his shirt as she held Robin's hand with the other. Robin stumbled along, bouncing off hips and shoulders until an angry, redheaded man grabbed one of the straps on Robin's duffle.

"Where are you going?"

Robin didn't answer as the man's forehead and cheeks became a darker shade of red than his hair. The man yelled to the crowd instead.

"Where's he going? I thought the trip was full."

"Yeah," called a large woman in an oversized summer dress from Robin's left. "Is Ramirez running a daycare out there?"

Phillip looked back only to urge his son along as they reached a pair of security guards at the edge of the gate.

"Mr. Visser," said one of the guards, bald and sweating in the sun.

Phillip pushed Robin into the man's arms, and turned to the trailing redhead and woman, blocking off his son.

"Everyone be at ease," said Phillip, his Dutch accent giving more pause than his words. "All our arrangements are in place. There is no line jumping going on here."

The redhead snapped back, "Like hell. How did this kid get a ticket? The fuck did he do? I'm a mechanic, twenty years' experience. I can fix anything you set in front of me. I should go before him." He met Phillip, reaching a hand over his shoulder to point at the security guard. "Tell Ramirez he needs me."

"Me too," cried the woman, crowding them against the gate like a rock concert. "I can sew, bake, and watch children. Don't leave me here."

Robin felt himself get pulled through the gate, his hand ripping free of his mother's, then it was locked shut.

"Dad?" Robin's eyes went wide with fear. One guard was on his arm, gripping it tight as if he meant to run back to them.

Phillip and Deborah stood, their faces getting smashed against the fencing as the crowd surged. The guard at the gate waved them to move. Robin felt like a cat outside a dog pound. Angry eyes pierced him, voices called, belittling everything about him, begging to take his place.

"Come on," said the guard at his shoulder. "We've got to move."

Robin met his mother's eyes first, full of fear and glistening with moisture.

"We love you, Robin."

Then his dad. "Make us proud."

He was bleeding from his cheek where it had been scraped against the fence, then he caught a shove from behind, his glasses falling off and immediately getting trampled. Phillip made no effort to retrieve them, only turned to fight off the crowd and shield Deborah.

Robin was dragged down the hot pavement toward the shuttle.

~ * ~

Robin was too heartsick to enjoy the wonder of the next three weeks. The shuttle was packed with as many people as would fit. It made everything a struggle, from eating the flavorless, synthesized food to sleeping in a packed bunk with barely enough room to move. Never mind the restroom and non-existent bathing regimen. He cried himself to sleep most nights, dreaming of his big room, soft bed, hot shower, his parents, and dog. What if they were wrong? What if the people of Earth figured out a way to get along? Would they send him back? Would his parents come get him? It was a silly thought, he knew, but what if all this wasn't *it* like they said?

Touchdown in the Belt was still exciting, anything to get out of the cramped quarters they shared.

They exited to an asteroid the size of Robin's yard in the Netherlands. Belters were there to meet them, helping direct everyone to their new living arrangements. Most were shipped off by early versions of the Rock-Hoppers. Robin waited until he saw Dr. Ramirez approaching with a black woman he'd never met, although he knew through stories from his parents. It was Dr. Gammen. She was the inventor of the food synthesizer that supplied them with the awful nutrients they needed on their ride over.

"How do you feel, Robin?" Dr. Ramirez asked.

Robin looked out at the endless universe at the edge of the TechBubble and shivered.

"A little overwhelmed, sir."

Dr. Gammen gave a warm smile and patted his shoulder. "You'll get used to it. I promise."

A Rock-Hopper landed, and a woman with flowing black hair stepped out, and a boy not much older than Robin ran over and hugged Dr. Ramirez.

"Dad," said the boy.

"Oscar," said Dr. Ramirez. "I want you to meet Robin Visser. His parents are a big part of why we were able to make it back. He'll be staying with us for a while."

"Cool," said Oscar, as his mother joined them.

"Oscar," she said, "show Robin to the Rock-Hopper."

Oscar waved him to follow as Robin tugged his bag over his shoulder, unable to take his eyes off the sky, or lack thereof. He wondered which direction Earth even was anymore.

~ * ~

It was coming up on a year in the Belt for Robin when Oscar and he landed at the government building. They were on their best behavior, hoping for Dr. Ramirez to grant their request to go exploring Ahuna Mons.

When they walked in, Doctors Ramirez and Gammen were huddled around a radio transmitter. They alternated staring at it, to each other, then back, as nothing but static provided an eerie soundtrack. Robin could feel the unease in the air. He wanted to turn back, go out the doors, back home and find anything else to do. Instead, Oscar stepped forward, catching the attention of his father.

"Dad?" said Oscar. "What's going on?"

Dr. Ramirez's face hung heavy as he said, "The war has started."

Robin felt a weight in his guts sink so hard and fast, he went to his knees. It was a weight he'd been holding since he first boarded the shuttle, held up by the faintest glimmer of hope.

Until now.

Now it felt like a cancerous tumor spreading throughout his body.

"They're not coming," said Robin. "Nobody's coming. We're it."

Chapter One

December 2091
Knox Shuttle
Inside a wormhole

Robin Visser lay in his bed aboard the Knox, unable to sleep, recalling memories of his parents abandoning him all those years ago. The last moments he could cherish were on the car ride from the airport to the launch site. When they were still a family, still working together for the greater good. After that, it was all chaos. He spent most his life in the Belt trying to prevent that kind of chaos from ever rearing its head again. When they'd finally found a good solution to the children of the Belt turning feral, he thought the Belt problems were finally solved. That he could rest if only a little, knowing he'd honored the legacy of Dr. Ramirez, the man who'd kept him when his parents wouldn't. But then, his own son was the chaos bringer. The one who helped throw a wrench into the entire machine. Marlow was the answer to the question they'd been asking for fifteen years, but Arjen was so quick to give it up.

Robin rubbed a hand straight back through his hair, thinking of the burned streak of skin on his son's head and cringing. He hadn't had time to at least do the fatherly thing and ask, "What the hell happened to you?" Keeping it cool when he could clearly see his remaining child had been through much physical and mental trauma. He'd prevented a scene on the alien planet. Now he wished he'd had a few more moments. Not to beg or demand, but just to talk, to make sure he listened, unlike his parents when they dropped him off. He shouldn't have given Arjen a choice, just like he hadn't had one. He should've lied to him, anything to get him on the ship and back to the Belt. Kaia was getting Isolde back. Maynard had Lana. Sure, their lives would be different than before, but they'd be able to see them again. *At this time in history,* Robin thought, *you take what you can get.*

There was a knock at his cabin door. Robin called that it was open, and Maynard stepped in, making sure it closed behind him before he began. He leaned a muscular arm on the wall. His hair was in the perfect car-crash style and his black goatee was trimmed to perfection.

"Glad you're up," said Maynard.

Robin slid his legs over the side of the bed and sighed. "Haven't had much luck so far."

"Speaking of that," Maynard looked back at the door and took a step closer, lowering his voice, "she's not pregnant."

Robin's face twisted slightly. "Lana?"

Maynard pursed his lips and nodded.

"What about Marlow?"

"Nope. Guess they were busy monster hunting after all."

"That's *good*, then we can put the plan in order the way we decide."

Maynard grunted. "Guess so."

Robin put his hands on the edge of the mattress to support himself. He felt tired from all the travel. Tired from losing his son again. Tired, thinking of the things they were going to have to do to get the Belt back in order before it became too late.

"It's not like *he* would've been the one to get them pregnant anyway. This is fine." Robin stared at Maynard, finally feeling ready to sleep. "If there's nothing else…" He nodded toward his pillow.

"Right." Maynard turned toward the door. "Lana's gonna want to discuss *her new job*," he made air-quotes at that, "sooner, rather than later. What should I tell her?"

Robin waved a hand. "Just give me a day to rest, and I'll have it all laid out. She'll buy it. No concerns there. A little power is all it takes to blind the foolish."

Maynard paused as if he meant to defend his daughter's honor, then shrugged and went out the door.

Chapter Two

A persistent wind whipped Arjen's tanned, sweating face. His hair was as short as the clippers Julie had rescued from the lab would allow her to trim, whilst his burns were still bright but not throbbing as they had been. He swung a hammer into the bent metal on the open ramp of the Pelosin ship. Amun, the alien owner of the ship, directed him to another section, while securing bolts for their makeshift repairs.

"Are we sure this is going to hold?" asked Julie.

She wore a thin, navy pullover with the word *Gap* circled and faded in the middle. Her hands explored her head and the cut she'd made on herself after she finished with Arjen. It didn't look great, but the disgusted looks she received from Captain Williams every time he saw it were just what she was going for. That ship had sailed. She only wished she'd taken Marlow's advice earlier.

"A short trip will be a good trial," said Amun.

His English was progressing rapidly in the short time they'd been together. Once he had the word translated, it was like he never forgot it. Williams mumbled one night that, "It's like he has a CPU inside that pumice stone of a head."

Amun was quick to ask what a pumice stone was so he could translate it, as the group broke into laughter. It was short lived though. The few days since everyone left them stranded on Wyan were focused and determined. While Williams felt slighted by his refusal to return and Julie was still processing everything, Arjen was more wrapped up in a mission than ever before. He'd stolen Marlow and Zane from Earth. He'd promised them a better chance on Wyan. He'd paired up with Lana, blinded by love that he'd never admit was more than infatuation. There were so many things he had to right in the universe, starting with his father. At least Amun shared his enthusiasm for getting the ship repaired. They'd agreed to look for his people first, then the Mack. After that, there was no guarantee of anything.

"Bah," said Amun, looking around as his bolt rolled down the ramp. Barchek scooped it up, tucking into a forward roll onto the ramp, landing on her back with a *clang*. She held out the bolt and Amun took it, patting her hand in thanks before she rolled back down.

Bruuth walked up with Cannie, Barchek's mom, pushing a wheelbarrow full of food.

"Break?" said Bruuth in the Wyan guttural.

Arjen looked to Amun, wiping sweat off his head and lowering his hammer. He raised his eyebrows.

"Let me try the seal." Amun went up the ramp for a minute, then came back down. The ramp closed behind him. "It will…test," he said, trying to find the right word, "while we eat."

They sat on the log seats at the humans' camp. Williams and Julie spaced themselves out, away from each other, while Arjen and Amun were side by side, sharing words and hopes for their journey. Barchek sat directly next to the wheelbarrow so she could pick through the food. Normally, Cannie would admonish her for this, but that meal, she was too busy laughing about something with Bruuth.

Williams whittled a stick with a knife. His mustache was being overrun with more than a week of no upkeep. He stripped another piece of wood free when he said, "We can't convince you to swing by the Mack first?"

Amun looked to him then Arjen for confirmation.

"Just saying," said Williams. "It's imperative that we determine if the Mack's working. This whole thing hinges on that."

Amun went to reply but Arjen stopped him.

"It's his ship," said Arjen. "His people were dropped and never picked back up. We owe it to him to let him get closure."

"They're probably all dead though, right?" asked Julie. "I mean, all of them. His people *and* ours."

"Probably," agreed Arjen, "but if we can get the Mack back in the air, we'll give ourselves a chance."

A breeze swept through, sending fallen leaves swirling across the camp. The giant trees surrounded them, backed by Ruh'la Peak and the darkness beyond. They could hear the crack of thunder over the mountains. Arjen felt a shiver go through him, thinking of his time on the dark side of the planet. If they couldn't get the ships working, the time would come again in four years. Would there be any Night Chasers invading? He couldn't be certain. He only held onto hope that he wouldn't be there to find out.

There was little noise beyond the wind and distant thunder. The camp lacked Percy playing some soothing music, or Lana discussing their next plan of action. It missed Admani's laughter at another one of Walters' harsh jokes, or Avani's giggles and cries. It had a shortage of *life*. When Arjen looked over the Wyans who shared a meal with them, he saw creatures who belonged in their place. Ones who would go back to their primitive lives long after the humans were gone or dead. They could be content with that. Arjen could not.

He stood at the same time as Amun. They shared a look.

"Should we check?" asked Arjen.

"Yes."

Amun was just as antsy as him. Being locked in a dehydrated sleep for four years would do that. He walked toward the ship and Arjen followed close to his side.

"Get a room," called Julie.

Barchek laughed at the joke she likely didn't understand and added, "Cunts."

~ * ~

As Bruuth and Cannie collected the food scraps, a smattering of rain began, mostly carried by the wind.

Arjen came jogging up to the camp. "Pack your things. We're heading to Melinger."

"But the weather," said Julie.

Arjen nodded. "This is the closest Melinger is going to be for six months. If we go now…"

Williams stood with a grunt, tucking his knife away and staring at the point of his freshly, whittled stick. "Then let's leave this hell hole."

Barchek perked up from laying on her back in a food coma. "Leave?"

Arjen paused before replying. "We have to go help your friend Marlow."

"Marlow." Barchek paused, then said, "Come." She started out of the circle of logs.

"No. That's not…" Arjen started.

Bruuth caught her shoulder to slow her down, grunting in Wyan with kind eyes. Barchek nodded for a second as he lowered his hand and Cannie joined. Then the little alien gave Bruuth a shove in the chest and ran for the ship.

Cannie and Bruuth shook their heads and started after her.

~ * ~

When the Pelosin ship was loaded, Arjen went down the hall into the furthest room on the left. He stood in the doorway as it opened, showing the little alien-girl tucked under a table with her hands over her head.

"Marlow always said you were good at hide and seek."

Barchek looked up. "Shit-bitch. Don't tell them."

Arjen smiled. The deal was that he'd try first, and if it came to it, a couple of them would drag her out. "I have to, Barchek. I know you want to see Marlow again, but you've got to stay here with your mom and Bruuth. The trip could kill you like it did the guys that came with Bruuth. Remember?"

Barchek began a coughing cry. "I have to…I have…"

Arjen stepped toward the table. He saw the Walkman with Pat Benatar's greatest hits inside. It must have been her idea of packing. He knelt next to her.

"You want to give me a message to give to her when I get back?"

Barchek sniffed, and snorted, then looked up at him with wide-set, brown eyes. "Yes." She said a few words Arjen didn't fully understand, but memorized, and stepped back as the alien crawled out from under the table.

They passed Amun and Williams at the ship's controls as Julie brought up a last box of stuff. Arjen saw an Arizona license plate poking out but figured he'd save that conversation for another time.

Barchek joined Cannie and Bruuth at the bottom of the ramp. Arjen met them, acknowledging Bruuth, the Wyan who fought by his side when the Night Chasers collapsed the Forge. The one who saved Zane from the well and nursed him back to health. Though the Wyans at the village turned their backs, Bruuth would remind him to always speak well about their species.

"If this goes well," Arjen started. E*ven if it doesn't,* he thought. "This is goodbye for good, friend."

Bruuth pulled him into a hug. "I am sorry about your friends." He motioned toward the mountains. They'd never had a true funeral for their fallen, only discussed them over dinner, sharing memories and details of their deaths.

"Without you, it would've been more." Arjen put a hand up to Bruuth's shoulder. "I'm sorry about the village." He didn't know how to better phrase his apology after getting the Wyan kicked out of his home.

Bruuth nodded but gave a quick glance at Cannie that may have said, "It all worked out."

Arjen looked up the ramp, then addressed the three Wyans. "In four years…in the next time of darkness, *go somewhere*, will you? You have nothing to protect here. Be safe, just in case. Promise me that. We don't know if they've forgotten us over there or if they're plotting. I don't want any of you," he paused, looking at Barchek, "*any* of you getting hurt."

"We will," said Cannie.

Arjen gave them one final goodbye as Julie came down the ramp. She held out a hand to Barchek. Four AA batteries sat in her palm that Barchek scooped up.

"I don't have anything these go to right now," said Julie, as

Barchek tucked them next to her Walkman in her pocket. "Those should keep Pat Benatar spinning until you wear out that tape."

Barchek had a big smile as she ran off, tucking the headphones over her head.

Arjen and Julie went up the ramp, realizing how temporary it all was. Four batteries could only last so long and then there would be no way to power the Walkman. If any component broke, it would be the same outcome. It went the same for humans on Wyan. In a few years, would anyone even talk about the humans? In ten, would anyone remember them?

The Pelosin ship sealed the recently repaired door and the Wyans backed off as the engines rumbled to life. Melinger was as close as they could ask for. The storm reached the edge of the mountain. It was time for them to leave Wyan for good.

Chapter Three

Knox Shuttle

Marlow paced the room, patting Avani's back as she cried. As far as she could tell, the baby was just bored, missing the open air of Wyan. It was always fresh and invigorating, not stale and recycled, locked behind the same walls. She had few toys on Wyan, but they'd all been left behind. Zane was working on a new version of Honey as he sat on the bed. His new leg casts prevented him from doing much else.

"How much of the sheet can I use?" he asked.

Marlow turned, rolling her eyes. "It doesn't matter. Without a needle and thread or something, you're going to have to make an origami version. She'll tear that apart in seconds."

"I just want to help. I feel so…useless. I'm just sitting here. Like I sat in that well while you all fought."

"You're hurt." Marlow took to hunching over and swinging Avani back and forth like a human cradle. "You were then. It's not your fault."

"But Percy—"

"Percy saved you. He did the right thing. We all made a lot of choices during those nights. I'm sorry it happened the way it did, but I'm glad he saved you."

Zane pursed his lips, the torn piece of sheet he'd started with just sitting in his idle hands. "Do you ever feel like we're bad luck? Not to each other, obviously, but everyone around us?"

Marlow craned her neck up while continuing to swing Avani. She knew where he was going with this. "Don't."

"Jason, Dad, your mom, the—"

"Stop, Zane. Things are just fucked up everywhere. We're not doing too great as a *species*. That's not our fault."

"Do you believe in karma?"

Marlow raised up, her back cracking in three places. "I don't know." She looked at the door. "But I feel like I'm going to find out pretty soon."

"What does that mean?"

"It was *him*. The guy that killed Honey and did what he did to Rami…he's on this ship."

Zane started wringing the fabric between his hands. "And he's Lana's dad, I know. We've been over this. You think karma's going to get him?"

"I hope, or—"

"I wouldn't count on it. Sometimes it feels like we're still alive so we can suffer a little more. Like, if I would've died at the same time as my dad, or Jason, maybe even before that…Sometimes it seems like it would've been better."

Marlow set Avani on the edge of the bed facing Zane, then knelt next to her to support her back.

"I'm still glad we've lived as long as we have. I've accepted we're never going to have a perfect house above ground with an endless food supply like they used to have on Earth. But we can still have moments of happiness. Wherever we can find them."

Zane lay back slowly, letting his body straighten out while his legs remained pointed.

"If you say so."

He tried to scratch a spot on the outside of his right leg, then gave up. They turned their heads to a slight knock at the door, then it slid open. Robin Visser stood; his hair tussled like he'd just woken up from a nap. His cheeks had lines in them they'd never noticed before. His tan was fading from months in travel.

"How is everyone?"

Zane took a deep breath to reply but stopped when Marlow grabbed his foot, giving a slight shake of her head.

"We're okay," she said. "Happy to be alive after all that."

Visser's eyebrows raised. "Oh really? A change of heart so soon?"

Marlow sighed. "Seeing Maynard brought back some bad

memories. I recognize that, but I'm ready to go back to the Belt."

"It's humbling to be wrong. We've all been there." He looked back at the door. "Well, I have a meeting I need to attend. If you need anything, let me know."

"One thing." Marlow raised her hand as he was halfway out. "Our friends, can we talk to them? Just to see that they're okay?"

Robin paused, not turning around. "Most of your friends…" He shook his head. "Stayed behind." The door closed behind him before Marlow could reply.

~ * ~

In the Knox meeting room, Lana sat with Maynard on one side, Lisa, the ship's gathering leader on the other, and Robin across. In the middle of the table was a display screen that Robin manipulated. *New Pangaea* headlined a model of the newest Belt Island. Robin zoomed it in to show the new home of the medical facility, the library, and the clothing manufacturer. There was a neighborhood in the north-west corner and a forest in the north-east.

"And the lake?" Lana leaned forward until her straight hair fell in front of her view. She pushed it back with one hand while pointing with the other. "Fresh or…?"

"Transported from Ceres," said Robin. "The water plant is going up soon. The plan is to be completely independent from Ceres. Like the original colony was." He intertwined his fingers. "Together. Working as one."

Lana pushed back and sniffed, crossing her arms. "You think that's possible?"

Robin matched her posture. "You're coming back, aren't you?"

"Yes, but—"

"We all have to move past what's only good for us," He patted his chest, "and do what's best for the Belt, the future."

"Your message hasn't changed, I see."

Maynard caught a glare from Robin, coughed, and said, "He's right, Lana, and we need you to help bring everyone back together."

She scoffed. "By telling them how well it went on Wyan?"

"By speaking at the christening," said Robin. "Tell them you were wrong for leaving. Repent for the lives lost and explain how you're ready to move forward, whatever it takes."

"What does all that mean to them? You want to move forward? You need Marlow up there, and you're not going to get her. You lock her up and you'll have a real civil war."

Maynard spoke low, "They won't know she's back. For all they know, she died."

Lana tilted her head, her eyes widening with each thought.

Lisa's chuckle came from a seat over like a cheese grater across Lana's skin. The best part about being Gathering Leaders in the past meant she rarely had to see Lisa. Now, the crooked faced, stringy blonde sat smirking. She loved being in the know and rubbing Lana's face in the fact that she wasn't.

Lana pulled her gaze from Lisa and asked, "What about Zane? Is he *dead* too? *Isolde*?"

Robin was straight-faced. "Isolde doesn't know about the Earthlings. She's in cryo-sleep. When she wakes, we'll be back and she'll get the same story everyone else will, those left behind are lost or dead."

"Jesus."

Lana brushed her hair back and kept her hands at her temples, staring at the slowly, rotating rock that was the next, 'Future of the Belt.' She shook the thoughts away. There was no time for a moralistic decision, only a choice to decide her place in the Belt hierarchy. Her next words would seal her verdict. "Okay." She put her hands out. "So, I get up there and make a speech. Then what?"

Robin smiled and motioned for Maynard to take over.

Lana's dad looked proud. "We need you to get up there and announce your pregnancy."

Chapter Four

Williams was back in his element for the first time since the night came. The Pelosin ship ripped through Wyan's atmosphere with minimal resistance. He let out a *whoop* as they hit open space. Wyan's star hung ahead to the left of their view as Williams squinted back at Arjen, behind him now that takeoff was over.

"Think it's too late to ask him if they have radiation shields?" Williams asked.

Arjen saw Amun tapping away at one of the monitors. He didn't bother him, only patted Williams on the shoulder. "I'm sure they do. If not, we're fucked either way."

Amun pointed at a flashing target on his screen. "The last communication was from here."

"So, show me how to program it." Williams leaned back and Amun stepped over, setting the course for Melinger. When he stepped back, a blurb of characters appeared at the top right corner.

"What's that?" asked Arjen.

"Time." Amun scrunched his ivory face. "How much time…from our conversations, I think it translates to about three weeks."

"Three weeks?" Julie squatted next to a crate with their food stores. "Are we going to have enough food for that?"

Arjen smacked his lips. "To *get* there. We're going to have to hope the 'Panel is working on the Mack or we'll be in trouble."

"So, you're saying it's not time for a snack?" Julie held up one of the bricks of dehydrated food Bruuth, Cannie, and Barchek spent days gathering while Amun processed them for long term storage.

"I…" Arjen looked to Williams then back. "We're going to have to be on a strict schedule. It would be nice to have something left over when we get there, so we don't have to scramble."

17

Julie dropped the brick on the pile with a dusty thump, then turned and dug through her bag for some nail polish.

"I can help with this," said Amun. "My room has my resting panel. Everything is in order with the ship. I do not need to be awake for the next…weeks."

"Jealous," said Julie. "Got room for more in there?"

Amun tilted his head at her.

"Just a joke."

She waved a hand, then unscrewed a *Raspberry Blue* color that had more than a little dried crust around the rim. It crackled when it opened, and the chemical smell seeped out. The Pelosin ship had an artificial gravity much like the TechBubble, and it kept the polish from floating into Julie's eyes.

Arjen followed Amun to his room, watching him slide out the panel and hit a few buttons.

"When we get close…" Amun showed him the button Marlow activated back on the dark side of Wyan.

"I will." Arjen stood with his hands on his hips. "Well, see you in a few weeks?"

Amun nodded, his eyes widening with one final thought. "My body will rest, but in there," He pointed to the panel, "my brain stays active with the ship. I would like to continue learning."

Arjen narrowed his eyes. "How can I help?"

Amun used the Wyan words for friends telling stories to each other. Arjen understood.

"You want me to come by and have story time? I can do that. Won't be much else going on."

Amun put a hand on his arm. "Thank you."

He turned and climbed into the panel. The process took only a minute as his body shrunk down into the seafoam-type substance. When it was complete, the panel slid shut. Arjen shook his head, wishing he too could rest inside the wall for the next three weeks instead of dealing with the awkward exchanges between Julie and Captain Williams. He went back out to watch the monitor and considered the first story he'd tell Amun later that day.

~ * ~

The following weeks dragged by on the Knox and the Pelosin ship. Arjen tried to keep his crew on some kind of routine. Meals in the morning and afternoon, cards in between, and bedtime stories for Amun before they'd all settle into restless sleep and insane dreams. After seeing what they saw on the dark side of Wyan, their subconscious minds kept up a consistent reminder that they would never be the same. The more distance they put between one planet only made the dreams transition to the terror they were likely to find on the next.

Meanwhile, Robin failed to find a good routine for those not in cryo-sleep, which was down to Maynard, the Earthlings, the pilot, and himself. He'd convinced Lisa, who was dead weight as a leader when they already had a government official and head of belt security aboard, to go into the chamber with the others.

Robin and Maynard rotated rounds of visiting the humans until Marlow begged him not to send Maynard back. Then it was just Robin, escorting them one at a time to their baths with a taser held in threat. For all the good things the NutrientPanel could do, Zane's legs felt like they were taking forever to heal. He'd been splinted by Bruuth in a cabin in the woods and hadn't exactly seen an orthopedist since. Marlow begged for a chance to take Avani out of their little room, just for a walk around as she'd done on the way to Wyan when Avani was a newborn. She wasn't granted her wish but was offered a gut-wrenching alternative. Robin would take Avani for a walk around. Marlow declined the offer over and over until she couldn't handle another minute in the room with a screaming child and crippled supporter. As soon as the door closed, she felt her stomach sink. She'd just given her baby over to the man that tried to steal her from Marlow's womb. What if he didn't bring her back? What if he took her to perform the tests, he hadn't been able to before she left for Wyan?

Then she'd claw his eyes out. That was what kept repeating in her brain until he showed up with a happy baby. It almost pissed her off more that Avani didn't scream his ear off the whole time. Zane sat on the bed watching and hearing her concerns, feeling his mind slowly slipping off an edge he wasn't sure if he could come back from.

Chapter Five

The approach to Melinger had them all glued to the monitors. Orange, hazy clouds swirled across the sky. It was beautiful from a distance, like an artist's rendering of a rust storm. But the thoughts of flying through the stratosphere of this unknown planet made Williams sweat.

"How do we know this won't eat up our ship?" Williams had a death grip on the controls as Amun put together his sentence.

"We safely dropped our companions on our first visit. The storms move fast. If we pick the right time…"

Amun leaned forward to bring up the weather patterns on the screen, then pointed as the storms simulated movement, clearing their path.

"I'm supposed to trust that?"

Arjen shared a look with Amun then addressed Williams. "Their instruments are more advanced than ours. They made it here before and out. Let's trust them."

"Easy for you to say." Williams slapped the controls then sighed. "Well, everyone who isn't shaped like a giant sponge, strap in."

Amun once again looked to Arjen.

"He wants you to sit by him," Arjen moved to his seat next to Julie.

As Amun predicted on screen, the swirling storms moved along the landscape below, giving way to craggy formations spreading through a carpet of sand. Amun tried to stand when he saw it, but his belt held him back. There was a circular, rocky formation around what had to be a lake. It was deep blue in parts, fading to a rusty brown on the edges where it met the shore.

"There." Amun pointed to the monitor showing a red icon on the map. It matched with the formation below. "Land there."

"Working on it," said Williams.

The ship shook as it pierced the atmosphere. They passed through the path the storm took only minutes before and felt the residual wind. Williams twisted the controls, growling at the shift of course. He righted the ship with little fight, a surprised smile crossing his face. "If we all survive this, we need to copy this tech for our own ships. The handling is incredible."

"How about you focus on the surviving part for now?" Julie's hands were locked over her straps and her eyes shut tight.

The lake came into clearer focus. The shore was mostly rock with a few smaller sandy areas. Amun pointed out a bigger patch of sand and Williams grunted at him, "I see it."

The Pelosin ship evened out, lowering slowly between the mountains and toward the ground. Black peaks rose around them, sending jagged shadows across the ship. There were caves reminiscent of those on the return path Arjen, Lana, and Admani took after the fight at the Night Chaser city. Arjen shivered when he saw the black holes in the sides of the mountain, feeling like they were staring back.

The lake rippled on the other side of the ship as they reached the landing spot in the sand. It was a location people on Earth would've turned into a resort. A private lake with mountains all around and a perfect patch of beach sand.

Amun was the first out of his seat, his hand on the lever to the ramp.

"Just hold on," said Williams.

"Yes." Arjen joined him. "We should scope it out first."

"But…" Amun pointed out the viewing window. Ahead, behind a boulder that looked like pure onyx, was a tire sticking out. It was an object just as foreign to the planet as the Pelosin ship. The crank of the ramp sounded, gears turning as Amun ran to ride it down. The humans stood watching, exchanging glances until Arjen spoke.

"I've gotta follow him. He could be finding the remains of his people."

"I don't know." Williams stood stroking his mustache down to where it met his developing beard. "Maybe you should let him have a minute with them."

Arjen considered it. "No. He might need support."

He headed down the ramp.

Julie crossed her arms over her breasts, looking at Williams' profile, remembering the times they spent together and feeling her stomach turn.

"Jules," he said, but she shook her head and took off after Arjen.

The sand was blazing, even through Arjen's shoes. The air was dry, dusty, and well over a hundred degrees. He plodded along, taking quick glances of the view. The lake was enticing. If he were anywhere but an unknown planet, he would've run straight in. After weeks aboard the ship, conserving water, and food, cramped even in a spacious ship, it felt good to be out. Even in the heat. Arjen dared a look into the caves, but they were dark. He'd have to get much closer to find out if they were empty, but he had no desire to do so. Amun reached the protruding wheel and turned the corner until he was out of sight behind the boulder. There was a sandy breeze that felt like a cyclone. Arjen shielded his eyes, slowing as he heard Julie cry out behind him. He turned to see her rubbing at her face with the sleeve of her *Gap* sweatshirt.

"Sand?" Arjen asked.

"Yeah." Julie's eyes watered as she caught up to him. "Hot as balls out here."

"Thought you knew that already."

"I did, and I would've changed first but you left me on the ship with Williams."

Arjen looked back. "Is he coming?" The ship was obscured by a swirl of sandy wind.

"Don't know," Julie said, but she was staring up at the rock face, pocked by caves, "but the sooner we're out of here, the better. That makes me think of your stories."

"Yeah. Come on."

They reached the boulder together. Amun sat in the cockpit of a rover vehicle. He was dead still. Arjen peered in the window and could hear him listening to a message. They waited for the message to finish, then knocked on the side of the rover.

Amun looked over slowly and popped the door open. "I don't know how…" He hit a few buttons on the dashboard, pulled on a control stick, then slapped it in anger. "to make it run again. I never learned back home."

"It's okay," said Arjen. "Was that a message? Are they…?"

Amun shook his head. "I don't know, but I know where they are." His face turned, looking up the mountain to a cave ten feet above them. Its ledge poked out like a toothless mouth waiting to devour them.

Arjen looked to Julie, his face contorting into pain, then back to Amun. "Would they even be alive at this point?"

"It's possible."

"Then, I guess we're going up."

Chapter Six

Zane sat on the floor next to the door. He'd lowered the lights to just above pitch black. Marlow hadn't argued as it helped Avani sleep, but she listened with wary ears from the bed. There was a clicking, one she recognized as his cast opening, then another as he closed it again.

"Zane," she whispered, looking from the sleeping baby to his shadowy figure across the room. "What are you doing?"

"Just trust me, Mar. I'm getting us out of here."

"What?"

"We're going to be free again. Like we were on Earth."

His voice was too whimsical for Marlow's comfort.

"Earth? We were almost dead on Earth. What are you saying?"

Zane looked back. She could barely see the whites of his eyes, though they were as wide as could be.

"When the family was still there, and Jason. Honey, Marvin, the cow…oh, what was the cow's name, Mar? You remember? I remember eating him, but I can't remember what we called him." Zane broke into laughter and Marlow shushed him.

"You're talking crazy, Zane. Put your cast back on and come lay down. But be quiet about it."

"It's fine. This is my good leg." He raised his right leg, bare, scrawny, and covered in scars.

"It needs to be—"

Zane shushed her, holding a finger to his lips, and pointing at the door. "Footsteps. Just act normal." He scooted against the wall, flattening himself as much as he could.

"Norm—" Marlow cut off as the door slid open.

Robin Visser stood, squinting at the darkness until he spotted Marlow on the bed.

"Nap time? Should I—?"

He cut off as Zane's loose cast smashed into his knee. Robin went down with a cry. Zane shoved him out of the doorway and waved to Marlow.

"Come on. This is our chance."

Marlow was up with Avani in her arms as she startled from the commotion. "Where are we—Zane, we're on a ship in the middle of a wormhole. Where are you planning to go?"

He frowned at her, struck by the logical question, then shook his head as his eyes lit up. "I'll come back for you." Zane hobbled out the door on one leg still in its cast, while using the other as a crutch.

Robin sat up, resting his back against the wall. "Don't think about it."

He pointed a taser toward Marlow, who was on the edge of the bed, watching the open doorway to the hall. Did Zane plan to hold the ship hostage for the next month? On two bad legs with no weapons? No, he didn't plan at all. He'd just had enough. She saw Robin's arm raise to his mouth.

"Please don't call Maynard," Marlow pleaded. "He'll hurt him."

"He hurt *me*," Robin snapped back.

"Let me get him. I can talk him back to the room. I'll make sure he never does something like this again. He's just stir crazy. He's traumatized from everything…" She couldn't finish her sentence as she broke into tears.

Zane wasn't the only one traumatized. Marlow just hadn't been able to let it out. Getting back Avani, no matter the rest of the circumstances, gave her the slightest bit of mental stability she needed to hold everything together a little longer. But thinking about what Maynard would do to Zane if he caught him trying to escape, she couldn't handle it. She became a sobbing mess, unable to see through her tears, but moving toward the door anyway.

Robin forced himself up, tucking the taser away as she held Avani to her chest. He limped in her way, blocking the door, holding a hand out.

"Don't." Robin lowered his eyes at her. "It will be worse for you. Let me go and maybe I can find Zane first. Where do you think he'd go?"

Marlow thought. Nothing came to her mind but the roof of the church in Inland. "I-I don't…" She hoped he wasn't far enough deranged that he'd try to go outside.

Robin grunted and backed through the door, keeping his hand up, then closed it in her face.

He went down the hall from their room. Thankfully there was no gravity as he floated along, feeling the throb from the blunt hit of the cast. Maynard would've just finished his morning bath. There was no telling where he'd be from there. With no agenda, he could be wandering any hall just to kill time.

Robin pulled himself along, recalling the first time he did so in Dr. Ramirez's Explorer Shuttle. He had few good memories of zero gravity and moved through it with minimal effort and enjoyment.

When he reached a junction, the right side led to the flight deck. It would be by data-pad access only and was currently closed. He turned left, floating down to another junction. The NutrientPanel room was to the right, nothing for him to do in there but sabotage. He hoped that wasn't the first thing on Zane's mind. Robin floated the other direction until he turned a corner and saw him. Zane's face was plastered in the cryo-room viewing window. One cast was on his left leg, the other tucked under his arm.

Robin stopped ten feet back. "Zane. I need you back in your room."

Zane turned, a crazed look crossing his eyes that Robin last saw in the astronaut Sam. "You lied to us. Ice is in there." He tilted his head and smashed his cheek harder against the glass. "Who else? Who else is still around? Is that Lana?"

"Zane, to your room." Robin held up the taser. "I don't want to do this the hard way."

"Free them." Zane slammed on the door, then the panel which required a code or data-pad to activate.

Robin approached slowly. "Enough of this."

His face was red with anger, but he was afraid as well. He didn't agree to be their sole caretaker to get attacked. He was trying to build relationships. To make the transition easier when they got back to the

Belt. A little cooperation moves everything along smoother. Now this boy thought he could break out his friends, and escape a ship floating in a wormhole.

Robin raised the taser, launching himself from one of the rungs on the ceiling. Zane turned and swung the cast at the last second, smacking the taser out of Robin's hand and sending them both spinning in circles.

"Hey," Robin yelled, watching his only weapon go floating away.

The fear was real at that moment. Zane had the cast and a deranged look that said he couldn't be persuaded away from his mission. Robin tried to stop the spinning, but he was too far from a wall, his hands reaching in any direction, hoping for contact. On his third rotation, he saw Zane catch a rung and lunge toward him. He covered his head, waiting to be bludgeoned. He felt a hand around his wrist instead. The cast floated above them as Zane reeled him in, next to the door. He yanked Robin's arm free from his body and held it up to the panel at the door.

"Make it open," Zane demanded.

Robin dared to take his other hand off guarding his head. "It's not just proximity. I have to enter a full string of commands. This isn't setup to be opened for another month." He hoped the lie would work but it didn't slow him.

"Then enter the commands." Zane shook Robin's arm on the panel, causing it to beep in error.

Robin wasn't sure what his next move was. If he opened the cryo-chamber and Zane saw Isolde, it would be no big deal, but if she saw Zane…he wasn't sure what the next actions would be. He caught a glimpse out of the corner of his eye and his plan fell into place.

"Right, right. Just help me read it. You've got me all flustered."

"Okay." Zane released his hand and stared at the panel. "It says 'enter user code.'"

"Give me a second." Robin clicked away on his data pad, holding it close to his face so Zane couldn't see him clicking around randomly through files to buy time. "Okay, now what does it say?"

"It hasn't changed."

Zane turned to Robin as if he meant to threaten again. He only had time to raise his arms as Maynard jabbed his taser out, catching Zane's elbow. His convulsions came quickly as Maynard and Robin backed away.

Zane's head floated, his eyelids in a sleepy, half-closed state. Maynard tucked the taser away and said to Robin, "What the fuck happened? What's he doing out here? Where's his—?" He stopped when he saw the cast floating near the ceiling. "Jesus."

Robin put his hands up in defense. "He's mentally unstable. We need to get him to his bath and see if there are any antipsychotics in the med bay. We'll introduce it to his NutrientPanel, and we'll be fine until we get back, then he's Dr. Vell's problem."

Maynard continued to frown and shake his head. "The future of the Belt," he muttered, grabbing Zane, and pushing off the wall. "I'll meet you down there."

Robin watched him go, then grabbed the floating cast, the taser, and headed toward the med bay.

~ * ~

It was an hour later when Marlow heard the door open. She left Avani on her back in the middle of the bed and went over to receive Zane. She led him to a chair in the corner, looking up at Robin as Maynard stood in the doorway, taser ready.

"What happened to him?" Marlow asked.

"He's fine now," said Robin. "He just needs to rest. He's had his 'Panel."

"Okay."

There was mistrust in her voice as she checked out Zane. He seemed lethargic and a bit loopy.

"Hey, Mar. I had a bit of a freak out. I'm good now."

"You are?" Marlow checked out his eyes. "You seem…off."

"Time for your 'Panel," said Maynard.

"I can't…" She looked over to the bed, then to Zane. "I can't leave him with Avani like this."

"I'll watch her," said Robin.

Marlow felt the conflicting thoughts spinning inside her. She needed her 'Panel. It would help her think and produce milk for Avani, but everything seemed wrong.

"Let's go." Maynard stepped forward to grab her arm and she pulled away.

"Okay," said Marlow. "Just give me a second." She turned to Zane, looking him in the face. "I'm just going to get my 'Panel, then I'll be back. Robin will watch Avani, okay?"

Zane squinted at her like he was in another world. "Yeah, cool, Mar."

She shook her head and went to Avani who smiled when she saw her, wiggling her arms, trying to turn over.

"She can crawl off the bed if she really sets her mind to it," she said to Robin, "but I have the gravity low enough that she won't hurt herself. Just…watch her."

He put a hand on Marlow's shoulder. "I will. She'll be fine."

Marlow went out the door with Maynard, her stomach cramping as it closed behind them. She hated the thought of him "monitoring" her bath. What was to stop him from sneaking a peek? She had to push the thought away and focus on getting it over with and getting back to Avani.

~ * ~

A half hour later, Marlow stepped through the door as soon as Maynard opened it. Avani was sleeping in her makeshift crib they had across from the bed. Zane was sleeping on the bed and Robin sat in the chair. He smiled and stood up.

Robin whispered, "We're all good here." He stepped out with Maynard and the door closed. Marlow did a quick check that both her roommates were breathing, amazed Robin got Avani to sleep. She slunk into the chair.

It was a minute later when Zane said, "She made it, Mar. Ice made it."

"On the ship?" Marlow sat up and saw Zane didn't have his eyes open.

"Yeah."

"What about everyone else?"

Zane's voice was dreamy. "I don't know yet." He yawned and turned over. "Robin Hood wouldn't let me into Sherwood Forest."

Chapter Seven

A low tune howled through the maw of the cave. Hot wind came out like monster breath, and Arjen could smell the damp earthy scent lingering on the surface, promising of more, deeper in. Amun pulled him onto the ledge, then Arjen reached back for Julie, still perched on the roof of the rover. They'd managed to roll it into place to act as their steppingstone. Williams remained on the ship as a sandstorm picked up. When Julie finished the climb, they all shielded their eyes to the storm, then Amun waved them to follow him in.

Amun carried a type of flashlight found in the rover that was still throwing light when he activated it. The cave was tall enough to stand fully upright. For Arjen, every shadow moved with pointed, crawling legs, but each curve showed nothing but algae and moss growing up the walls. He swallowed his fear and Amun led on.

Soon, the cave opened to an enormous cathedral. Huge walls rose on all sides, carved out by billions of years of natural progression. Orange and blue moss snaked up the sides and a centerpiece of rising cylindrical formations met a hundred feet in. A tunnel of light spilled in from high above. The wind screamed through it, playing a disturbing soundtrack. It was breathtaking and terrifying all at once. Julie covered her ears as she moved but Arjen felt himself standing in place, taking it all in. It was a sight he'd never forget in his life. A sight he would've rushed to tell Lana about only a week ago, but something inside him said it didn't matter. He could enjoy it for what it was, raw, natural beauty that he may never top in all his future travels. He took in the moment, hoping it wasn't his last.

Julie came to a stop after she passed him, looking back, when Amun pointed at the centerpieces, further ahead, like pedestals.

"There."

Amun took off, moving as fast as he could along the slick rocks.

Arjen and Julie followed. As they rose, the pedestals moved further to the center. A drop off stood between them with a river running below. They continued up, along the right side until the path looped around, finally connecting with the center. Amun jogged ahead across a narrow formation until he stopped on the platform. Arjen and Julie were just behind, seeing what he saw. An arrangement of four, solid white cases sat in a semi-circle. They were each the size of a large, rectangular desktop and two inches thick. Amun stopped just before them, lowering to his knees, and letting out a happy cry.

Julie grabbed Arjen's arm and leaned her head against him. "Those are his…people?"

Arjen nodded. "I think so."

"Are they…?"

Amun turned back. "We need water."

Arjen raised his eyebrows. "You can revive them?"

Amun smiled. "Just like you did to me."

"I think I saw a pool further up ahead." Julie threw a thumb behind her.

"Okay." Amun stood and grabbed the end of the case on the left of the semi-circle.

Arjen came over and took the other end. Julie helped guide as they crossed the narrow path back. Where the light came through, there was a small pool. They lowered the Pelosin into the water and Amun clicked open what they learned was just a case. Inside was the foam-type substance Arjen had first encountered when he accidentally *tasted* Amun, not knowing what he was.

"So, we just leave it there?" asked Julie.

The foam began to grow and Amun nodded. "Keep it in the light and water. It will help." Then he waved Arjen to follow, and they went back for a second. Julie watched them, then looked back at the growing foam.

"Uh, seriously?"

Parts began taking shape. She could make out limbs and a face forming right before her. She hoped they'd hurry. She didn't speak Pelosin and was afraid her face, wild haircut, and blue-raspberry nails might freak it out. Julie chewed on a nail while giving nervous glances back down the path.

Soon, Arjen and Amun returned with the second, repeating the process in another part of the pool. The first Pelosin was puffing out in a way that made Julie uncomfortable. As Arjen and Amun turned to get a third, she said,

"What do I say if it comes alive?"

Amun turned back, using a language so foreign, she'd have an easier time with Mandarin Chinese, though she'd never heard it. "It means, welcome," he said, then continued away.

When the guys were on their way back for the final Pelosin, the eyes of the first sprang open and it sat up, blinking, and taking in its surroundings.

Julie had been trying to practice the word Amun used but each time sounded more like a dying witch than a Pelosin. Finally, she said, "Uh-uh, welcome." Then cursed herself for using the English word that could have just as well been, "dried beans," for all it meant to the alien.

The Pelosin reared its head back, then looked to see its companions bulging in the pool next to it. It tilted its head at her.

"Friend," said Julie, putting a hand to her chest. "Damnit. You're not a gorilla. Um…Amun. Your…brother, Amun is with me." She pointed down where the heads of Arjen and Amun were just popping up into sight.

The Pelosin stood, getting a better view of where she directed. Amun almost dropped the last case when they caught up. He left Arjen to open it as he squeezed the shoulder area of the newly hydrated friend of his.

"Nihca," Amun said, then spewed out a rambling of his own language, pointing at Arjen, then Julie, then the cave as he explained at least some of the events leading to his discovery of them.

Nihca and Amun sat, still conversing as the others came around, one by one. There were few defining marks to separate one Pelosin from another. Nothing gave a clear gender or even area of Pelosia they may have been from.

They dried out in the beam of light coming from the ceiling as

Amun told them the full story of his time on Wyan. He went into details of how things turned for the worst with his exploration team, then about Arjen and friends saving him and losing companions as they collected a piece of crystal to power their ship. Amun ended with the explanation about the Mack ship and how the humans were on a similar mission to find their people. The Pelosins stood, taking in the story after a four-year sleep. They were dazed but went along as Amun led everyone back out of the cave, relishing in the fact he was not the last of his kind.

~ * ~

As the Pelosins came out of their dehydrated state, the Knox ship was passing through one wormhole and setting course for the next.

Marlow was led to her bath by Maynard. She paused at a viewing window.

"Earth…" Marlow stood staring at her old home.

"That's right," said Maynard. "Miss it?"

Sometimes, she thought.

Like Zane said, the times it was all of them still together, still finding enough food, still able to throw in the occasional joke. She missed those times. It seemed like the Belt could be that for some, but not for her.

"Eh," she said, shrugging her shoulders and walking on. She'd learned early on not to show weakness around Maynard. He thrived on it like some kind of sick tiger.

Marlow stepped into the bathhouse, recalling the memory of sharing a steak from the nameless cow with Jason and her mom for the last time.

~ * ~

The sandstorm died down as Amun led the group to the mouth of the cave. They had a panoramic view of the lake and the mountains across the way. Arjen shielded his eyes against the star, pouring down golden light against the waves of the lake.

"Waves?" Arjen mumbled, holding a finger up to feel for a breeze but there was nothing.

"Are we going?" asked Julie.

Arjen pointed to ripples in the water. "Look."

Amun and his group watched as a black mass moved to the shoreline.

Julie jumped back. "What the hell is that?"

One of the Pelosins said something that Amun translated. "A creature. It goes to those caves, then back to the water. Looking for food."

They all took a step back as the creature slid out of the water. Its head and body were shaped like a wide torpedo with one big eye on either side. When it hit the beach, it propped up on six crab-like legs. Behind it trailed four tentacles dragging like slimy dreadlocks. It crawled along the sand. Every few feet, the tentacles spread out, feeling around for anything of interest. It made its way to one of the caves near the bottom, feeling along the opening before squeezing itself inside. The crab legs tucked up into its body as it went.

When the last tentacle was out of sight, Arjen asked the group, "Is it going to come back out soon, or should we go?"

The Pelosins conversed, then Amun reported, "It's a cycle. More are coming. Soon, all the holes will be filled."

"Oh, Jesus," said Julie.

"Then we need to get to the ship," said Arjen. "Can one of your friends get that thing driving?"

He pointed down to the rover. Amun spoke and one of the Pelosins, Asiv, stepped forward, looking down but not going further. He might have been the youngest of the group, but it was hard to tell.

"He's scared," said Amun.

"So are we." Arjen watched the water. "That's why we need to go now. Tell him I'll come with him and once we get it running, everyone else will jump down, then we drive to the ship."

Amun relayed the message. Asiv nodded and they stepped to the edge together. Arjen dropped out of the cave onto the roof of the rover. He rolled off to the sand, waiting for Asiv to land next, but instead saw Julie at the edge with her hands to her mouth. She gasped.

"Hide," Julie whispered. Another creature slid onto the shore just on the other side of the onyx boulder. Arjen ducked behind the rover, squatting down to keep an eye on the creature. It scuttled up the sand, tentacles reaching out, feeling along the boulder, then the rover, as it reached the caves. It picked a lower one, giving one last look around. Arjen fell to the ground, panting, as the giant eye passed over him. The creature secreted a black, slimy substance along the edge of the cave, then pulled itself in, smearing the slime across like it was marking its territory. Arjen let out a deep breath, standing up, as the rest of his group peered over at the cave the creature just entered. Arjen waved on Asiv and with a little encouragement, he jumped down. Arjen stood watch at the door of the rover as Asiv got in and started clicking buttons. After about thirty seconds, he jumped out, mumbling to himself and slipping underneath to continue his work. Arjen spotted another creature further down, poking out of the water. He froze in place, hoping it would keep on its path. The creature moved along the sand, and all was well until Asiv connected something that made a loud, electrical pop. The creature looked their way. Arjen saw Asiv coming out from under the rover and grabbed his arm to speed up the process. He pointed down the beach as the creature made a beeline for them. Asiv let out a screech, then yanked at the door and dove in. Arjen ran around to get to the other side. The panels clicked and illuminated.

Asiv was frantic, trying to get them moving when a tentacle stuck to the front of the vehicle. It shook them when it landed, then a second hit Asiv's door. He jumped over toward Arjen, the vehicle still not running. Arjen could see the giant head raise up in the window, the eye training in on him and Asiv, practically hugging each other.

There was a thump, then a clunk as a rock bounced off the creature and landed on the hood. Arjen looked up to see Julie yelling. Amun came forward with a big chunk of jagged rock. He raised it over his head with two hands and launched it into the side of the creature. It turned, moving the tentacles off the vehicle, and sticking them against the side of the rocks, just below the cave entrance.

Julie screamed and launched another rock directly into its eye. The Pelosins showered it with anything they could throw. The creature twisted back, shielding its eyes with its tentacles, then backing away.

Arjen and Asiv watched from the rover as it retreated and found another cave, dipping in quickly, leaving streaks of black slime behind. Arjen tapped Asiv, bringing him out of his daze. He went back to his work and this time the engine clicked to life. It ran quiet, but when Arjen gave a questioning look, Asiv moved a control that made the rover rock forward. Arjen held up a hand for him to wait, then got out to help receive the others.

More creatures spilled onto the beach. The "cycle" as the Pelosins described it, had officially started. One by one, the group dropped down. Only four Pelosins fit inside the rover as Amun, Arjen, and Julie climbed on top, linking arms, and holding on through the windows. The rover spun sand, then lunged forward. One of the creatures appeared in the water on their left. Its eyes raised enough to watch the rover, but it didn't surface onto the sand. Asiv drove them slowly ahead. There were two creatures ahead crossing toward the caves and one coming out, heading back for the water. The lake bubbled with action. There was no telling how many of the creatures would continue pouring out of it. They had to cross the sand now, get back to the ship and get out while they still could. Only, Asiv had frozen up again. The rover was parked. One creature to their left, three ahead and the ship still far away.

"Go," Arjen screamed from the roof as another creature appeared from a cave on the right. It paused as it examined the rover full of people hanging off it.

Amun called in Pelosin from the roof. Nothing changed but his voice, growing more intense as they stayed stationary. He switched to yelling something that may have been Pelosin curse words.

Finally, as the creature on the left was testing the sand, and the one on the right was fully emerged from the cave, the rover started moving. Asiv steered toward the middle of the sand, keeping an even speed that felt like crawling with all the action around. The spinning wheels and hum of the electric engine was enough to give pause to the creatures.

They moved along the beach, coming up on the last two creatures, one heading in and one out. Asiv steered behind the one going toward a cave. It lashed back a tentacle that just missed the rover. They picked up speed, Asiv driving with fear guiding him after the close call. The rover dug in, throwing up sand as the last creature stopped in their path, perched on its crab legs, with its tentacles spread like scorpion tails.

They were in an awful game of chicken. Amun yelled in Pelosin. Asiv tugged on the controls, swerving to miss the creature, but the momentum carried Arjen into Julie, who lost her grip and went flying off. She hit the sand in a sideways roll. Arjen fell next with Amun just behind. The sand burned their uncovered skin as they scrambled to their feet, taking the left side around the creature as it was focused on the rover. They moved toward the edge of the lake.

The Pelosin ship was only twenty feet ahead as the creature latched onto the rover, dragging behind it in the sand. Two tentacles held tight on the windows where the roof riders had been hanging on. A third came up and caught onto a back wheel. The suction and spinning wheel created a fishing reel action. The creature was sucked up toward the rover until it dragged to a halt, screeching out an awful cry as its tentacle was mangled under the axel. The rover spun sand but couldn't get moving. The Pelosins jumped out the doors, stumbling to their feet. Asiv was the last out and was caught from behind by the creature. He screamed for help. The creature pulled him in toward a wide mouth none of them had witnessed until then.

The other Pelosins turned, one grabbing Asiv in a tug-of-war, the other two began stomping on the tentacle. The creature tried to lunge at them with its black hole of a mouth, but the rover stopped its progress. It was still tangled in the undercarriage and trying to drag the vehicle like a ball and chain. They broke Asiv free with a popping sound, everyone landing in the sand and scrambling to their feet. The group joined together, sprinting toward the ship. Arjen waved and screamed for Williams to lower the ramp.

Williams, who'd witnessed the whole thing, was ready with the lever. He met them at the top of the ramp, marveling at the others as they passed him, then he closed them in before anything else could follow. Their action stirred a parade of the creatures around the ship. Williams got the engines fired up. The heat thrown sizzled a few brave tentacles and bought them just enough space to take off. The Pelosin ship raised among the mountains as a gathering of the creatures circled their landing place.

"Goddamn." Williams watched the monitors. "This is why we should've gone to the Mack first. The weapons are on it."

"Just fly." Arjen looked down and hoped Captain Davis and Peter hadn't suffered a fate like the one below.

Soon the lake was just a spot of blue and orange below. Arjen sat next to Williams at the pilot's seat. He was plotting their next course.

"I'm pretty certain that's where Percy projected their landing." Williams pointed at a layout of the planet. "See the mountains and that river?"

Arjen squinted at it, remembering Percy's incessant telescope watching when Davis and Peter abandoned them. Arjen hadn't been as worried about those details at the time. They still had their date with the Night Chasers to come. He was glad Williams had been listening.

"I hope you're right." Arjen stood. "How long?"

Williams eyed the map again, bringing up the weather patterns as Amun showed him. "The storms are clear if we take this way." He traced his finger across the digital map. "I'd say a couple hours at most."

Arjen moved to a seat to strap in. They hadn't even had time for introductions before they were on their next stop on the hostile planet.

Chapter Eight

Robin Visser and Maynard Royal stared at each other across the meeting table. Time aboard the Knox was wearing on them. Neither were sleeping well. Their shared duties of making sure the Earthlings were getting their nutrients and not killing each other was another point of contention. Robin made a call in the heat of the moment during the first wormhole, then, on their contact with Dr. Vell back in the Belt during the stretch between wormholes, she explained why it was the wrong call.

"We can't just keep him handcuffed to a chair," said Robin, after they'd ended communications with Dr. Vell.

Maynard tapped the table with his fingernails in no perceivable rhythm. "You want him to take out your other knee? You've been limping ever since."

Robin shook his head. His knee was a slight bother, but the thing he couldn't handle any more of was the tapping. Every time they were in the same room, it was the tapping. Sometimes he could even hear it down the hall.

"No, but—"

"You take him off those meds and—"

"Stop it." Robin pointed at Maynard's thrumming fingers.

Maynard's hand froze, mid-tapping, like he'd been caught stealing Robin's underwear. He pushed himself out of the chair. "Then what do you suggest?"

Robin stood as well. "What about a camera?"

"Who's going to watch that? You and me? All day, every day? You know Captain Miller isn't going to help. He's been hitting the med-bay a bit himself."

Robin held up a hand to push away the problem of Captain Miller's dependency issues. It couldn't be on his radar right then. "We wouldn't have to watch it all the time, just before we get them for baths. To make sure there are no ill intentions for us."

"Oh, I'm sure there are plenty of ill intentions. You seen the look on the girl's face lately?"

"Yes, I've seen it. That's why a camera—"

Maynard interrupted, "What's to prevent them from tampering with it? What are the repercussions for doing so?" Maynard pounded the table. "We've got no power here, Visser. We can't harm them, or this trip's been a waste. You brought me to uphold rules I'm not allowed to enforce."

Robin turned away, knowing what he said was true but finding no comfort in it. "Well, we're not going to handcuff him to a chair. That would only worsen his condition once the meds are out of his system."

"That quack doesn't know for sure those meds will even affect his swimmers, and she's not here to test it or deal with him when he's straight. I say we do what we need to do, then when we get back, he goes clean again, and it'll probably be fine."

Robin went for the door. "I can't live with probably. I've got to do what the doctors are requesting. Just meet me there in the morning and I'll have a solution."

~ * ~

Marlow woke to Avani fussing. Zane was passed out cold still. She went to the bathroom, letting the baby wiggle and cry, closing the door to soften the sound. She splashed water on her face in the mirror, hoping the next dose would shock away the thoughts she'd been having. It started with a dream, handing Avani off to Cannie and Barchek, then heading to the Belt Forest to meet up with Wesley's ghost. It was a perfect scene, though when she considered it, did it mean she was also dead? Like Wesley? Or just able to see him in the place they'd both remember? Why would she give her baby to the Wyans and not the people of the Belt? Trust. Intentions. Lots of thoughts came to her about that one. She'd wanted to discuss her dreams with Zane, but he was doped up around the clock. Whatever they were giving him was working for their purposes, but it left her even more alone. Soon, the dreams started coming during the day as her own thoughts. What if she handed Avani off? What if she just walked away? Gave Robin Visser what he wanted? What if she let her cry until she stopped? What if Avani wouldn't stop?

She could hear her through the door. The fussing had become wailing. What if she grabbed a pillow from the bed to muffle the sound? What if—?

Marlow splashed the water directly in her eyes. The contact stung but was enough to pull her off that rabbit trail. She took three deep breaths, water still dripping down her face and some in her hair, then stepped out of the bathroom.

Zane was sitting up in a dazed stupor, his default state of late. If she'd waited another minute, it was possible she would've gotten some help from him.

He saw her and gave a lazy, yet concerned, look at the crib.

"Don't worry, I've got her," Marlow said, in a voice thick with sarcasm that went right over his head.

Avani clung to her, banging her little head against Marlow's chest. Marlow sat to feed her as Zane lay back.

An hour passed slowly, as all hours did aboard the Knox. A knock came at the usual time. Robin and Maynard took turns playing hall monitors, escorting them to their baths separately. Marlow considered asking them for a hit of whatever they were giving Zane, but then who would take care of Avani?

When they finished the routine, Marlow waited for the men—their oppressors, in her mind—to leave. But Maynard stopped in the doorway, closing it, and turning to stand guard. Robin sat in the chair and motioned them toward the bed. "Let's have a little talk."

"What about?" Zane seemed more with it than usual after a bath.

"After a consult with Dr. Vell, we've decided to take you off your medication. We don't want to risk any long-term effects."

Marlow nodded, her eyes narrowing in thought as if they were speaking to her.

Robin lowered his eyes at Zane. "We also don't want a repeat of last time."

Zane's mouth was open, but he had no reply. The fog wasn't completely clear from his brain. He still knew there wasn't a good lie *or* truth to tell about his attack on Robin.

Robin threw a thumb over toward Maynard. "*He* wants to handcuff you to this chair. I told him it wouldn't come to that, that we can be civil during these last three weeks." Robin held out his hands, fingers splayed as if he meant to choke anyone who disagreed. "Can we do that? We all want to make it to the Belt, but we have to cooperate."

"Yeah, okay," said Zane.

"Hold on." Marlow bounced Avani on her knee as the bags under her eyes felt like they had ball bearings in them. "We're going crazy sitting in this room. You have to let us out. Give us something."

Robin gave a prudish shake of his chin. "We all know how that went last time. I'm afraid not."

Marlow pursed her lips. "Then we starve."

She knew they were being taken back for a reason. They wanted them healthy, to *serve the Belt*. A food strike would—

Maynard chuckled and muttered, "Stupid bitch."

Marlow stood. "What was that?"

Robin played mediator, standing between them with a hand in each direction. "What he's trying to say is, the NutrientPanel isn't like sealing your lips and refusing to eat your vegetables. You *will* eat or we will drag you to the bath house and throw you in."

Marlow stumbled over her next words, realizing how poor of a threat it had been. "Well then, I'll…"

She looked down at Avani. She had not received hagfish DNA. She was solely reliant on Marlow breastfeeding her until they were back in the Belt.

Robin hunched down to meet her eyes. "I wouldn't say that threat aloud. You'll regret it later."

Marlow stared at him with fiery eyes. She could feel her cheeks getting flushed as she growled and turned away. "Then what?"

Zane stood with a hand on his chin. "Don't you have anything we can do? I can't read another book."

Robin looked around the room as if he'd find something they

hadn't seen a thousand times over the last month. He began a sentence or two with no real solutions when Maynard jumped in.

"Hold that thought. I might have something." He went out the door, leaving the others behind.

It was ten minutes later, as Robin was getting more suggestions rejected by the Earthlings, the door slid open, and Maynard stood with a monitor and a tangle of wires.

"What is that?" asked Robin.

Maynard set the monitor up across from the chair and struggled with the wires.

"Where did you get that?" Robin pressed.

Maynard didn't look up. "Lisa's room."

"Really? Just tore it out of the wall?"

"Desperate times." Maynard stood, punching buttons on a small controller as a coin spun on the screen with a *ding*. He handed off the control to Zane. "Lisa loved her Super Nintendo emulator. I'll apologize when she wakes up."

"Awesome," said Zane.

He scrolled through a list of games enjoyed many years before he was born and settled on Super Mario World. His attention was locked as Robin nodded in approval and went for the exit.

"So that's it?" asked Marlow. "You take him off his meds, hand him a video game and you're done with us?"

"It's the best we can do right now." Robin leaned in, doing his *personal* voice. The one that said he cared deeply about you and meant bullshit would be spewing from his mouth shortly. "We've all got to hunker down for these last three weeks."

With that, Maynard brushed his hands of the dust from the monitor and was out the door.

Robin followed when Marlow said, "We were on a nice planet with friends…"

Her voice trailed off, quickly flashing from the good times around the firepit with the full group to the desperate battles they had, just to escape the dark side alive. It wasn't a nice planet. There was no future for them there after all. They'd lost most of their friends and it was back to her and Zane again. She stared at the side of his head, watching him find a way to cope with all the trauma they'd been through by jumping a plump, Italian, plumber down a hole. It wouldn't last, but the smile on his face gave her a brief pause. To see any expression was a welcomed sight. As the door closed behind their captors, she remembered Isolde, and longed for a conversation with her. Even the short, blunt kinds she would provide. They should've bargained for that. Send Maynard into cryosleep and pull Ice out. But she knew Robin would've never gone for that. She settled in next to Zane.

"Next time you die, it's my turn." Marlow turned Avani around to distract her with the colors from the screen. Zane gave a quick glance over.

"Okay, but…damnit. Those mushroom guys…" He handed over the controller. "Your turn."

"That was quick."

Marlow took over, feeling the glow wash over her. Maybe they'd be okay with something to distract them. At least for a few days. After that…well, she wasn't going to think about that just yet. She had to keep the plumber out of the hole.

Chapter Nine

The landscapes of Melinger had a rugged sort of beauty to them. When the Pelosin ship left the lakeside mountains, there were miles of rusty plains ahead. Sand swirled around dry riverbeds, but pockets of green popped up sporadically. Williams kept a high enough altitude to stay out of any further sandstorms. Arjen felt his stomach churning. Sure, he was hungry, and not exactly sure where their next food supplies were going to come from, but more, he worried what they'd find. If the Mack was unsalvageable, what would happen next? There were now five Pelosins to go with the three humans. The trip to the Belt would be eight weeks. If they didn't have the NutrientPanel as an option, things were about to get a lot more complicated.

Julie was next to him, watching the window, then his face. "You think they're dead, don't you? I mean, there's no way they'd still be alive."

Arjen watched the scenery streaming below. "The odds are against them."

Melinger reminded him of what Venus might have been a billion years ago, before its atmosphere became so thick, and temperatures rose so drastically. It was likely the same future for this planet. If things went differently on Earth, and they knew about the wormhole and the planets out there, all efforts would've been made to travel and take over the solar system. Wyans wouldn't have had to worry about the Night Chasers, only the bombs raining down on their heads. If wormholes were on the map, a lot of human history would've turned out differently. Instead of fighting over Earth, they could've fought over Wyan and Melinger.

Amun and the other Pelosins finished a conversation that he turned to translate.

"They were hiding out in that cave for all this time. After they lost communication with us, they knew it was the only way to survive in the chance that we could retrieve them. I explained to them, it is thanks to you for reviving me and getting us out of the awful capture of those beasts. Without that, our species…"

"We're all teetering," said Arjen. "Right on the edge of eternity it seems."

"But we're still here." Amun seemed euphoric knowing he wasn't going to die the last of his kind.

"Whoa," said Julie. "Look."

Williams started a low chuckle as he honed in on a familiar hunk of metal. "There she is. Just waiting for us."

"Let's be careful," said Arjen, giving a quick look to Amun. "This time we stay on the ship until we know it's clear."

A small river snaked past the Mack. Patches of plants grew around and against the side of the ship. Williams landed them close, once again marveling at the maneuverability of the Pelosin ship. The humans stood at the viewing window, watching their stolen transport as if it would come alive at any minute. It sat, an eyesore among the flowing water. The swaying plants stood tall, clicking together in places, welcoming them with song. Everything was calm and peaceful, compared to their first experience on the planet.

"It looks clear," said Julie, then caught Arjen's raised eyebrow and followed with, "but so did the last place."

"We go quickly to the ship. Williams, can you—?" Arjen stopped when the captain raised his data-pad, useless for the last few months, and showed its display. It was connecting to the Mack's mainframe.

"I think it's online," Williams stood, "but there's only one way to find out."

Arjen nodded as they headed to the ramp. Julie followed, then Amun.

"We will wait here?" Amun said as a question to Arjen.

"Yes. Let us check it out first."

Arjen, Julie, and Captain Williams stepped off the Pelosin ship. There were a few feet of burning sand before a patch of grass leading to the Mack. They took it slow, feeling the balmy breeze, smelling the fresh water. The only sounds were the plants softly clicking. The open savannas surrounding left them feeling exposed, but compared to the claustrophobic, black caves, it was a welcomed exposure.

Arjen and Julie stared up at the Mack together, a recent alien relic they hoped would be their salvation from not just Melinger, but the solar system. Williams clicked around the codes to unlock the ramp. There was a bellowing thump, then mechanical whirring as the ramp descended. Williams turned.

"Good thing you brought the captain."

A wave of stale, sweltering air awaited them inside. Running lights glowed in the halls as the solar panels read a full charge from sitting in the almost constant sun.

"I'll get the air moving." Julie connected her data-pad as she waved away the thick air to no avail. Arjen went deeper inside as Williams turned off toward the flight deck.

Each room was empty, giving no clues of the two-person crew's fate. Arjen stepped into the weapons stash. The one Walters was supposed to have moved from the Mack to their supply on Wyan. He wondered how different it all would've been if they had their full supply of defenses. *And if the Wyans hadn't betrayed them, that is.* Arjen tucked a pistol into his pants, feeling like a sheriff from one of the old western movies his dad would watch when he and Wesley were little. He wondered if Julie's cowboy hat was still aboard or if it had stayed on Wyan.

His data-pad lit up with a message. *No signs of anyone. Any luck on your end?*

Arjen replied to Williams and kept on, following a loop around the ship.

On his way back toward the bridge, he was getting lightheaded from the heat. Julie got some airflow to kick in, but it was an uphill battle. The med bay was on his right before he hit the main path back out. He needed some fresh air and maybe a splash of water from the lake. Arjen did a quick door check and was about to shut it again when the smell hit him. Death. Decay. Rot. He covered his face with his shirt. The conditions were enough on their own, but this added a new level. Still, he had to see. Around an exam table was a rack of medications secured in place. On the other side was Peter. He was slumped against a cabinet, his chin in his chest. His red hair was the only thing still recognizable, and it was more than Arjen could handle. His stomach lurched. He stumbled out of the room, hitting the door to close behind him, then down the hall toward the exit.

Julie and Williams saw him holding a hand over his mouth as he went, his eyes fixed on the ramp.

"Arjen?" said Julie.

He pushed past her, considering at least saying the name of the deceased, but his stomach disagreed. He went outside, sucking in the hot air. It wasn't the refreshing breaths he'd hoped for. He dry heaved toward the grass. When nothing came, he focused on the river.

The water flowed in a crystal-clear stream and Arjen was ankle-deep before he considered if it was safe to drink. They could test it on the Mack, so he settled for splashing it on his face. It was warm but at least wet, helping to cool his skin even in the slightest. He stood as the stream passed around him. Wyan rejected them, now Melinger wasn't looking better. It was time to go back to the Belt.

~ * ~

An hour later, Arjen and Julie sat in the shade of the Mack with Amun, as the other Pelosins harvested a nearby grain they deemed edible. The good thing was the GammenVat aboard the Mack didn't discriminate. It would pull out the nutrients and turn them into a 'Panel, and for Julie, Arjen, and Williams, it should be enough to keep them alive for the long trip back.

Julie passed a container of freshly filtered water. Arjen drank with pleasure, watching the rusty plains for any signs of life. They'd seen a small herd of lumbering creatures in the distance ten minutes prior, but nothing since. The creatures on this side of Melinger seemed to want to have nothing to do with them.

"Have you decided?" Arjen asked Amun.

Amun glanced to his group foraging. They were the longest survivors of Melinger, despite being in a dehydrated state most of the time.

"We are…without a leader." His eyes darted, then tilted his head toward the sky. "They look to me because of my father, but I'm not the same. Their expedition leader was the one who left the instructions to find them, but he is gone."

"That's tough." Julie smiled at the alien. "I wouldn't want to be in your…shoes." She looked down, realizing the Pelosin didn't wear shoes, then shrugged it off and continued anyway, "I'm glad old baldy over here makes the decisions for us."

Amun was confused at the word, "baldy," but got the gist of the message. "Yes. Maybe we will try Wyan again. Do you think the Night Chasers are…done?"

"Not *done*," said Arjen, "but maybe deterred for a while. Who's to say in four years?"

Amun looked down, contemplating.

"At least you know people there," said Julie. "Bruuth would make sure you guys were okay."

The sound of footsteps came down the ramp and Williams peered over, not stepping into the grass. Arjen never saw him so disheveled and equally determined. His mustache faded into a scraggly beard and he had a wild look in his eyes. Arjen imagined the rejection from his father and Maynard replayed in the old pilot's mind every night since. It was the fuel for his rage. The revenge story he was plotting. And Arjen was just fine with that.

"Still no sign of Davis," said Williams, "but he was so close. The damn fool. He led me right to it. I wish he was around so I could thank his corpse."

"Jesus," said Julie, then, "What did he do?"

"The thrusters. That's where it went wrong for them. He had it figured out. A couple more steps and they would've been out of here. Anyway, I need help with this next part. Arjen."

He motioned to follow, then disappeared back into the ship.

Arjen handed back the water container and stood.

"You're still gonna help me with Peter, right?" Julie gave a half smile, half wince.

"Yeah. Unless you can convince Amun to help."

He winked at the Pelosin, then walked up the ramp, heading toward the engine room. He knew almost everything about his ship, the Iris. This one wasn't much different, but the engines were always beyond his reach. Captain Davis and his co-pilot were always on top of those details. Arjen hadn't had to worry. He could focus on the overall mission. Now his hopes rested on Williams and his desire for revenge.

The engine room was even warmer than the others. The sweat poured off the men as they worked and cursed together for the next few hours. They emerged for water at Arjen's urging. After a few swallows, Williams was back up.

"A few more tweaks and we can give it a trial."

Arjen exhaled slowly. "Can we take five at least? The daylight's not going anywhere and that heat…"

Williams waved a hand. "Take your rest, pansy. I can do this next part without you."

"Where's the fire?" said Julie. "Shouldn't we get Peter out first?"

Williams let out a condescending chuckle. "No, this is more important. The sooner it's fixed, the sooner we're out of here, the sooner I get to see the looks on their faces when I return."

Julie shrugged and turned to watch the river. Williams scoffed and was gone.

Arjen stood watching the ramp. "He's right."

"Just sit," said Julie. "You've been through a lot lately. We all have. And you *don't* want to be around him when he's like this. Trust me."

Arjen plopped down, reluctant. "Twenty minutes. Then we take care of Peter and go help Williams finish up with the thrusters."

Julie shrugged again. She was in no rush to get back on a ship for almost two months, or to the Belt for that matter.

Arjen's twenty minutes turned into an hour as the Pelosins joined them, sharing some of the edible plants they'd discovered.

"It's not pretty like this." Julie stuck out her arms at the landscape around them. She was telling stories of the Belt that Amun was doing his best to translate. "It's different. Weird. Not like this. There *is* the Belt

Forest. That's pretty cool."

Arjen finished a plant root that reminded him of the stalks even the Wyans didn't eat. His teeth were getting a workout like never before. He looked at Julie as she finished trying to explain how tall the trees were. "Peter?" he asked.

"Yeah…" Julie stood and pointed to the Pelosins. "To be conti—" She stopped and exchanged a glance with Arjen. "Was that…?" She didn't have time to finish her question as alarms started going off in the Mack. Arjen jumped up and they ran inside.

He led them back to the engine room where Williams was likely to be. The door was sealed but residual smoke hung in the hallway. A panel outside alerted of a fire within. Safety protocols had taken over and locked it down while the fire retardant dispersed.

"Thomas," Julie yelled, banging a fist on the door.

She tapped at her data-pad, trying to override the lockdown to no avail.

After a grueling couple minutes, Arjen was pacing, checking his data-pad for a return message from Williams. The door finally opened to a room covered in sticky foam. Williams lay just beside the thruster he and Arjen had been working on together. He was white with foam, including the piece of engine shrapnel protruding from his forehead.

"Oh god." Julie threw her hands to her face as Arjen went to him.

Williams's eyes were open, coated with foam; his mouth in a terror-filled, fixed gaze on the engine that betrayed him.

Before Arjen could kneel beside him, Julie ran past, slipping in the foam and sliding on her knees to Williams. She cradled his head, giving a delicate examination of the object in his skull. Any movement caused the waterfall of blood to increase velocity across his cheek. She let it go and wept. Arjen knelt beside her, putting a hand on her heaving back. When a minute passed, she turned and hugged him. They shared a final moment with their companion. The human population now down to two.

~ * ~

The four, recently revived Pelosins waited outside, murmuring amongst themselves as Amun reappeared. His expression was a flat line that told them enough. Arjen and Julie came out next, taking their places back in the shade, sharing the filtered water and staring off to the distance.

Amun addressed the Pelosins in their language. "They have lost their pilot. Their ship will no longer fly. Like us, they have no home in this system. This planet has rejected us, as well as that one." He pointed to the sky. "But there is another system where they were headed that could give us one more chance. The *best* chance."

"What about Wyan?" asked Nihca. "We're a short journey away. We could try again."

Amun shook his head. "But the Night Chasers are many."

Rezih pointed a pale, chalky hand at Julie. "She says you killed most of them. We could set up a camp. Try to finish what your father started."

"But the humans…" Amun tilted his head at his two grieving friends.

Rezih stepped closer. He was six inches taller than Amun and made sure to let him know it from his posture. "What is your obsession with these bags of meat?"

Amun pulled away. "They saved me. They saved *you*. That one," He pointed at Arjen, "braved a treacherous mountain and an army of Night Chasers to collect the crystal that powers our ship. I…*we* owe him transportation home."

Rezih shook his head. "If it were truly home, they would've never left."

~ * ~

Through their grief, Arjen and Julie could tell there was a heated conversation going on around them and *about* them. Arjen wanted to stand up and defend himself, but the only one who understood him seemed to already be doing that.

There was a closing statement from the tallest one, then the group of four turned and walked toward their ship. Arjen observed Amun, who watched his people go.

"So…" said Arjen, hoping to get a few details, like, if the ship was about to take off without them.

"They want to stay on Wyan." Amun turned, "but they're still deciding. They don't want to be back on the ship for all that time, to a new system. You have to understand."

"I…"

Arjen was at a loss for words. He wasn't above begging at that point. He felt the wave of icy regret wash over him. He should've taken his father's offer. His defiance left him stranded. But if he went, he would've stranded Julie and Williams. He looked over at the chopped, red hair, the distraught expression, and chipping nail polish. Was his loyalty to her what sealed his fate? All he'd done to Marlow and Zane and now he'd have no chance to make it right. He hoped, at that moment, Ice would. That she'd find a way to get free and do what he couldn't.

Julie snapped out of her thoughts of Williams and addressed Amun. "You can't leave us here. Not after—"

"No, no." Amun held up his hands. "We will take you back to Wyan. If you want." He turned away. "But I know that is not where you want to go."

Arjen paced as Amun went back to his people.

"We can't…we *can't*…" Arjen muttered.

"Wyan's not that bad." Julie sat, picking at a fingernail. "Especially now that there's four years without Night Chasers."

Arjen stopped, frowning at her, trying to read her face for any signs of sarcasm. He found none. "You serious?"

"I'm just saying, we lived there on and off for years. It's habitable." She motioned toward the ship. "Hell, even they know that."

"Because *you've* been telling them."

She looked away, avoiding eye contact. "It's a nice planet."

Arjen huffed in frustration, keeping one eye on Julie and another on the ship, afraid they might just take off without him if he didn't. "You know you and I can't repopulate, right? Just the two of us."

Julie's hands were open, palms up, resting on her knees. "I know. I can't even get pregnant." She squinted up at the bright sky, then to her shoes. "That's why your dad left me here."

"You what? Why would he…?"

"Never mind. I'm just blabbing." She picked up a leftover root vegetable to chew on.

Arjen sat next to her and sighed. "Why don't you want to go back to the Belt?"

Julie blew a raspberry and waved a hand. Her cheeks were flushed a darker red than her hair.

Arjen pressed, "Julie? It's just us now. You can tell me."

Julie searched the sky for answers. "Okay, but you might not like this."

He put his arms out. "I don't like much of this. Try me."

Julie took a drink to wash out the husk she'd attempted to eat, spit, then began, "I'm the last generation before they started figuring it out. Most of my peers are feral. Once they learned I wasn't, their interest piqued. They ran all kinds of tests. My ovaries were everyone's favorite topic in the lab."

"So, one of your parents was from Earth, then?"

"No. That's why it was such a big deal. They tried to figure it out. They tried to impregnate me. To find the missing gene. I was—"

"You were the original Marlow." Arjen rubbed his head, the former habit of brushing back his hair, still happening. "I didn't know."

"Don't be surprised. They kept me out of the public a lot. Didn't want me meeting someone and getting pregnant with the wrong person." She shook her head. "But I failed the trial. I miscarried. I don't know if it was from all the tests or what, but instead of calling it good there, your father told them to try again. Dr. Ramirez commissioned him to find a solution, then turned a blind eye. He didn't want to see what your dad and his son, Oscar, were doing. He just wanted the Belt to go on, and you can't blame him. That's why they impregnated me a second time. I miscarried that one too, and it almost killed me. I remember everyone freaking out about blood loss, or blood pressure, or…I don't know. It wasn't good. I woke up later to my dad. Apparently, I'd stabilized enough for him to take me home to recover.

"Those were good memories actually. We watched a lot of

nineties TV shows and music videos he'd gotten on a hard drive from work. We hung out in a way we hadn't before.

"Then, as I was almost fully recovered, he told me the news. He wasn't my dad. Mom had an affair she'd never told him about. Said it was a onetime thing but…are they ever though? Didn't matter. What mattered was after all the testing they'd done to that point, they finally tested what they should've before they started. Turns out my biological father was older."

Arjen's mouth was hanging open. "He was born on Earth." The full picture became clear to him. "Shit."

"Yep. All that testing. Everything to find out through a simple paternity test that I was just a normal, non-feral kid."

Arjen had a hand over his mouth. "Jesus, Julie. Did they…so what then?"

She shrugged. "I was useless to them, then. I could just go back about my business. At that point, I was heading on a career path to be a doctor, only now I wanted nothing to do with that group. I ran into Lana outside the medical center one day after clinicals. She could tell I'd been crying. She listened to my story, but instead of giving me pity like anyone else would've, she gave me an opportunity. She said, 'I bet you'd like to get out of here, wouldn't you? Have you thought of gathering?' I didn't realize she was recruiting me for the Mack. She told me that the ship medic program would be on the same path I was on but much shorter and then I could get out of the Belt, at least for a little bit at a time. It was the best idea I'd heard. My family was torn apart. I couldn't look at my mom anymore. Not when she knew about the affair and didn't bring it up as they tested and test—"

Julie stopped to compose herself. "She didn't truly apologize. She just said she didn't think it could've been from that *one time* with the other man. My dad…well, the guy I grew up thinking was my dad, let's just say we started drifting after that. Those times during my recovery made me think everything was going to be okay, but I was wrong. I didn't want to see those I'd been working under. If I switched career paths, I'd switch mentors as well. It all just made sense. It's not like Earth was. You know how in those shows or movies when someone was having a tough time, they'd move across the country, or the world, to try a different situation? That was never an option for me. I couldn't go far enough away. Until I started gathering that is. Until we found that wormhole. It felt like fate finally smiled on me. Then we lost half the team on that mission. We had to come back and get more support. I hated it. I wanted to stay, but the promise of another Earth trip. The chance to gather a few more things. It balanced out for me. But now it's all gone to hell again, Arjen. I don't know where I belong anymore, but it sure isn't the Belt. If we're stuck on Wyan, I say it's fate. You can't fight that."

Arjen finished pondering her story. He probably knew her parents in passing but didn't want to make her say more than she wanted to. They sat in silence for a few moments until he said, "I can, and I'm not leaving you here to die."

Julie rolled her eyes at him. "We're all going to die soon enough. The odds are pretty much against us."

Amun descended the ramp to the Pelosin ship alone. He approached slowly, raising a finger, speaking quietly to himself, then lowering the finger as he walked. Finally, he stopped a few feet away, the light reflecting off him like a beacon. The humans had to shield their eyes.

"We've talked." Amun glanced back at the ship. "We're going to set up a mobile colony on Wyan. The land is fertile. With the abundance of that crystal, we feel we'll be able to keep our machines powered and even build more. We'll be ready for the next attack. We'll know what to do. Where to hide. We'll—"

Arjen cut him off. "Amun…" He stood, looking between him and Julie, ready to lower to his knees and beg for a ride home.

"I know." Amun put out his hands. "I know, but please hear me. We want you to be part of our colony. Both of you. We can live in harmony together." He put out a smile that was not returned. "Okay. Let us gather what you need from your ship, then we'll be on our way."

Julie smiled a fake grin at Arjen, patted him on the shoulder and said, "Fate."

Chapter Ten

"Put it down, Mar." Zane's voice was shaky with fear.

His bloodshot eyes locked in on the controller gripped in her hand. She stood on the edge of the bed, dramatically holding the game controller as high as her short frame would allow, threatening to drop it. Avani cried in her crib.

"I *will* put it down," Marlow said in a rasp, "but it won't be gently."

Zane edged to his left, holding his hands up. "Just wait. *Wait*. Let's talk about it."

"I've tried, Zane. Every fucking day, I've tried but you're too interested in goddamn Metroid."

"It's—"

Zane stopped himself from correcting her that he'd beaten *Super Metroid* and moved on to *The Legend of Zelda: A Link to the Past*. If she busted the controller, he may never find the Titan's Mitt and be able to lift heavier objects and rescue the Dwarven Swordsmith from the Dark World. His whole sense of purpose was wrapped up in the plastic Marlow held way too high up. If it fell…

Zane had a thought, fumbling with the panel near the door as quickly as he could.

"What are you—?"

Marlow stopped herself, realizing. The anger pushed her over the edge. She cocked back to throw the controller and found it just floating out of her hand, slowly toward the ground. Zane kicked off the wall, his hands out to catch the object of his obsession, though the threat of it breaking against the ground was neutralized. He'd turned off the gravity and threw off Marlow's attempt. Zane overshot it by just enough to watch his fingers come up short as he headed for the wall near the bathroom.

59

Marlow wasted no time, using the bed to leverage herself to the floor. She grabbed the controller and raised it to smash on the ground. Her momentum sent her into a one-eighty. She spun to see Zane aimed at her like a missile. She ducked, cradling the controller, and caught him in the chest with the top of her head.

Zane grabbed her sides as he flipped over her. Together, they became a spinning blob, heading for the door. Zane's back took the brunt of the hit. Marlow used the moment, breaking free as he tried to catch his breath. She pushed off the chair Robin loved to lecture them from and went straight at the screen full of a bright colored world, with Link standing in a field in his green hat, his blue sword drawn. Marlow felt Zane smack her foot, trying to redirect her path, but it wasn't enough. She shifted sideways, grabbing the edge of the monitor with her left hand, and driving the controller directly into it with the other.

Zane cried out. Avani wailed as she floated out of her bed. Marlow perched against the wall like Spiderman, slipping into a fit of wicked giggles.

~ * ~

Robin put his head in his hands, gripping his hair and considering pulling it out. He'd caught the tail end of the fight from his data-pad. The alert came up with the changes to the wall unit. Maynard had been sly getting the camera into the monitor. It gave them the option to watch for any issues without alerting the Earthlings of its presence. Until they smashed it that is. He looked at the time. The goddamn, meaningless time. Ten days. That was all that mattered. Ten days and they could all be back in the Belt getting their plans into motion. He'd told Maynard repeatedly that the trip was the easy part. Once they were back, they'd have to quell a civil war, begin the impregnation process, and help establish New Pangaea. Well, Robin and Oscar would. Maynard would just be there for crowd control. Thinking of crowd control, he hit his-data pad to message Maynard. He hated to wake him. They were doing their best to split shifts but this one would likely require both of them.

The men met at the door to the Earthling's room. Maynard's

spiked hair was going in every which direction. He rubbed at his eyes and patted his taser.

"Haven't had the chance to review the incident yet. Think I need this?"

Robin pursed his lips. "Just be ready for anything."

He nodded and hit the door controls. The scene inside gave them both pause. The Earthlings sat on the floor, knees to their chests with their backs resting against each other. Avani was on the floor next to them on a blanket, crying as Marlow half-heartedly patted her leg and wiped tears from her own eyes.

Zane looked up from his knees. "Not a good time, Bird." Then put his head back down.

Maynard blinked a couple times and whispered to Robin, "Did he just call you Bird?"

Robin huffed. "Well, it surely wasn't directed at you." He stepped in as Marlow raised a middle finger straight in the air while facing away from them.

"Fuck off, Goonies."

Maynard's nostrils flared. "Okay now." He went toward them, but Robin put a hand on his chest.

"Tell me what happened here." Robin kept his arms at the ready in case they had any projectiles he hadn't considered.

Zane started, "She said I was playing the Nintendo too much. She took the controller and—"

Marlow cut him off, "No, Zane. Don't confuse them with any big words. Let me translate." She switched to a mocking, lower tone. "Pew, pew. Boom, bang. Too much. Me not like. Me smash screen." She swirled a finger over their heads. "We no friends now."

Robin's face twisted but he replied in rhythm. "Why do you sit so close if you're not friends anymore?"

Marlow tossed up both arms, Avani watched like it was a game. "Nowhere to go. Our abductors are too busy blowing each other to think of a better solution."

Robin pleaded to Zane with his eyes. "Care to embellish?"

Zane let out a groan, looking over at the smashed monitor and controller lying next to it. He shook his head. "We're back in the bunker mentality. When we'd get mad, we still needed each other to stay warm. So, we'd sleep back-to-back. It's just what we do. You wouldn't understand."

"No," Robin admitted, "but I know all about tough situations that you've got to find a way through. It's why we're all going back to the Belt. It's why Maynard and I came all the way out to that god-forsaken planet to collect you again. You're important to us, but you still have to serve your purpose, and this is not a good situation." Robin examined the room, then looked down at Zane. "Get up. Get your things. We're separating you two."

"What?" Zane said. "Really?"

"Yes. Now get up before I make you get up. We have ten days left and by god we're all going to make it there alive. Do you understand?"

Zane stood slowly, looked back at Marlow. "Okay…"

Marlow twisted around to face them. "You're going to leave me here alone with Avani?"

Robin crossed his arms. "I'll come by and give you a break. But you two," he pointed at Zane, then her, "need to spend some time apart. At least until we get back to the Belt." He tilted his head at Zane. "Now, move it."

Zane began collecting his clothes as Maynard cleaned up the broken monitor and took it out of the room.

Robin oversaw everything until Zane was at the door. Marlow stayed on the floor, looking up, shocked that it was all happening. Then the door closed, and she was alone with Avani.

~ * ~

They were three days away from the Belt when Marlow heard the door. Robin came in and she held a finger to her lips, showing him the sleeping baby. Robin nodded and whispered, "I'll be here."

Marlow forced a smile at him as she went out the door. Maynard waited as he always did, just outside, hand near his taser, leering down at her. She went ahead without acknowledging him. The bathhouse was a few turns ahead. They stepped in and he locked the door behind them. Marlow went behind the privacy wall. It irked her every time she had to undress around the head of security, but she wasn't in a position to argue, or even stall. It would only fuel his temper. She quickly disrobed and jumped in, feeling the warmth of the nutrient-filled bath wash around her tingling skin.

After a minute, she called out, "Maynard. Maynard! Help. Something's wrong."

He stepped around the wall; eyes narrowed. Before he could ask, she yelled, "It's burning. Burning my skin. Help."

Marlow's head went under, then popped up just enough to scream again. Maynard ran around the tub to her position. He got ahold under her armpits and pulled her out. She was slick from the water, turning in his grasp. It wasn't until the last second that he saw the flash of black in her hand as she swung it straight into his neck. Maynard fell back with Marlow on top of him. His arms flailed, trying to pull her hand away, while instinctively reaching for his taser. He caught it just as she did, knocking it loose to clatter onto the floor. Stars flashed in his vision, before things started going dark. He managed one solid blow to her chest and Marlow fell back. The blood poured from his neck as he freed the object, she'd stabbed him with; a sharpened piece of computer monitor. Lisa's monitor. He'd barely had the time to think back if he'd accounted for all the pieces or just thrown the thing out. The answer was clear. He'd slipped up and was paying the price.

Marlow stood over him, pointing at a scar on her abdomen. "You did this to me. How does it feel?"

Maynard blinked away the stars, holding tight to his neck to stop the blood, but in turn, cutting off his air supply. He wanted to tell her he didn't do the cutting but didn't think it would help. She knew he was one of the ones that took her that day on the Belt. He was the one who beat up on her boyfriend.

Then, as his breaths were growing raspy, Maynard saw the door open. He needed to buy just a few seconds and he knew just how.

His words were barely coherent, but they did what he needed. "S-snapped your duck's fucking neck."

He followed it with a grin as her face lit up in a rage. Maynard braced for a kick to his balls when she stepped past him and retrieved the taser. She did a quick examination of the button she needed to press, then lowered it toward him, but her time had run out. The shock went through Marlow's body and she crumpled to the floor, dropping Maynard's taser as she landed beside him in convulsions. Captain Miller stood over both of them, wide eyed with pupils too dilated for the room's light.

"What the hell happened here?"

Chapter Eleven

Lisa, the ship's usual leader, sat at the meeting table across from a jittery Robin Visser, and bandaged Maynard Royal. Captain Miller was back at the bridge, keeping an eye out for the end of the worm hole.

"Shoulda woke me up earlier," said Lisa. She brushed some blonde hairs that had strayed from her ponytail out of her face. "With all due respect, that kind of thing doesn't happen under my watch."

"Doesn't happen on my watch either," said Maynard. He threw a thumb toward Robin. "But his rules don't exactly lend to being able to keep any order."

Robin pointed at him with his whole hand. "You were the one that brought them that monitor. You were the one who disposed of it. If I'd done it, I would've checked."

"Maybe you should've then. Maybe it would be your neck instead."

"Wait," said Lisa. "What monitor? The one missing from my room?"

Robin crossed his arms and sat back. "I told you to leave it."

Maynard slammed his hands on the table. "It bought us a couple weeks. *You're* the one who saw the video. You should've warned me she made a shiv out of the monitor."

"The video obviously wasn't working at that point. The—"

"Hold on." Lisa stood up. "This is getting us nowhere. I'm the one that should be mad. You stole my gaming setup from my room, and it was destroyed while I was in cryo-sleep. I should've stayed awake. This is my ship."

Robin frowned at her. "It's the Belt's ship, and we're almost back. Why don't you lead us the rest of the way while we go take a nap?"

"That's fine with me. What's the plan for the rest of them?" Lisa motioned in the direction of the cryo-room down the hall.

"No one else wakes up until after we land. We take the kids home first undercover. Then Maynard takes Isolde to prison, and I take Lana to debrief with Oscar."

"You got it." Lisa eyed both men, lucky to have survived the return flight. "You gonna go nap then?"

"I doubt I'll be able to sleep, but I will go lay down." Robin stood and left the meeting room.

Maynard grunted to stand. "I'll be in my room as well."

~ * ~

A few hours later, Captain Miller and Lisa watched the wormhole reach its end and the Belt come into view. The first islands appeared, the TechBubbles no longer around them. Their buildings were cleared out and what remained had floated off into space. The Belt Forest still stood tall but had thinned out compared to only six months prior. The workers were on a double shift, trying to hit quotas for the demand of New Pangaea. A hauling ship was docked and being loaded. Club Earth was further up, only, the parking lot and building like a ghost town, despite the dim 'Bubble around it. Then came Ceres. Huge water tankers were being filled with resources from the oceans. In the shipyard sat the Iris, the gathering ship that once picked up two kids from Earth and changed the course of the Belt in one way or another. Though most of its crew were dead, the other vacant landing place for the Mack signified the rest wouldn't be coming back.

The Knox landed.

Just off the horizon of Ceres, there was light and movement. In its orbit was New Pangaea. The consolidated community of most of the remaining humans in the Belt.

Lisa patted Captain Miller on his shoulder after a successful landing.

"Trip as bad as they said it was?" she asked.

He tilted his head at her. His pupils, abnormally large and without blinking, said, "No. It was just fine."

Part II

Chapter One

Lana gazed out the window of her new apartment on New Pangaea. It was small and claustrophobic, obviously put together in a hurry, but with no threat of weather and no need for a kitchen, what more was required than a bed and bathroom? Everything else was digital and the bathhouse behind the apartment provided all her nutritional needs. It was everything she hated about the Belt. The "new object" her father and Robin sold her on Wyan, turned out to be just one of the oddly shaped, larger belt objects. She couldn't remember the name, but she was quite certain it was classified hundreds of years ago.

She stepped out onto the gravel made from smooth asteroid rock. There was a less than obvious road heading to her right. The medical facility had been transported there. The incredible foresight of the initial builders made everything mobile. Detach the foundation, throw a TechBubble around it, and haul it to its new location. Lana eyed it with conflicted thoughts. She had an appointment there later. One that was going to change a lot. She was indifferent about being a mother, despite her plans. Her mother was weak. She'd died in childbirth, which, on the Belt, was extremely rare. A true sign of her weakness, according to Lana. She got all her domineering traits from her father, but her looks gave her a different level of persuasion he didn't possess. She could even persuade him if needed. And she would need to.

After the events on Wyan, there was much regrouping to be done. She had a hard realization when she lost Arjen's allegiance. Regardless of the turnout, they didn't have enough to recover and rule Wyan. This was only compounded by Karath's betrayal. Lana felt a vein throbbing in her neck just thinking about that purple-faced traitor. It could've worked.

If not for Davis and Peter taking off, it would've. She'd be ruling Wyan right then. Once things were settled after the war, she would've gotten pregnant on her own terms. Her child would've been the first human birth on Wyan. The first heir. Not Avani, as everyone talked about in their camp. Avani was born in the Belt. Lana's child would've…

It didn't matter now. Her plans were set back, but only by a year or so. She'd get pregnant; say the right things at the right gatherings and all the while she'd be preparing. Her father would work for her. With a little convincing, he'd build her army. It wouldn't need to be large. Just enough to go back to Wyan and take over the village that was rightfully hers. That would be the first wave. The second would be the mothers. A group carrying the next generation of Wyan children.

Lana stopped on the path, looking over the row of mostly vacant apartments. This is where they would incubate. Robin Visser had no idea how well he'd set her up to put this plan in motion. She could improvise on the fly. When they'd told her she was going to get pregnant to be the symbol for these other women, that she'd have to repent for what she'd done on Wyan, for abandoning her people in the Belt, her first response was rage. But now, it was retribution. They say people don't dream in cryo-sleep, but Lana had. She awoke with plans bigger than Robin, Oscar, and her father could even imagine.

~ * ~

The medical center was as Lana remembered it, though her last memory was a violent one of her and Bruuth breaking Marlow out. The girl was fresh off a c-section and all Lana knew about her was she was important to Arjen. She remembered the fear on her father's face as he cowered against the wall in a heap. He didn't know how docile the Wyans truly were at the time. She'd left the room, flown away, and though she'd been with him again, they'd never spoken of that day. She'd bested him and maybe he was a little proud. Maybe he thought, "I'll get you next time." She didn't know his feelings, and that's how their relationship worked.

Her exam room was just down from Marlow's on that fateful day.

"Are you planning to tell stories of your travels during your speech?" Dr. Vell asked as she finished the procedure.

"I'm not sure yet." Lana dressed herself as Dr. Vell stared her down.

"My advice? Don't. Nobody cares where you've been. They all just want to know how you had the audacity to come back." She turned her back and busied herself around the room. "See you in two weeks."

Lana felt a shiver go down her spine, hoping the doctor would hold to her medical ethics before any feelings about Lana's actions.

On the way out, a woman looked up at her from the waiting room. She was in her mid-twenties with perfect, light-brown hair, bobbed at the ends, and doe eyes that somehow made Lana sad for her. She stood as Lana reached the door.

"Miss Royal," she said, and Lana paused in the doorway.

"Yes?" Lana tried to place the girl's face but couldn't.

The girl stood, looked to the hall Lana came down, then said, "I just wanted to say, it's really brave what you're doing." She was bubbling over with nervous excitement. "Inspiring, really." Her hands were clasped in front of her.

Lana tilted her head. "What I'm—What do you think I'm doing?"

Her face froze for a second. "T-the new mother initiative. You're leading that, aren't you?"

"Right. Yes. I didn't know the word was out. I haven't even given my speech yet."

"Oh, no, no. I don't think others know yet. I just do since my dad is Dr. Crouch. He'll be overseeing some of the inseminations." She stuck out a hand. "I'm Darcy, by-the-way."

"Hi Darcy. Call me Lana, please." She checked the girl out, seeing how clearly, she fit the profile. "So, you're next in line?"

Darcy checked the hall again. "Yep. Just waiting my turn, but I'll definitely be at your speech tonight. It's going to be a great opportunity for a lot of us. I'm probably the youngest but I feel like I've been waiting the longest."

"That's…exciting." Lana managed a smile at her as they heard footsteps coming down the hall. "I'll see you tonight then." She dipped out the door before Dr. Crouch appeared.

~ * ~

The podium looked too formal, like Lana was planning to announce her campaign for mayor of New Pangaea. She tucked away from the window of her apartment as people started gathering out front. There weren't even curtains yet. The whole thing was so new and so last minute. It was as if Robin and Oscar threw it together to distract people from a true civil war. Can't fight when you're building, can you? Lana knew they could fight if they wanted to and some in the crowd looked like they'd come to do just that.

There was a knock on her door, then the reassuring voice of her father.

"Time, Lan."

She released a deep breath and stepped out with him escorting. He kept the bandage on his neck tucked behind his collar and refused to go into detail about how he'd gotten it.

Robin waited for them at the podium with Oscar beside him. He gripped Lana's shoulders when she reached him.

"Let me start, then keep it quick and to the point."

Lana nodded, trying to avoid looking around at the distrusting glares coming from the two hundred or so gathered. Two thirds of the Belt population.

Robin raised his hands for silence, then began, "When I was thirteen, Dr. Ramirez took me in as his own. He helped raise me like his family. His son," He turned to nod at Oscar, "treated me like his brother. All he ever wanted was for us to thrive in the Belt. And we have. We've had many good years. Most of a lifetime for some of us, but we all know the problem of the next generation. Some of the…extreme measures we've had to go to, to try to resolve this problem.

"On his death bed, Dr. Ramirez asked just one thing of me." Robin held up a finger. "One thing. To find a solution for our kids. And I'll admit, I haven't always gone about that with a clear conscience. A lot of these decisions weighed on me, and in turn, split our people down the middle. So, Maynard and I," he pointed back to the head of security, "took a trip to mend fences. To work toward our future together, rather than everyone going their own way. We can't afford that, people." Robin raised his arms. "We're it. We must find a way. This is why I've brought our next guest to discuss a new initiative. Please give her your attention. Please hear her out before you pass any judgement." He turned and waved Lana up to the podium. "Lana Royal."

She was greeted with murmuring. People crossing their arms and whispering to each other. There was the sound of clapping from the left side of the audience. Lana dared a glance to see Darcy with a wide smile. She gave a quick smile back, then addressed the crowd.

"I'm Lana Royal. I'll give a quick history for those that don't know. I was raised in the Belt, became a gathering leader, and took many trips collecting useful materials for the houses you live in and the medicines you use. On one of these trips, my team discovered a wormhole to a new world. This world is a lot like a primitive Earth as we understand it. I worked with the people, learned their language, and tried to live in peace with them. I even came back to recruit others to join me. In retrospect, I was wrong. I was blinded by the thought of colonizing a new planet. We cannot live in peace with the Wyan people as I once thought. Our home is here. I cannot begin to apologize for the pain I've caused for any of those who did not return. They all went of their free will. They all wanted what I wanted."

Lana tried to slow her breathing. She could tell she was losing the crowd at the mention of their dead friends and family.

"Get to it," Robin whispered, then stepped back.

"This is why I want to be the first to offer myself as part of the solution. As you all know, we tried different methods to solve the problem of our children, but now we're taking a new approach. The apartments you see behind me will be housed with the Motherhood Initiative. Starting with myself, we'll be fertilizing women of reproductive age with stored samples of Zane from Earth. I probably don't need to explain that this will prevent the children from becoming feral. It will buy us more time without halting the next generation. Each pregnancy will be examined to determine if we can track down the missing gene. I'll let the scientists explain the rest." She took a slight step back, did a short bow and said, "Thank you."

Immediately, questions started raining down, drowning out the applause from Darcy and a few others.

"What happened to Marlow?"

"Did Arjen die?"

"Why is she walking free? She should be in prison."

More came as Robin tried to quiet the crowd while Maynard stood by Lana.

It took two hours for Robin and Oscar to answer all the questions. Their responses were: Arjen was dead. The Earthlings were, too. They recovered what they could but, in the end, the war on Wyan took its toll. Lana had been tried for her crimes, stripped of her power, but it would do no good to have her rot in a jail cell.

The last of the crowd trickled out, most by the hum of Rock-Hoppers, and Darcy came over to congratulate Lana on her great speech.

"I don't know about that," said Lana. "I'm surprised I wasn't lynched."

"Oh." Darcy waved a hand. "They'll come around. You're on the right team now."

Dr. Crouch waved her on from a Rock-Hopper.

"I'll see you around soon. I'm packing up for the move tomorrow."

"See you then." Lana watched her leave, then walked back to her apartment with her father.

Maynard gave a look around as she opened the door.

"Looks good. I think we appeased them for now. Do you want me to stay?"

Lana shook her head. "I can handle myself. If someone shows up to give me a firm, fact-based argument, I'll give you a call." She ended it with a smirk.

Maynard patted her shoulder. "Night then."

Lana closed the door, clicked the lock, then headed to the bathroom. She badly needed to relieve herself, then drink some water. Her throat was dry from her speech. She reached for the sliding door handle and a hand caught her wrist. Before she could scream, it spun her around, pushing her arm too far up her back. A second hand clamped her other wrist and tightened it up around her neck.

"Ah-ah-Ice," Lana forced out the words.

"Where are the kids?" Isolde's breath was hot against Lana's ear.

"The what?" Her arm jammed higher and Lana let out a muffled scream.

"Don't play dumb with me. Where are they? Where's my sister? What happened on the dark side?"

"Let me go and I'll tell you. You don't have to threaten."

There was a pause from behind her. Lana's arms begged to be released and finally Ice appeased. Lana stumbled forward, turning around to see the shadow standing in the doorway of her bathroom. There were multiple scars on her face and arms that Lana never saw before. Ice's mouth hung open like an animal deciding when to pounce.

Lana held up her hands, taking breath after breath. "I…please just listen to me. Things went bad on the dark side. They took us. They wanted us to—" Lana cut herself off. "They wanted to kill us all. We got split up. Arjen, Admani, and I escaped to the mountains, but things were even worse out there. I was the only one that made it back. I never saw the rest of the group again."

Ice tilted her head and narrowed her gaze. "You're the only one who made it out of the entire group? Bullshit."

"No, listen. The Wyans betrayed us. Didn't you see that? They set us up. After Davis and Peter left, they never trusted us again. They made a deal with the Night Chasers. They knew our every move. I only made it out because of Arjen. You know how he felt about me. He tried to save me, and Admani, but she got poisoned by some nasty creature in the mountains."

Ice was slowly shaking her head but didn't reply.

"I'm telling the truth." Lana dared a step forward. "Don't you think Robin would've made every effort to take his own son back? And your sister? What about the kids? Of course, he would've taken them."

"Where's Avani then?" Isolde's glare was bordering on demonic. "I know she made it because she was with me. I didn't see her at your little press conference. And don't tell me—"

Lana waved a hand. "They've probably got her in some lab. You really think they want to tell that to the crowd? 'Don't worry, we did find a baby to do some more testing on.'"

Ice stepped forward, unamused. "I want to see her. I hid out in that hole, half dead, trying to protect her until her mother got back, and now you're telling me she's dead? I want to see Avani, and she probably wants to see me. A familiar face."

Lana shrugged. "So, take it up with Visser."

Ice considered pressing her more, then said, "Okay," and went down the small hall, heading for the door. "I'll do that. But if I find out any of this isn't what you say…"

"Spare me the tough talk."

The women spent a long moment locking eyes. Lana with her peachy skin, straight hair and commanding eyes met Isolde's brown gaze, midnight dark coloring, and shaved head with the twirled-up bun on top.

Isolde broke it and opened the door. "Enjoy your pregnancy. It's a good thing you won't be the only one out here. I have a feeling you're going to be a terrible mother."

Chapter Two

There was a forest at the base of Ahuna Mons on Ceres. It grew in a sporadic tangle of trees and shrubbery. It was a trial plot for anything and everything they'd engineered to grow, to make sure the specimens would integrate well with other plants before being introduced to the Belt Forest. The result was little more than a jungle of organized chaos with the mountains standing tall behind.

In the shade of a mountain ash/cypress tree hybrid, a rectangular house blended into its surroundings. Made from the same wood, it bridged the gap from the giant abomination with its confused leaves to a jagged row of bushes. There were no windows in the front. For the casual passer-by, whom there were none of on this side of the mountain, it looked like just another Frankensteined timber.

Inside the soundproofed walls, Zane sat watching his Armageddon partner, once again under lock and key. She marched to the bolted door, then back past the couch. She stopped at the barred windows, looking deep into the forest behind them, and imagined running until she could run no more.

Marlow slammed her fists against the bars, hot tears burning down her cheeks. "They took her. I left so they could never get ahold of her again and look now." She turned, swinging her open hands around the minimalistic room.

"Mar." Zane leaned his head back in a lazy fashion. "They were always going to take her. You knew that as soon as we got on the ship."

"But the plan—" Marlow stopped next to the couch. "We were supposed to play it cool. Just get along, and when we got back, they'd let their guard down. Then…"

"Well, it didn't work that way, did it?"

"All 'cause *you* couldn't hold it together."

Zane sat up and turned to look at her. "I was…*we* were almost killed. We lost everyone—most everyone. I just didn't—" Zane broke into tears, holding his face in his hands and weeping.

Marlow leaned over the couch, putting a hand on his shoulder. "I'm sorry." She held the other to her mouth, trying to hold back the sobs. "I couldn't hold it together either. That ship did something to us."

"It wasn't just the ship." Zane shook his head. "It was everything we lost. Wyan was supposed to be it, our stroke of good luck. Instead, look, we're like a death stroke for everyone we get close to. Peter, Percy…"

Marlow nodded in agreement. "Rami," she said aloud, then thought, *Wesley*. Even though his death didn't have anything to do with her.

Zane kept on. "And we haven't seen the others. Everyone you came back from the dark side with, where do you think they are?"

"Visser says they're dead."

"But you—"

"I know, Zane, but you saw into the cryo-room, not me."

"It was hard to see. We know Ice and Lana came back, but I didn't see Arjen or the others."

"No way Visser would leave his own son." Marlow absentmindedly felt the scar on her abdomen, then found her eyes drifting to the bars on the windows. *No*, she thought. *There's no telling what that man would do. Something inside him had been broken a long time ago.*

~ * ~

Robin, Oscar, and Kaia, the judges of the Belt, met in the government building on Ceres. They reviewed a case brought to them by Maynard who'd been sent to wait outside.

Kaia met Robin's eyes with a hard look. Her braids hung down around her and there were dark shadows in her gaze. Robin broke away, talking aloud to the room.

"How are we supposed to defend her?" he asked. "The deal was, I get your daughters back whatever it takes, and they stay out of trouble.

Now, I'm sorry about Admani. I truly am, but you'll remember who tried to stop that first trip from ever happening."

"It wasn't about the trip," said Kaia. "You know that. It was about the choice. We don't run a dictatorship here."

"Maybe we should at this point," said Oscar. He caught a look from the other two judges. "I'm saying, all this free will, all these choices have led to our division. We need to pull back together."

"You may need a history lesson," said Kaia, "but a dictatorship is not how you pull together."

Oscar shook his head at her. "That's not what I meant, and you know it."

"Both of you, please." Robin raised his arms. "Let's discuss the matter at hand. An assault on Lana Royal by Isolde Gammen."

~ * ~

They didn't hear the hum of the Rock-Hopper until it landed outside their window. Marlow was up first, followed by Zane. They watched as Admani's old partner, Mateo Ramirez, stepped out onto the forest floor. Next came a woman they didn't recognize and an obvious security guard carrying a taser armed and ready.

Marlow whimpered when she saw Avani in the woman's arms. She smiled and talked to the baby, *Marlow's* baby, as they walked up.

The guard reached the house first, commanding them to step away from the door, then the party entered. Marlow wanted to rush them and take Avani back, but she knew she'd get tased if she made any sudden advancements. Instead, she stood biting her bottom lip as Mateo smiled.

"Hey guys. It's been a while." He sounded as if they were long lost friends reunited during a trip through town.

Marlow stared at the woman, then tore her eyes away long enough to say, "Your partner's dead."

Mateo's smile drooped into a prepared frown. "I heard. It's terrible. Admani was one of a kind."

Marlow reached out her arms. "Can I have my baby now?"

"Right, yes." Mateo motioned to the woman. "This is my wife,

Layla. If you remember when we first met, I told you about our son, Antonio."

"He's one of the feral children," said Zane.

"Yes, and with the help of you three, we were going to try to solve that, along with potential future pregnancies." Mateo shook his head. "But then you guys took off. That put a major damper on our research."

"Sorry to have inconvenienced you," Marlow said. "Avani, please."

The baby struggled in Layla's arms, trying to get to her mother. Mateo held up a hand to wait.

"Please, guys. I'm trying to work with you. We've had enough tragedy. Can you just cooperate this time? We're so close with the research."

It was evident he could see Marlow was paying him no mind. He sighed and waved Layla to hand over Avani. Marlow took her with a great wave of relief, cuddling her chubby cheeks against her own.

Mateo gave them their moment, then said, "She was able to help a child of the Belt. Not ours, mind you, but with the cord blood we were able to introduce the correct developmental gene in a newborn before it was too late." He watched Marlow coo at Avani like he wasn't a few feet away, talking directly to her. "We need to do better than one for one, though. In the next pregnancy, we hope to have more time to trace and replicate the gene. Then a simple shot would do it."

He crossed his fingers, squinting dark eyebrows that Layla probably found attractive but made Marlow want to strap a thick piece of Duct Tape over and pull free. "Hopefully for ours."

"Next pregnancy?" Marlow looked up, just processing what he'd said.

Mateo's smile returned. "Glad to know you're paying attention."

"You said Avani helped someone, a baby?"

"Yes, your old teacher's baby. Hopefully she can help more. Another pregnancy would tell us best if we…" Mateo went on, but Marlow and Zane were facing each other, saying the same name, "Tiffany."

Chapter Three

The Motherhood Initiative Village was buzzing with activity. Though, Lana hoped that wouldn't be the official name. The apartments were filling up one by one with freshly fertilized females. Lana cracked a half smile, picturing those words on a sign above the apartments, as she went out the sliding back door. It had been repaired and reinforced since her former teammate busted in for her violent interrogation.

Lana understood. Isolde came to Wyan with her sister, promised a new life and returned alone. If she could keep her anger there; they could work it out. But if she kept asking about the kids, she was going to find herself in more trouble. Lana was undecided on them. When the time came, did she want either of them back on Wyan with her? Zane was resourceful, generally easy to get along with, but lacked the fire that Marlow had. The fire that would also be the main root of her problems. Lana could afford to stay undecided. The next year would make the choice for her.

Behind the apartments was the gathering area. A circle of reclining chairs faced each other like a posh A.A. meeting. Tree branches extended over them, thinning as they stopped just short of the apartments. Two women were hanging multi-colored, paper lanterns from the branches. One was standing on a chair, stretching out, the other stabilizing her with a concerned expression. Darcy.

"Hey," said Lana.

"Oh, hey." Darcy gripped the chair the best she could.

"You any taller?" the other woman called back. "This one's—" She stopped when she saw it was Lana.

Lana eyed the chair. "We could probably get a ladder."

The woman jumped down, still holding the last lantern. "Eh, that's okay. Just trying to spruce it up back here." She motioned at the circle of chairs. "This is where we're going to talk about our *feelings*. We may as well make it a nice place to sit."

Lana admired the setting. It would be perfect. *Perfect* if it were on Wyan. Not this floating space object.

"Good work." She stuck out a hand. "I'm Lana."

The woman chuckled. "Oh, I know who you are." She met her hand. "Zelda."

Her haircut bordered on a dirty brown mullet, and her clothes signified she'd just come from work. Wherever that was.

A few others straggled over, and an older woman urged them to sit. She held a tablet and clicked away at it.

Lana narrowed her eyes at the woman, sliding in next to Darcy and Zelda.

The woman gave a warm smile. "Looks like we're all here. I'm Dr. Ianesso and you're here because you've volunteered to be part of the Motherhood Initiative." She brushed a long tangle of gray hair over her shoulder, her face holding a sheen like she'd just put on lotion. "For these next nine months, you'll be together, sharing the joys and pains of pregnancy. I want you to get to know one another, support each other, and be prepared to be part of history." She tapped on her tablet. "Now, I'll be running these weekly meetings to check in with all of you, to make sure we all stay the course. "Why don't we start by going around the circle and giving a little background?" She scanned the faces. "Darcy, would you like to start us off?"

Darcy gave a shy smile, adjusted the hem of her dress and began, "Okay, I'm Darcy Crouch. Some of you probably already met my dad."

A few laughs broke out at the mention of the Doctor who performed the procedures to give the village its name. Whatever that name was going to be. "I work in clothing which is…" She looked off, then smacked her lips and made a face. "Right down there now." Darcy pointed down the path opposite from the medical facility. "I keep forgetting. We just got the water hooked up. It's been nice. If you need anything fixed or taken out," She widened her hands around her body, "let me know."

"Thank you, Darcy." Dr. Ianesso took over. "She'll be helping with all your maternity clothing needs, it sounds like. Who's next?"

A black woman with violet extensions raised a hand.

"I'll go. I'm Erika Johns. I work with the 'Panel. I'll be making sure we all hit our nutrient needs."

Zelda went next. She was on a further branch of one of the founding families. "…and you bunch of mothers keep drinking it, so we keep processing it. I'm glad we have a plant on this rock so I can keep it close to home. Am I the only one who hates taking a 'Hopper everywhere?"

Others agreed with her, then the rest shared their stories. There were six in all, not including the doctor, who Lana still didn't quite trust. All the other ladies brought something to the table. They all served a purpose on the Belt, but they could serve a purpose elsewhere too. Lana knew it. When she took her turn, saved for last, which felt purposeful, she fought the urge to say, "I'm Lana Royal. I will be your leader, and together, we'll conquer a new land."

~ * ~

When the meeting ended, Lana snuck off to her room. She kept an eye out for Dr. Ianesso to leave. She was the only one who didn't live on New Pangaea. She'd obviously been commissioned by someone in the government. Lana didn't have to guess it would be Robin or Oscar, but likely Robin, to keep an eye on her. She heard the Rock-Hopper fly off and casually strolled back to the circle of chairs. Darcy and Erika were listening to one of Zelda's stories. She was going off about a water main break from early in her career, and how she tried to block the flow with her hands. She was animated, gruff, and perfect for Lana's plans. She took a chair across from Zelda and watched the show.

"Luckily I didn't try my mouth." Zelda busted out laughing, egging on her audience. "Though, my mom would've said I could handle it." She pointed at her lips. "You know, big mouth and all." She glanced at Lana and shifted in her seat. "So, the queen of the skies came back to join us?"

Lana shrugged. "Sounded like a good story."

"It was." Erika crossed her legs and adjusted a bright, blue dress she wore, "but I'd like to hear more about that place you've been living in the past couple years. What'd you call it?"

"Wyan." Lana leaned forward. "What do you wanna know?"

"I don't know. You just made it sound so…exotic. So beautiful."

"It is." Lana looked up at the branches that hung over them. "Like this. This is nice, but it's not the same. There're trees as wide as your entire apartment and not genetically altered to be that way. There's a breeze that comes through the village bringing the smell of the wood, the soil, the water. You can't—" She bent down and tore off a handful of the grass they'd laid down to give the apartments a less desolate feel. She smelled it and wrinkled her nose, tossing the blades into the air. "Smells like a chemical. Not real. Not like Wyan." She leaned back in her chair.

Erika raised her eyebrows. "Sounds like you miss it. You never told us why you left." She looked around, lowering her voice, "Did they make you?"

Lana smiled a knowing smile. "No. I was betrayed by a couple men that couldn't handle a woman being in charge. Ever met one of those?"

"Uh huh." Erika bobbed her head in unison with her words.

Zelda chimed in, "It's hard to find one that doesn't have that problem."

"They're not all like that," Darcy said. "I know some—"

"Honey," Zelda lowered her eyes at Darcy, "your dad don't count."

Erika giggled. "Got that right."

Lana could see Darcy was about one comment away from heading in for the night. "I know what she's saying. There were men that worked with me, side by side. Fought with me. I wouldn't be alive if not for them. But things didn't end how I'd imagined it."

"Do you ever think you'll go back?" Erika's eyes oozed with wonder.

Lana scanned the women, two of them excitedly hanging on her words, the other, intrigued but afraid. "Talk like that would just be treasonous." Lana smirked. "Dr. Ianesso reminded us after I shared my story, remember?"

That was when Lana knew her true purpose was to keep an eye on things and prevent discussions like the very one they were having.

"It's just talk," said Zelda. "No harm in it."

"Right." Erika pulled her head back, looking around. "Just a bunch of pregnant ladies shooting the shit."

Lana nodded, standing slowly. "It's true, and I'm always up for talking about life out there. Just, let's not bring these things up around the good doctor, okay? I'm afraid she wouldn't see it the same way."

Erika and Zelda quickly agreed, while Darcy sat with slightly widened eyes, staring at the spot in the grass Lana had plucked.

"Darcy?" said Lana. "All good?"

"What? Yeah." Darcy forced a smile. "Just getting tired I think." She stood. "See you ladies tomorrow." And she headed for her apartment.

Chapter Four

Marlow rode in the back of a Rock-Hopper next to a security guard. It was unlike the others as the viewing window was only in the front. She understood why and it infuriated her even more. No one knew she was alive, and they intended to keep it that way. Worse was, the woman she'd been through hell with, was out there somewhere. Lana knew the truth, but so far, it seemed like she wasn't saying anything. What about Ice? Marlow was desperate to see anyone but another branch of her captors. She needed a familiar face that wasn't Zane.

Mateo was a scientist, but so far, reasoning with him wasn't working.

"You think Admani went because she was *bored*?" Marlow said to the back of Mateo's head. "She was guilty for what you two did to me. She told me as soon as we got there. She wanted a chance to do something that would make her mother proud. Don't you want the same?"

Mateo's voice was even. "We didn't *do* anything to you. You were already pregnant when you got to us. Remember?"

"But you knew. You kept the secret and locked me up in that little house, thinking I had free will all along."

Mateo turned around. "You did have free will. All we wanted was the baby. The whole Belt was counting on that, and instead, you took off. Admani would've seen it clearer if she had a child like mine."

Marlow huffed and sat back. "So, what's this trip about then? If I'm such a secret, why do I get to leave our hole in the forest? You gonna experiment on me some more?"

"I'm going to give us the chance that you tried to steal from us."

He looked forward as the ship started to slow, then motioned to the security guard. Marlow would've put up a better fight if her hands weren't tied, but soon felt the needle in her neck. As the inside of the ship started to go out of focus, she saw Mateo's face over the seat. He eyed her with pity, then said, "I'm going to give Layla the baby she's always wanted."

~ * ~

A few days later, Marlow and Zane were lounging in chairs they'd dragged outside. There was a fence, not unlike the one they had at the back of the Bride of Christ Church they'd lived at on Earth. Only, this one wasn't for keeping others out, but for keeping them in. Avani entertained them by rolling from place to place. She would reach the edge of the blanket Marlow laid out for her, then look up with a mischievous smile, knowing her mother didn't want her rolling onto the forest floor and picking up leaves and sticks to cram into her mouth.

"Uh ah."

Marlow waved a finger and watched the baby with Zane's eyes squint in delight as she thrust her arm, sending her crunching across fallen leaves. Marlow sighed and pushed herself out of her chair, picking up Avani and brushing off the onesie she'd already spit up on.

A Rock-Hopper landed out front, though they couldn't see it under the cover of the forest on their side. Footsteps sounded alongside the house and Marlow watched, bouncing the baby as she did.

Robin Visser appeared, holding a baby, with a guard behind carrying a big box. They stopped outside the fence. Robin couldn't hide his smile and Marlow couldn't help but see Arjen in it. She felt a wave of remorse. Arjen was the one that saved her on Earth. He lied to her, set her up for a pregnancy and convinced her it was her decision, but then he made it right, giving her another opportunity. She wanted to talk to him, have a drink with him and take the politician out of his voice after he'd had a couple.

"Who's that?" Zane stood next to her.

"My grandchild. Wes Junior." Robin kissed the baby on the head. He was beaming with pride, with love for the child, as he greeted the people he kept locked up around the clock, sanctioned experiments on, and impregnated against their will. Marlow found it amazing how he could separate the two.

"Why is he here?" asked Marlow. "We're not running a day care."

"Well, it's my day to play Grandpa. I thought we could have a little playdate. At the moment, Wes and Avani are the only non-feral children in the Belt. Thanks to you."

"A playdate?" Marlow's mouth hung open, shaking her head, then she stepped back. "Well, come on in then. We don't have anything else going on. We're prisoners, remember?"

Robin ignored the comment, stepping to the electronic lock on the gate to their fence. He raised his data-pad, then paused. "We're not going to have any trouble, are we?" He looked over the Earthling's faces, then motioned to the guard behind him, still holding the box. "You'll notice I haven't been bringing Maynard out with me. Mateo, either. After your little *incident* on the Knox, I felt it best if you two stayed away from each other."

"I'm sorry," said Marlow. "Are you trying to say you're doing me a favor? I couldn't hear it through all your bullshit."

Zane grabbed her shoulder and pulled her back before she could say more. "We're fine." He said, "A playdate will be fine."

"Good."

Robin unlocked the door, stepping in first. The guard followed, bumping the gate closed behind them. It locked on its own.

"What's in the box?" asked Zane. "Christmas presents?"

"Close." Robin motioned for the guard to set it down. "Take a look."

Zane opened the top with hesitation, then his eyes lit up. "My suit." He pulled out his pin striped suit made for him by Carol, the dead wife of Captain Williams. Marlow peered in next. Her suit was folded just below Zane's. She'd barely gotten a chance to wear it before she was too pregnant to do so. Then it was left behind when they fled the Belt. She still remembered the night she wore it to movie night at Wesley and Tiffany's house. How he'd complemented it, then turned bright red when Tiffany came back from the bathroom much quicker than he'd expected. It wasn't long after that he kissed her and then, of course, his death. Now his child sat on the blanket she'd prepared, staring up at her with blue eyes and a sweet giggle as his tyrant of a grandfather tickled him.

Marlow set Avani down so she could get back to rolling around. Zane pulled out more treasures.

"My first stool." He held up a slightly off-centered footstool. It was solid wood but painted a bright orange. He paused, looking at Wes Junior, bouncing on his diapered butt while Robin held his arms. "Your dad taught me how to make this. I swear his always turned out way better than this."

Marlow rummaged through other clothes of hers that hadn't made the cut. There were a few of her favorite leaves plucked from the banyan trees behind the medical facility when she used to take her walks. Next, she found a deck of cards Marlin left with her. She held it, feeling her stomach knot up, remembering how the claws dug into him, pulling him into the darkness of the cellar, the door slamming, his last scream. Then she'd run. For the sake of Avani, she took off, leaving her traveling card buddy to a brutal death trillions of miles from home. She tucked the cards in her pocket, steeling herself to keep the tears at bay, when Zane pulled out the next item and she burst out crying. Zane pursed his lips, slowly nodding as he held out Honey's nest.

~ * ~

The playdate ended up being a minor success. The children didn't exactly play together, but they did keep one another entertained as they rolled in opposite directions, sometimes into each other in passing. Robin was cordial and delightful. In any other scenario, it would've been a fully pleasant afternoon. Only, as he picked up his grandson and the guard opened the gate, reality crashed down. They were still slaves of the Belt, locked away in a hodge-podge forest to continue breeding until they died, or worse, couldn't produce offspring anymore. Then what? Marlow wondered. When the time came that she was no longer useful, what would they do with her?

"I want you to know," Robin was safely locked on the outside of the gate, "that you did this." He patted Wesley's back. "Because of you, we were able to save my grandchild, and I never got to thank you. Just think of the others you're going to help."

Marlow's face tightened. She wanted to say a lot of things, but, "Go fuck yourself" was at the top of her list, so she kept her mouth shut. She wanted another playdate. They were so desperate for company, she'd take her enslaver, his grandchild, and the mute guard. Was that considered Stockholm Syndrome? She thought probably not.

The Rock-Hopper left the base of the mountain and Marlow picked up Zane's stool. The wood felt solid despite its crooked design. "Perfect," she said, and went inside to get to work.

Chapter Five

Gilbert looked across the play area he guarded. The feral kids, some as old as twenty, found rocks and logs to climb, play on, and generally entertain themselves with. It made his job easier. They were seeing progress. Not the kind they wanted, but the kids learned to live with each other. There were almost no fights to break up. All Gilbert had to do was oversee the play area while Tiffany Visser continued to try to teach them, and transport them, with security, for lab testing. It was way better than his last job of TechBubble maintenance. His only mistake on that job had cost two people their lives. If it weren't for the Belt being so short on workers, he wasn't sure what they would've done with him.

As he gazed up at the banyan trees and Ahuna Mons in the distance, he leaned on the back of the government building with a sigh. Gilbert understood why others didn't want the job of watching the children, but it fit him just right. All he had left to do was get them in for the night. He checked his data-pad and pushed himself off the wall. It was showtime.

"Hey guys." Gilbert waved a hand in the air frantically. "The birds are coming. Get inside." He projected a soundtrack of crows cawing to a speaker, and one by one the kids looked to the sky in terror. Some ran, almost tripping over themselves to get to the door.

"No shoving." Gilbert ushered them in, taking a false, fearful look around as they went.

He knew Tiffany was opposed to scare tactics, but it always got him the quickest results. The area was clear as the last one made it inside. He didn't need any do-gooders telling on him for his methods. He killed the crows and locked the door. The last step was the headcount. Gilbert checked the rooms and ticked off eighteen. He paused, remembering the couple Tiffany brought for testing earlier. Had she mentioned needing to keep them overnight? Were they with her when she came back? It happened from time to time and he usually was on the ball with it but today he was drawing a blank. He did a recount of the rooms, landing on eighteen again. He checked his data-pad, considering messaging Tiffany, who would be annoyed at his poor memory, then saw a message from Gwen, his girlfriend of the last two weeks. She was asking how soon he'd be off work. Gilbert smiled, knowing what that meant. The first month was always the best for his relationships. He left the room, and replied, *Right now.*

~ * ~

Zane's footstool made a cracking sound as it struck the wall. Marlow pulled it away, seeing a nearly perfect split down the middle. "Damnit," she said. "What did you make this out of?"

Zane bounced Avani on his hip, pacing nervously in front of the couch Marlow had pushed away from the wall.

"It wasn't meant for bludgeoning your way through a wall, Mar. Why don't you try the fence?"

Marlow looked up, sweat pouring down her face despite only making a small dent in the wall. "Because it will alert them. You've seen the lock system they have for all the entry points. I'm sure there's some kind of alarm, camera or something."

"That's a stretch. Remember what Visser said to that guard? They can't have a camera. I think it's so no one else could intercept the feed and find out about us."

Marlow stood, groaning as she did. "I'm just…there's no way they plan for us to go through the wall."

Zane narrowed his eyes at her. "Yes. I'm sure you're right about that."

She cocked the footstool back and swung with all her might. It exploded into pieces of legs and top as it hit the wall. She began giggling maniacally, perched on her knees as Zane came over. He put a hand on her shoulder.

"Maybe you should take a break."

Marlow shook her head, still laughing like a lunatic. Her finger raised to a split in the wall. She pulled on Zane to help herself stand, then stepped back and kicked the damaged wall. They backed up and admired her work.

"It's working." Marlow smiled at Zane who had his head tilted sideways.

"Is it?"

"Just…move."

Marlow pushed him aside and lined up another kick. She struck the wall hard, sending a shock up her body.

Zane looked on, worried, as she unleashed another blow. The crack was growing, but slowly, and he wondered which would break first, the wall or his friend.

After a few more hits, Zane drifted to the window, unable to watch as Avani's face grew concerned at the pure rage fueling her mother.

"It's okay." Zane patted the baby's back. "Should we go play on the blanket some more?" As he started for the door, he caught movement outside the window. Zane craned his neck back to see the security guard, usually with Robin, at the gate. He was tapping on his data pad to unlock it.

"Shit. *Shit*." Zane froze for a second, looking for a place for Avani. He dumped her in her crib in the corner of the room to surprised protests from their child, then got down and lowered his shoulder into the couch.

"What's happening?" Marlow watched him with intense eyes.

"Visitors." Zane pushed. "Help."

Marlow joined him as they heard the gate open outside.

~ * ~

As he closed himself inside the fence, Desi unhooked his taser from his belt. It felt silly. The Earthlings had never shown any violent tendencies since he'd been around them. He hardly knew why he escorted Robin for his visits, only that his Boss, Maynard, had a history with the girl and it wasn't a good one. He was told to never let his guard down, so even on a simple delivery, he stayed ready. The case of NutrientPanels in his right hand felt heavy and it was the first thing he'd throw if they tried anything. Desi took a deep breath, looking around the small, fenced-in area. He was clearly alone as he approached the door. He used the case of 'Panels to tap a few times, then backed away. There was no answer at first, so he called out, "Hello. I've got your 'Panels for the next few days." He tapped again, then heard movement and a muffled, "Sorry." From the other side.

Zane answered looking a bit frantic. He was smiling at Desi. He'd never smiled at him before. Desi narrowed his eyes, feeling the button on his taser with his thumb, one quick flick would be all it took to take down the skinny guy in front of him. He glanced over Zane's shoulder. Marlow sat on the couch with a blanket obscuring most of her body. She looked more out of sorts than Zane, sweaty and flustered. There was crying from the baby. Desi knew something was off. "Everything okay?" he asked.

"Oh, um." Zane looked back at the couch. "Avani's just been fighting her nap, you know?" He made an exaggerated laugh. "She's just trying to…feed her." He stepped to the side and motioned. "Did you need to come in, or…?"

Desi remembered Maynard's story, how he'd choked her to within an inch of her life for the cut she gave him. How he would've done worse if not for Robin. Then he thought about the limp Robin walked with and how the story was that it'd been given to him by Zane. He shivered and thrust out the case.

"Your 'Panels are here." He stepped back when Zane took them, keeping one eye on Marlow for any sudden movements. "Any questions?"

"Questions?" repeated Zane.

"No? Good then." Desi backed toward the gate. He managed to deactivate the lock and snuck through, closing it in a quick motion. Zane waved at him and closed the door to the house. Desi wiped the cold sweat from his forehead on his sleeve. They were plotting something. Likely to jump him. He would advise Maynard and Robin to not send him alone again.

~ * ~

Marlow waited to get the signal from Zane. She was sweating worse than when she was kicking the wall. The blanket and squirming child that was in no mood to breastfeed were not helping. She had the pieces of the stool poking into her sides and lap.

"Kinda can't breathe over here," she said.

"Just another minute." Zane opened the door and stepped out to the fence. He came back and slammed it behind him. "Okay, we're clear. I saw him flying off."

Marlow kicked the blanket off, pieces of wood hitting the floor as she stood with Avani. She held her out to Zane.

"Seriously?" said Zane. "Back to kicking the wall?"

Marlow just nodded and pushed Avani into his chest.

~ * ~

Tiffany got Wesley back into his crib, then sat on the edge of her bed, sticking her splayed fingers into her hair. He never graced her with a full night sleep but some nights it felt like he was making every effort to destroy her REM cycles one at a time. She looked at her data-pad, checking into the child center notes she shared with Gilbert. She hated micro-managing him and had purposely taken the night off from checking up on him. But it wasn't technically night anymore, it was early morning.

The notes Gilbert entered were short and pointless. He rarely documented more than a few details about scuffles and how they were resolved. That was the case for the previous night along with the headcount. She blinked and rubbed her eyes, confirming what she saw, before she called him in a panic.

~ * ~

"Mar, you have to stop." Zane stood, hours later as Marlow's leg disappeared inside the wall. With each strike, he'd hear the resulting pain in her voice. "We all need to rest and…" He looked down at their baby. "We kinda *can't* with you doing this."

Marlow rested her hands on her thighs, her hair in loose, sweaty strands matted to her face. "I can't. I've made too much progress and we can't hide it now if they come back."

Zane knew it too but was powerless to do much about it. He'd tried to take a turn a few hours earlier, but his recently healed legs were no good for kicking through the solid wood of the wall and his stool was busted to pieces.

Marlow groaned and hopped away from the wall after another strike. She'd made it through to the second and final panel but was having no luck from there.

"There's something on the other side. I can see a little daylight but it's like trying to break through a mountain."

She stared into the gap she'd made, and Zane joined her. Avani's head drooped on his shoulder.

"You can't really hit it from another angle, can you?" He spoke low, backing away, stroking the baby's head.

"No," Marlow shook her head, tears forming on her cheeks, "but if I move spots, I've got to start all over." Her breaths were shallow. "I don't know if I can…"

"I know, but we've tried everything. The stool is dead. We can't get enough momentum on the couch to do any real damage. They haven't left us with any other tools."

Marlow sighed, holding her shaky hands to her temples, then stepped outside. Zane rocked Avani for another minute, then laid her in her crib. He joined Marlow outside if only to not have to look at the wall anymore. It wasn't going to be a fun explanation to Visser, and he wondered what the repercussions would be.

Marlow sat in one of the chairs, looking deep into the forest. Zane did the same in the other. He waited to hear the hum of the Rock-Hopper landing and their next punishment to be laid out. Instead, they sat for what felt like an hour without speaking. The silence of the baby and the forest was soothing after the day they'd had.

Zane felt his head nod to his chest, then flinched awake. He looked to Marlow, who'd scooted down in the chair softly sleeping in an uncomfortable pose. Zane considered moving her inside to the mattress but figured as soon as she was awake, she'd be back at it inside. He let her rest. The door was open for him to hear Avani if she cried. Zane leaned his head back. His eyes were just closing when he heard the snapping of a twig. In the forest ahead, Zane saw movement, just shadows at his distance, but it made him think. Ceres didn't have wild animals. That meant the only thing moving out there could be people. He stood and went to the fence to get a better look. The shadows closed in, darting behind one tree, then the next.

"Mar," he whispered. "Look."

She shook awake. "What?" And saw him staring off.

After a groan to get out of the chair, she joined him at the fence. There was a grunting sound only a few trees away. Marlow smashed her face against the fence. "Hello? Who's there?"

A head popped out from one of the branches of the tangled tree nearest to the fence. Marlow immediately recognized it as the feral kid they'd found up in the banyan tree the day Sam, the crazy astronaut, let them all out. She couldn't remember his name, but it seemed that he recognized her as well. He approached with caution, his eyes darting in every direction, obviously looking for those that kept him captive.

"Friend." Marlow patted her chest. "Remember?"

The boy reached the fence and pointed at her. "You. Friend."

"Yes. Remember? We tried to help you. I'm sorry you've been locked up again." She saw movement behind him. "Wait. How many of you are there?"

The boy waved over a girl. They both looked between eighteen and twenty. She may have been the one they saw get hog-tied on that same day, but it was hard to tell. Her hair was wild and full of leaves.

"Friend," the boy said to her, pointing to Marlow, then he looked up at the sprawling fence. "Take from family?" He rattled the chain links.

Marlow and Zane shared a look. "Yes," she said, then pointed, "You help?"

The boy shook the fence and shrugged. "Too strong."

Marlow's face lit up. She pointed around the corner of the house. "Come around that way. I'll show you."

It took a good deal of explaining, but eventually, the feral boy and girl were on the other side of the wall, peering through the crack Marlow made.

"Is something there?" Marlow knocked on the wall which was more of a thud. "I can't get through."

The boy's voice was muffled on the other side. "Big rock."

"Oh, I knew it," she said to Zane, then turned back. "Can you move it? Push…out of the way?"

"We try."

There was grunting from both kids for the next minute or so, then nothing. Marlow tried to see anything through the crack but there was just dark forest. Worse was the silence.

"Do you think they left?" Zane was behind her holding Avani.

"I don't…" Marlow waved at him. "Go check outside."

As she finished her sentence, there was a cracking a few inches from her face. Marlow pulled her head out of the hole. Another hit came, splinters of wood falling inward. After a few more, there was a hole the size of her head with a feral boy staring at her through it.

"Yes." Marlow pumped a fist. "You did it." She squatted to look up through the hole on her side. "Bigger?" She widened her hands.

The boy nodded and went to work. He was using a rock the size of a basketball, breaking off chunks of wood at a time. When the hole looked big enough, she looked back at Zane.

"We need to find help. All it takes is the right person seeing us and this," she motioned around the house, "is all over."

"I know, but where?"

"I'm pretty sure the shipyard is on the other side of the mountain. If we don't find a good option there, we could try to find Kaia at the government building a little further down."

Zane bounced Avani. "But how far is that, Mar?"

"I don't know. A few miles through the mountainside I think." She pursed her lips, looking at her little family, then leaned in and kissed each of them. "Let me go. I'll be as fast as I can. We can't afford to go slow with her. They're likely looking for the kids already. If they come here…"

Zane was uncertain but nodded. "Okay." He kissed her forehead.

"Hurry but be careful."

"Right." She slipped through the first opening. "Can you give me a boost?"

Zane stuck his knee through so she could step off it and reach the higher hole the kids made. Marlow pushed through, pulling herself on top of a boulder, the thing she'd tried to kick her way through hours before. The size of it made her laugh as she jumped off. The fact the kids even tried to move it was humorous. They waited on either side of her, watching her face for cues.

"We've got to go find help."

Marlow started toward the trees. She could map her directions by the view of Ahuna Mons as soon as they got to a thinner point in the forest. When she looked back, the children waited, hesitant to go back into the forest. "Please." Marlow waved. If her calculations were correct, the front side of the house led toward the ocean. It would be a dead end for them, potentially a drowning hazard for the kids and worst of all, unpopulated. The only ones that would be looking for anyone there would be their captors. She waved in rapid succession, pleading the kids to follow, when they all heard it, the Rock-Hopper flying toward them. The kids finally moved further under the canopy as the 'Hopper touched down on the other side of the house.

"We've got to move," she whispered, pointing. "They will lock you up again."

Marlow decided that was their last warning and took off running. Within ten seconds of dodging roots and jumping over branches, she heard the kids next to her, fear on their faces as they followed deeper into Frankenstein's Forest.

Chapter Six

Oscar paced in his house on Ceres, staring out a second-floor window at the mountain range. He felt a weight on him that he was getting too old to carry. His father made it look so easy, even until his death in his nineties. Even Robin, after all he went through with the retrieval of the Earthlings, carried it better. Oscar just wanted it to go back to the good days of his thirties, when Mateo was young, the Belt was thriving, and he didn't have a feral grandson yet. He was tired of the constant struggle. He sat at his desk, propping up his head as he called Robin.

"Visser," Robin answered.

"A couple kids got out last night."

"Damn it." There was a short pause, Robin's breath huffed out on the other end. "Does Kaia know?"

"She's the one who told me, but listen, they haven't found them in the usual places. She's thinking of searching the mountains."

"She what?" Robin lowered his voice. "You told her no, right?"

"I told her we'd have Maynard's team on it in case things took a turn we didn't like. It's a couple of the older kids, too. So, she's accepted it for now, but you've gotta—"

"I'll get him on it. Just keep me up to date and keep her away from that mountain." Robin hung up before Oscar could reply.

~ * ~

The security team of Maynard and Desi landed at the house tucked into the side of the forest. Maynard was calm despite the circumstances. He turned to Desi and pointed a finger an inch from his nose.

"Our job is to check on the Earthlings first. After that, we'll see."

"But the message said—"

"I know what the message said." Maynard ran his palm up the front of his hair, making sure it was still pointing directly to the sky. "You've gotta be able to read between the lines on these things. We secure the house…this side of the mountain so nobody else comes looking. The kids will find their way back on their own. You clear?"

"Yes, Sir."

The men walked around the house, tasers ready. They let themselves in the fence as Zane came out, closing the door behind him and patting the baby on the back.

"Oh, hey," he said. "I was just going to let her roll around while Marlow takes a nap. She's been a struggle lately." He sat Avani on her butt on the blanket while holding her arms. "We got our 'Panel already, remember?"

"See anything interesting lately?" asked Maynard. "Either of you?"

"Interesting?"

"Any action out here? Out of the ordinary?"

Zane took his time thinking. "Huh, no. I mean, nothing ever happens out here you know."

"What about Marlow?" Maynard crossed his arms.

"Like I said," Zane was starting to sweat, "she's napping inside."

"I'll ask her myself then." Maynard started for the door.

"Wait." Zane stood, leaving Avani on her back. "We heard a sound toward the front of the house." He approached Maynard. "You didn't see anything when you landed, did you?"

Maynard frowned at him. "See what?"

"Not sure," Zane was talking too fast. "It's just, we don't hear much out here except for your visits, or Robin's, you know? So, we thought maybe it was something else out that way."

Maynard gave a look to Desi and for a second, contemplated sending him to go take a look, then said, "Let me just check on your girlfriend inside a minute. Haven't seen much of her since we landed. I'm sure she misses me."

When his hand gripped the doorknob, Zane grabbed his shoulder.

"I really think—" Was all Zane could get out before Maynard

swung an elbow back into his stomach. Zane doubled over and Maynard gave him a shove to send him to the ground.

"Don't ever touch me." Maynard signaled at Desi. "Watch him. I'm gonna check on her."

Desi nodded and stood with his taser ready as Avani rolled off the blanket. She made it into the dirt, picking up leaves on her onesie as Zane lay on his side.

Maynard burst in the house. He first noticed the blanket hanging on the wall over the couch. Then, the unnatural lump in the mattress. He walked over and stomped on it, half wishing it was Marlow underneath the blanket, but found it to just be pillows and clothes. He tore off the covers, growled and went to the couch next. The blanket came down with little effort. Maynard roared as he saw the hole. He ran back out, pulling Zane off the ground by his shirt.

"Where did she go? How did she get out?"

Zane shook his head but saw Maynard's fist raise. He held up his hands to defend himself. "To the…to the ocean."

"Bullshit."

"She thought there might be a boat or something. She was gonna check it out, then we were all gonna go."

Maynard contemplated Zane's lies, shifting his eyes to Desi for thoughts. Desi only looked down at the baby, raising a dried-up leaf to cram into her mouth.

"Uh…"

"Damn it." Maynard dropped Zane and went to the gate. "Watch them." He cleared the lock and went around the house to the rock Marlow climbed out on.

Desi looked from Avani to Zane. "She's uh…she's eating leaves."

Avani blew a raspberry at the bitter, dusty taste and threw the leaf, reaching for another one. Zane kept his eyes on Maynard until he was out of sight, then picked up the baby and wrestled a large, green leaf from her. She kept a torn corner of it in her fist.

Maynard came back into sight, watching the ground, following the path the feral kids took with Marlow. The footsteps were obvious in a normally undisturbed forest. His eyes stopped on the dark entrance.

"Fuck." Maynard patted his taser, then pointed at Desi. "Stay here. Don't let him leave." He started off. "And call Visser, now." Then he was gone.

~ * ~

Marlow and the kids ran through the trees. There were roots along the dark path, low hanging branches, and vines of all kinds. It was like working through a TV show jungle with no machete and no lights. Each of them took a spill during the first hundred yards where it was thickest. Marlow was limping, with blood coming from her palms from catching herself on her recent fall. Her legs throbbed from all her work getting out of the house, but she needed them to just give her a little more, a few miles and they could start righting all the wrongs.

Light spilled on the path further ahead. The forest spun into a final tangle before releasing them into the open. There was the sound of running water. The sun exposed them, but it didn't matter. The path was still treacherous. There was nowhere to land a Rock-Hopper. They were teetering along a cliffside next to a river. Marlow stopped, looking up to the mountain peak where they "buried" their dead. Below them was a large pipe and the sounds of a pump. She followed it down the river. The pipe continued through the next part of the range. It didn't look like they could follow it through, but if they went over the mountain, there had to be civilization. The shipyard, from her memory. She straddled the path and kept on, slowly. The kids followed.

~ * ~

Zane pleaded with Desi as they watched the forest. "He'll kill her. You have to stop him. You have to tell somebody who has a fucking conscience in their head."

Desi's reply was delayed and faltering when it came, "She knows what she did."

Zane paused, wondering how much this guard knew about what happened on the Knox. *Probably everything,* he thought, but likely only

Maynard's side.

"She was trying to survive. That's all we've ever done." The emotion was strong in his voice, barely getting the last words out. "Don't you get it? We're like animals to them."

Desi sighed, only looking to the forest, unable to meet Zane's eyes. The sound of another 'Hopper coming in stole their attention. Soon, Robin Visser came around the house. He was followed by Mateo. They wielded tasers as they joined the others inside the fence. Robin held the door for Desi.

"Get out there. Get her under control and get her back here. Don't worry about the others. Marlow cannot be seen."

"Right." Desi took off in a sprint. He knew he had ground to make up, but he was fast, and he'd been climbing the mountains his whole life.

Robin watched him go, then turned to Zane, still holding Avani. "You didn't want to leave?"

Zane had considered leaving. He knew Avani would slow him down, but she would've been a diversion, even if he just headed toward the ocean. He also considered leaving the baby in her crib. Someone would've shown up to take care of her, but it didn't feel right at the time. He could never live with himself if she climbed out of her crib and got hurt.

"We drew straws," he said, finally.

Mateo went inside as they continued their conversation.

"This is no different than the ship, Zane. If you behave, you get me. If you don't, you get Maynard. You two have made your choice again and again. I can't promise she's going to come back in one piece."

Zane swallowed down the fear he had for Marlow. He wished he had any way to communicate to her that Maynard was on her trail, but in the end, he knew she would do what she had to. Marlow would find a way.

"Just wait," said Zane.

"Excuse me?"

"When Marlow spreads the word of what you're doing to us out here, you're going to be overthrown."

Robin let out a chuckle. "By whom? You remember that I run the

Belt, don't you?"

"There are good people. I've met them. I've worked with them. They're not going to let this go on."

"And those people will never know this day even happened."

Mateo came back out, his brows knitted. "They had help."

Robin turned from Zane. "What?"

Mateo waved him inside. "Look at this hole." He pointed to the second hole above the boulder outside. "See how it's broken inward at points?"

Robin looked back as Zane stood in the doorway laughing.

"Who helped her?" asked Robin, his eyes on fire.

"A fucking army," Zane lied. "Your men out there are in trouble."

He walked back outside, his face twisting into a deranged smile. He didn't know if they'd buy any of what he said, but it felt good to see a small wave of fear cross their faces.

~ * ~

Marlow's chest heaved. Her legs protested every step. She wondered how many microfractures she had in her bones from her battle with the wall. None of it mattered, because they were cresting a hill just over the pipe they'd been following, and she was certain the other side was the shipyard. She'd roll down the hill if she had to.

The last portion was the hardest. There were few rocks to offer a handhold, and they were far between one to the next. Marlow stretched her five-foot-two frame as far as it would go. She felt a nudge from the boy behind her, helping to get her to the next ledge. As she pulled herself up, the dread sank deep into her stomach as a Rock-Hopper swooped overtop them and landed on the peak they were aiming for. She stopped, looking up and hoping, as the feral kids joined her, huddled on the side of the ledge. It didn't have to be someone bad. It could be a simple rescue party searching for the kids, that would bring her back as well, unaware of the civil war they were about to cause.

Then she saw his face. The permanent sneer she'd come to recognize, the car-crash hairdo, and the scar on his neck.

"Where do you think you're going?" Maynard called down.

Marlow waved her hands. "I've got kids here. They're scared. They're lost. Just let me take them home."

Maynard rubbed his chin. "How about you and I head back to your place real quick, then we'll worry about the kids." He pointed behind him. "Besides, they're on the right path. Almost made it to the shipyard, but that was the goal, now, wasn't it?"

"We're not going with you."

"I'm not here to give you a choice." He squatted and came up holding a rock the size of his fist. "You wanna fight? I start *accidentally* dropping these. You come up; we work things out."

As he finished his sentence, a rock went whizzing over his head. Marlow cursed her aim and started ushering the kids back down the way they'd just climbed. The girl nodded and went first, then the boy. Marlow covered her head just in time for a rock to skim off her arm. The hit burned, but she was thankful it wasn't direct. They moved down in a hurry, undoing the climb that took them the last ten minutes of their journey. A shower of stones rained down on them, gashing their arms and heads. The girl was ten feet from the ground when she lost her footing. She took the rest of the trip by air, landing with an awful popping sound and a scream. Marlow and the boy raced to help her. She was holding her leg as her knee looked unnaturally bent.

"We'll get you help." Marlow stroked the girl's head with one hand and covered her own with the other. The boy started growling, looking back down the path. Marlow followed his gaze to see Desi, their mostly-silent security detail. He slowed his sprint, stopping ten feet away as Maynard descended the cliff.

"She's hurt," yelled Marlow, hoping to pull some humanity from Desi at least. "We've got to get her help. I'll cooperate. Let's just—"

But the boy took off running with another growl. Maynard saw him coming, loosed another rock, but the boy ducked. Maynard timed it just right, jumping down as the boy got close, dropping his full weight onto the skinny frame of the child. They hit the ground together, rolling. The boy clawed at his face, trying to take a bite out of any part of the bigger man. Maynard managed to push him away. The boy slid on his back in the dirt but was up quickly as Maynard drew from his belt.

"No," Marlow yelled, but the boy lunged forward as Maynard stepped to the side, jamming his taser into the boy's belly. He convulsed on the ground and Maynard gave him a kick for good measure.

Marlow stood, knowing she couldn't outrun the two of them. The girl next to her moaned in pain, but it was like they didn't hear it.

"Just surrender and we can go back," said Desi.

Marlow was about to reply when Maynard called, "No. There is no surrender now. She needs to pay for a few things first."

"But…" Desi stood. "Robin says the future of the Belt—"

Maynard forced out a laugh. "Yeah, yeah. We've heard it. I'm not going to kill her." But his smile told her death might be a better way out.

Marlow balled her fists and ran for Desi. He couldn't hide the look of surprise, but still readied his taser. Marlow knew one touch would do it. She went hard into a false attack. A kick meant to go wide right. It worked to perfection as Desi took the bait, thrusting the taser at her, which she countered and chopped down on his wrist, causing him to lose his weapon. He turned just in time to see the heel of her hand connect with his nose. His head rocked back, but he held his ground. Marlow reached for the taser, wanting to end things quickly, but he kicked it away. Marlow rose up with a shoulder to his chest. Desi stumbled back, keeping his footing, but stunned. She turned to see Maynard bearing down. He blocked her kick and countered with his taser. Marlow caught his arm, keeping it a few inches from her chest. She went to push off her back foot for a kick to his midsection when she was hit from behind by Desi. The shock shot through her body and she fell to the ground.

Maynard and Desi took a second to recover, then they cuffed Marlow and dragged her to her feet. The feral boy had recovered from the shock, but he stumbled off into the hills defeated. The girl dragged herself in the same direction. It was a pitiful sight watching the first generation of belt children left in that state, like soldiers from a forgotten war.

"Now what?" asked Desi.

Maynard looked up the mountainside. "Damn. I'm not carrying her ass up that. Looks like we're hiking it."

They went back the way Desi had just come, Maynard dragging

Marlow by the cuffs, not worrying about rough patches.

A quarter mile in and there was the sound of feet on the hill behind them.

Maynard turned and patted Desi. "That damn boy trying to be a hero. Take care of him."

Desi armed himself and waited. When the figure crested the hill, Desi stopped dead.

"Shit," said Maynard.

"Marlow?" Isolde stood on the hill in disbelief. "You're alive. You're here. I knew it." She narrowed her focus to the handcuffs and who had a hold of her. "Get your filthy hands off my friend."

"Now, now," said Maynard. "You wouldn't want to violate your parole. You shouldn't even be out here."

Ice shook her head. "I was out here looking for the missing children, but then I followed your tracks, and boy am I glad I did." She switched to her fighting stance. "Now, let go of my friend before I make you regret it."

Maynard wrenched Marlow's arm and pushed her against a tree. She didn't have time to catch her breath before he handcuffed her to a branch, then, he joined Desi, tasers drawn.

Isolde looked over their heads. "Marlow, are Zane and Avani…?"

Marlow called, "Yes, they're okay, but I haven't seen Arjen or the others. Only Lana."

"Same, but we're going to get the truth out of them." She lowered her eyes to the approaching men.

"No," Marlow yelled. "Just run. Tell everybody. I'll be okay until then."

"No. I'm not letting them take you again."

She started down the hill, cautious in her movement. Maynard came first, keeping his weapon back, guarding his face with his other arm. Ice bounced on her feet, light, ready to strike at the right moment. Maynard made quick flinches toward her, trying to get her to bite when Desi rushed her from the side. Ice sidestepped and sent a spinning kick to the side of his head, sending him sprawling to the dirt. Maynard struck, throwing a handful of dust into her face. Ice swatted at the air, backing up and just missing the snap of his taser. Maynard kept after her, but she'd switched her course, now backing toward Marlow, rubbing at her eyes as she did. Maynard charged, shielding his head, and taking a solid body blow as he led with the crackling sparks directed at her face. Ice dislodged his weapon with a knee to his elbow, but his weight fell forward, knocking her onto her back. She felt the breath leave her as Maynard's fist pounded at the side of her head. She caught the second hit and flipped him into a kimura submission hold. His face was planted in the dirt, his arm bent behind his body with her legs scissored around his torso. Maynard screamed, fighting her from breaking his arm but powerless to stop her.

Then there was another cry. Ice couldn't see from her position on the ground, but Marlow gave it away.

"Lana," said Marlow.

Lana breezed past her and screamed at Isolde. "Get off him."

"He was kidnapping Marlow. Holding her hostage somewhere." Ice wrestled Maynard back into submission. He was whimpering now. "I told you if I found out—"

"Shut up," said Lana. "This is not the time. The Belt needs her to get this process going. We can all discuss this. Just get off my father."

"Lana," said Marlow. "You can't be serious. Help me."

"I'm sorry, Marlow. Just a little longer and we can—" Lana stopped at the sound of her father's arm breaking. He screamed. Lana screamed and Ice tried to squirm free of his body. She just got her legs out when she felt Maynard's taser at the back of her neck, only Lana was holding it.

"You shouldn't have done that." Lana clicked the button and Isolde's fight was over.

Chapter Seven

In the basement below the government building, the cells normally filled by the missing children, held the remaining members of the Gammen family: Kaia and Isolde. A family that once held a fifty-percent stake in the Belt that shrunk to a third as the Visser family rose to power and the desire for balance was requested by the inhabitants. Petra Gammen passed on her leadership to her daughter Macalla, who gave birth to Kaia. When Kaia stepped into her governmental role, Macalla stepped out, leading a simpler life until her passing just a year ago. Neither Isolde nor Admani showed any interest in the bigger decision making for the Belt. When they left for Wyan, any inheritance of power was forfeit. That left Kaia as the sole remaining Gammen still eligible for duty. Without her, Robin and Oscar held the monopoly. The man who knew that fact better than anyone, stood just outside the bars of her cell.

"Why was she out there, Kaia?" Robin paced, visibly frustrated as Desi stood watch at the stairwell. "I told you we'd handle it. Now you've—"

"She was fulfilling her duty to the Belt," Kaia's voice boomed off the basement walls. "You won't let her do anything else."

Robin stuck a hand toward Isolde. "Because she abandoned the Belt, then came back and assaulted someone."

"I—" Ice started but felt her mother's hand on her, letting Ice know she would handle it.

"May I remind you who it was? Or have you forgotten the part where *Lana* led the rebellion? And now, she comes back, and you have her in a position of power. Power she'll without a doubt abuse."

"She has no power." Robin sneered. "She's just another child carrier. All she had to do was fall in line when she got back. She did. Your daughter on the other hand..."

Kaia slammed the bars and Robin flinched. "She uncovered the truth. You've come back with Marlow, Zane, and their baby and you've enslaved them. Hidden them away like some unholy affair." Kaia took a step back to breathe. "My daughter did nothing but hold you accountable to the standard you preach to our people. We all serve, we all work together for a better Belt. Did you forget that?"

"No," Robin turned away, "but I also haven't forgotten that we must preserve our species. Without that, we have nothing to work for."

He reached the stairwell, took one more look at the Gammens, then shook his head and left them in the dungeon.

~ * ~

The next day, Robin commended his security team for rescuing the missing children, calling off the search through a broadcast message to all active data-pads. During the delivery of his speech, Maynard Royal interrupted him, appearing on camera with his arm in a sling, presumably from his heroics the day before. Robin nodded, then paused before returning his gaze to his people.

"I'm sorry. We've just learned of some tragic news. One of our Rock-Hoppers went off course and collided with a dead island." He turned and whispered loud enough for all to hear, "Track the data-pads, that will tell you." Then turned back. "I'm so sorry. Bear with me for just a moment."

Maynard came back, whispering in his ear and Robin asked, "Are you sure about that?" He nodded and left the view of the camera. Robin's face scrunched up. "This is just awful. I…" He held a fist to his mouth, taking in a deep breath. "We've found that two people were aboard the Rock-Hopper that crashed. Isolde and Kaia Gammen." He put his hands to his face, mumbling obscenities as he walked off camera. The feed cut. The people of the Belt left to put together what just happened in the broadcast.

Maynard met Robin in his office, raising a hand to high-five him. Robin moved past him and slumped into the chair behind his desk.

Maynard slowly lowered his hand. "We did it. Great

performance."

Robin was searching his drawers until he came out with a bottle, taking a drink straight from it.

"Hell. Pour me one too." Maynard saw Robin had no intention to share, so he continued talking, "I still think we should've put them on it. Lot less chance of anyone finding them."

Robin glared at Maynard with bloodshot eyes. "Kaia is one of my oldest friends. I feel sick just having her locked up as it is. I don't want her dead. I didn't want any of this. Oscar and I could've just out voted her. Now, she knows too much. I don't know how long we can keep her there, but I don't see a time in the future to let her out. I can only hope enough time will change her mind about what we're doing."

"It will." Maynard patted the desk. "Hey, I've got a lot going on with the Gammens and the Earthlings. I'd better get out there and relieve Desi."

Robin shooed him off with a wave. Left to his drink and his regret.

Chapter Eight

19 years ago, 2072
Government Building, Ceres

Dr. Ramirez stood at the head of the table, observing the deep contemplation across the face of his longtime partner, Petra Gammen. Her dark wrinkles folded in on themselves. Life had been a beautiful challenge for both of them. They'd accomplished things no other humans could claim. They'd started a colony in the asteroid belt that was not only succeeding, but thriving. With their combined tech, they were able to liberate themselves from Earth and its wars. They'd only just started seeing abnormalities in their children, but it was nothing their company of scientists couldn't figure out in their minds. With all their knowledge, they knew time would still catch up to them eventually.

Their biggest decision since the last ship arrived lay in front of them. A proposal from some of Earth's leaders. A trial union. Just like in early times, there was a laundry list of those ready to board a ship headed for the Belt. Only Earth, in all its wars, destroyed any potential for space flight. Whereas the Belt had done nothing but advance theirs. They'd started gathering trips aboard their three shuttles, the Iris, the Knox, and the Mack. Dr. Ramirez didn't divulge this information when the communication began. He knew he was in a position of power. He had all the leverage against the planet that fought to keep him. It wasn't that they couldn't support more inhabitants. Especially useful ones.

"They want us to give them a number?" Dr. Gammen asked. "How much do they know about our means?"

Dr. Ramirez shook his head. "Only that we can get there and back and take a bunch of them with us."

Robin Visser, silent until then, watching his mentor work, spoke up, "I think it's worth considering."

Oscar chimed in, "How do we know they'd send us anyone worthwhile? Not just political jumpers?" Then he nudged the man that was the closest thing to a brother he had. "We've already got one of those."

Robin took the ribbing in silence.

Dr. Gammen said, "It's a good point." She motioned a spiraled, wooden cane toward Robin. "His parents did what they did. They paid his way. God rest their souls, but what's to stop us from picking up a load of bloated politicians and billionaires?"

"Exactly my point," said Oscar.

"To truly expand," said Dr. Ramirez, "we need an insurgence of strong, healthy workers. We've given them almost twenty-eight years to resolve their differences. A trial of just twenty or so could test the hypothesis."

"That's a long way to go for twenty people," said Dr. Gammen.

"And what if it doesn't go well?" asked Oscar. "Do we just take them back home?"

"I don't see why not." Dr. Ramirez scrolled through Earth's proposal on a screen in front of them.

"It's been many years," said Dr. Gammen, "but don't forget how they felt about us leaving the first time. No matter what's happened on Earth, some will still feel we abandoned them. They always do. Remember the Mars Rover? There was always the question of tying up finances in exploration instead of the planet we inhabited. We came out on the end that proved it all worthwhile, but they may not see it that way."

"Yes…" Dr. Ramirez stroked a hand across his lips repeatedly, a gesture Dr. Gammen had grown accustomed to, knowing it meant he was about to make a decision. Robin knew it as well. Before Dr. Ramirez could speak, Robin said, "We should just try. One ship. A small, controlled group. We could trial it and see."

Dr. Ramirez observed the man put in his care those years ago. "This means a lot to you, but you have to know, you're not going to find your parents alive. We lost contact with them after the third war."

Robin hung his head. "I know, but we could try. What if this is the push that we need to reach the next stage out here?"

The group let his words hang in the air. The Belt was at a crossroads. Doing so well on their own all those years but still having a low population. The TechBubbles were expanding. NutrientPanel was more advanced than ever. They could feed and house twenty, but not without risks.

Dr. Ramirez clicked on the proposal, shaking his head. "Petra's right. There may not be loyalty to be found, no matter their kind words. If we went, there'd be no guarantee that ship would ever make it back. We stay the course. *Our* course. Going back could run the risk of losing it all."

Robin accepted his decision, leaving the government building to get home and find his wife had moved out with another man. His heart hardened a little more that day.

Chapter Nine

The next six months passed with a shift the Belt had not seen since Lana's group of deserters flew off to Wyan. Tensions were high in the beginning. The change of power. Uncertainty. But with Kaia and Isolde locked away, Marlow, Zane, and Avani's house reinforced with brick and stone, soon, troubles faded into the back of everyone's minds. As bellies grew in the Motherhood Initiative Village, so did hope. But the mothers of the village weren't the only ones. Layla Ramirez and Tiffany Visser also grew special deliveries inside them. They carried eggs taken from Marlow. It was another route, another angle for scientists like Mateo to study. They would figure out the missing gene, and while they may not be able to save the children already born feral, they had a whole new generation of kids that would not be, on the way.

But while many had hopes in the next generation, others still questioned if the Belt was the best place to raise them.

After their most recent session with Dr. Ianesso, some of the Motherhood Initiative took a stroll to the New Belt Forest, located just past the clothing factory. Near the center, under fifty-foot redwoods, the others waited.

Fleta and Nigel, a proficient rock hauling couple. Amelia and Shirley, the builders who'd made the apartments on New Pangaea. Luis from agriculture, Hudson from NutrientPanel, Lavinia who repaired Rock-Hoppers, Desi from security, and Roel, the oldest member, a bit of a drifter, and most notably, Admani's father.

Lana approached with cautious eyes darting around. She was flanked by Erika and Zelda, so far, the only two mothers she could subtly convince to join.

"Anyone followed?" Lana asked the group.

Most looked around, shaking their heads, and grunting negative replies.

Lana stepped to the middle. "We're at four months and counting. How are preparations coming for everyone? Hudson?"

"Good, good." The short, stubby man nodded. "I'm slowly stocking away in my cellar. I'm on track for double the required servings as you requested."

"Good to hear. We want to have room for others that decide to jump ship...or *rock,* at the last minute." She turned to a woman with a tan complexion covered in dark freckles. "Lavinia, how's the Iris?"

The woman leaned against one of the redwoods, her arms crossed, wearing blue overalls and just a spandex bra underneath. "I sneak in when I can. It's hard to test engines but everything looks to be in working order. Bunks are stocked; bay's ready to be loaded."

"What about you?" Luis pulled off a straw hat to reveal salt and pepper hair. "Last time there were four of you." He motioned to the bumps on their bellies. "Are we losing mothers?"

Lana switched her hips and frowned at him. "Darcy may not be cut out for this life, but we're working on the others. Plus, we always have Marlow in our back pocket."

Luis tilted his head in surprise. "But according to you, she's locked up. How do you plan to get her away from them without your father's help?"

"I'm working on it. Just trust me."

~ * ~

The mothers-to-be strolled back the long way around the water plant to avoid any suspicion. They discussed their future plans as they went.

"Do you think Jameer will really come?" Zelda asked Erika.

Erika smacked her lips. "He'd better. He said he wants my next kid to be his, but we don't know how that works out there, do we?"

Lana shook her head. "You could be the first to try it. Remember, we may learn a lot from all the pregnancies coming up. We may find a way to fix it for the next ones, then, they'll all be Wyan babies."

Erika's smile was big and bright. "I'm so excited. You said they have rain? I want to stand in the rain. Have a party at the lake. Live free, girl."

Lana laughed. "If only I could get you to talk to everyone for me."

"Just say the word."

"I will," Lana sighed, "but this next recruit is going to have to be on me."

~ * ~

Lana's Rock-Hopper landed next to the government building. The feral children played in their cage while Gilbert sat back watching, leaned against the back wall, his thick eyebrows drooping.

"Hey," Lana said, a little louder than needed.

Gilbert sprung off the wall. "Whuah? I—hey Lana."

"Tiffany around?"

Gilbert pointed down the path to the trees that separated the government building and the shipyard. "Took a stroll with the baby. Want me to call her?" He raised his arm and his data-pad with it.

"No." Lana started off. "I'll catch up to her."

Lana found Tiffany power walking back from the shipyard. She wore shorts that showed off her legs and let her strawberry blonde hair hang down. Her belly was becoming obvious, six months into her second pregnancy. Wesley was strapped to her back, his cheeks jiggling with her movement. Lana raised a hand and she slowed to a stop.

"Lana? What brings you out here? Everything okay?"

"I just…" Lana paused, giving a slight shake of her head. "I had a moment. A memory that I could only share with you."

"Oh really?" Tiffany gave a cautious smile. "What about?"

"You remember that double date we went on with Arjen and Wes back…oh, probably seven or eight years ago?"

Tiffany squinted at her, a bit confused. "Like…"

"To the forest," Lana added.

"The forest…" Tiffany's face scrunched up, pulling details out of her brain. "Yes. I remember. You didn't want it to be called a double date.

You said it was just a hang out."

Lana blushed, looking at her feet. "Yeah, I did. I didn't want Arjen thinking…well, you know. But he brought that bottle…"

"Yes." Tiffany broke into a big smile. "He always found Robin's stash. You'd think he would've wised up to it at some point."

"Do you remember…" Lana coaxed her.

"Spin the bottle? How could I forget, because," Tiffany threw up some air quotes, "'the bottle has to be empty before we can spin it.' According to those Visser boys at least."

Lana was laughing. "Right? I think they were just trying to get us loose enough to even play that game."

"I know." Tiffany reached back a hand for baby Wesley to grab. "Joke was on them though because there was a magnet in that bottle or something. I landed on Arjen almost every time until—"

"Until Wes suggested we change seats."

Tiffany laughed loudly, then her face shrunk into a tight smile. "He was always…I don't know, a bit jealous of Arjen."

"I don't know. I think each brother wanted to be the other brother at times."

"Yes, and I remember the walk back most of all. Wes was holding my hand, Arjen kept drifting closer to you but you never…"

Lana held up her hands. "I had a big trip the next day. My first Mars gathering trip. I was leading it. I couldn't be distracted."

Tiffany put a hand on her arm. "We knew, Lana. Wes and I did at least. I don't think Arjen could ever accept that excuse."

"I know…"

Tiffany wiped at her eyes. "Hey, sorry, not trying to ruin your memory. I really appreciate you thinking of me."

"Yeah. You know, I just miss those two sometimes."

"Me too. What I wouldn't give to be back out there with those two dummies, drinking and joking. Life's sure changed out here."

"It has," Lana agreed, "but can I tell you a secret that you can't repeat to anyone, especially your father-in-law?"

Tiffany looked nervous. "Oh, Lana, I—"

"No. I think you deserve to know."

Tiffany stopped bouncing Wesley Jr. and met Lana's eyes. "Know what?"

"He's still alive out there."

Tiffany's mouth dropped open. She whispered, "Arjen?"

Lana nodded. "Visser left him. I didn't know if he'd find a way back, but it's been too long. I'm afraid he's stranded."

"Are you serious? Why haven't we sent a ship?"

Lana shrugged. "Family feud? They're playing an awful game of chicken that nobody wins. I was powerless at the time, but I have a plan to go back out there. To be with Arjen. And you…" She put a hand on Tiffany's shoulder. "You should come too."

"Oh, I don't know. Are you talking about defecting again? Living out there? With those…things?"

"Not with. Not anymore. It would be our planet. We neutralized the threat out there last time. We just needed to regroup. Now it's ours for the taking."

"I don't know what you expect of me. I have responsibilities here."

Lana stepped back, putting her hands on her hips. "You like to teach, right? Who are you teaching here? How many of those kids actually listen to you? I'm planning," Lana looked around to confirm they were still alone, "I'm planning to have a village out there. We're talking a bunch of babies growing into kids, growing into teens, all needing somebody to show them the way."

"Oh, stop." Tiffany blushed and looked away. "This is a big deal, you know. Robin will be…I don't even know. It would destroy him. And your father?"

"He had his chance. He's got his own grudge against me, same as Robin, but they're old, Tiff. They can't see a future outside of here. I can. I *have*. We just needed this regroup, this reset. Now it's time to get out there and do something different."

Tiffany's cheeks were fully blushed. She put a hand over her heart like she was having palpitations. "The whole Belt…our way of life here…"

Lana picked up her intensity. "It will be gone. After this

generation. Kaia's gone now. Robin has no heir. You want Wesley to grow up in a Belt run by Mateo?"

"No, I—"

"I'm not trying to play hero. We've all seen where their leadership has led."

Tiffany studied her feet, ignoring Wesley as he pulled on her hair. "I…I'll think about it, okay? That's all I can promise."

Lana put a hand on her arm and looked her in the eye. "It would be good for you."

"I—"

"And I need you to promise on Wesley's life you're not going to tell anyone, okay?"

Tiffany's eyebrows knotted up. "Lana."

Lana shook her head. "Sorry. It's just important. Visser's off the rails. You've seen him."

Tiffany gave a reluctant nod. "I-I won't say anything."

"Good." Lana hugged her gently, then put on a smirk. "Because otherwise I'm telling the end of the double date story to the whole Belt. The part where you puked on Wes when he was trying to kiss you on the Rock-Hopper ride home."

Tiffany burst out laughing. "Don't you dare. It was that booze that did it."

Lana and Tiffany walked back to the government building together. When they broke off, Lana said, "Talk to you soon."

Tiffany nodded but didn't reply. She was too deep in thought.

Chapter Ten

Lana swung her legs over the exam table, happy to get dressed again as Dr. Crouch tossed his gloves and washed his hands.

"Darcy said she's enjoying the village." He watched her, as if waiting for a reaction.

"Good." Lana finished adjusting her maternity pants. "I am too."

"She really looks up to you, you know?"

"Okay. Are we—"

He took a step closer, the constant two days of stubble on his chin showed a few speckles of gray. "I just hope you're giving her good advice. Pointing her in the right direction." He put on a toothy smile.

"Well, she's already pregnant." Lana moved toward the door. "Hopefully she doesn't need me to tell her how to raise it."

She left the exam room, not looking back as Dr. Crouch stood in the doorway.

~ * ~

The Motherhood Initiative Village was quiet during the day. The other ladies worked the first shift. Lana's job had been gathering. Supposedly, her current job was helping oversee New Pangaea, but Robin Visser made all the real decisions. She was a figurehead. An example mother and nothing more. She felt a sympathy for Marlow that she lacked on their first encounter.

But Lana was much more than a queen bee. She had plans. The first thing she was going to do was casually stroll past the clothing factory as Darcy's shift ended.

She moved faster than she meant and had to continue to the forest, then make a U-turn. When Darcy came out, Lana was far enough back that she had to pick up the pace. She wanted to have this conversation before they reached the village. Her ankles were beginning to ache at the movement. She looked down and cursed them. She hadn't even gained that much extra weight. How could her body betray her already?

"Darc," Lana called, trying to sound casual. "Is that you?"

Darcy turned, her face brightening into a big smile. "Hey. You just out for a walk?"

Lana nodded. "Yeah, but my legs are feeling it."

"Tell me about it."

"Right. A full day of work must be hard on you."

Darcy linked arms with Lana, and they walked together. "We can support each other."

When they were a quarter of the way home, Lana said, "Saw your dad today."

"Checkup?"

"Yeah. He said some things about you too."

Darcy turned, her hair bobbing with the movement. "Did he?"

"Just that he hopes I'm giving you good advice. Any idea what *that* means?"

"Oh, um…" Darcy's brow furrowed.

Lana stopped their little train, holding Darcy's arm still, not for support but for control. "You didn't tell him anything you shouldn't have, did you?"

Darcy waved her free hand. "No, Lana, I swear. We were just talking. I just said you were encouraging me to try new things. When he inquired as to what new things, I lied." She put her hand to her mouth. "I hate lying to him. He always sees right through it."

"What did you tell him, Darcy?"

"Just that you thought I could be the head of the clothing factory. Like Carol used to be. It wasn't completely a lie, I guess. You think I could if I came with you, right?"

Lana squeezed her arm and started walking again. "I do. You absolutely have what it takes."

Now Lana was lying, but having a young enough mother with a child and the ability to help clothe her new colony of people was valuable.

Even if she was a little shy about it. "But you're going to have to lie to him again if we want to pull this off. Just be ready."

They reached the front of the apartments and broke their link. Lana started toward her unit.

"I will," Darcy called after her. "I'll be ready."

Lana looked back. "Good."

~ * ~

At their next group meeting behind the apartments, the paper lanterns glowed their different shades of the rainbow, the trees hung in their perfect canopy, and Dr. Ianesso's conversation starters were being stone-walled by every mother to be.

"How about a word," said the doctor. "Any word to describe your feelings about the upcoming pregnancy."

Darcy held her hands over her face, trying to avoid looking at Lana. "I…apprehensive, I guess. I don't know."

"Apprehensive," Dr. Ianesso repeated, her neck bending as her eyes probed Darcy's face. like a bird seeing a worm emerging from the dirt. "Would you like to share with the group why you're feeling apprehensive? I'm sure others—"

"No," Darcy cut her off, shaking her head.

Lana could see her about to crack. She didn't think Darcy would blab their plans, but she didn't need to get too deep into her feelings with the Narc Doctor.

"I feel apprehensive, too," said Lana, catching the tilted head now eying her. "The whole Belt is counting on us. We just don't want to let them down." She looked over at her recent Wyan convert. "I'm not sure if Darcy is feeling the same or…"

Darcy nodded thoroughly. "It's a lot of pressure, and every day it gets closer. I hope it works out."

Lana pursed her lips into a smile. *And that's enough*, she thought.

"Thank you both for sharing." Dr. Ianesso looked around the group. "Who here can think of things we can do when we're feeling apprehensive about the upcoming birth?"

"Focus on our breathing," said Kiki, one of the ladies who worked at the medical facility.

"Yes." Dr. Ianesso's face was lighting up. "More, more."

"Do a meditation," said Monica from engineering.

"Read the entire birth plan," laughed Zelda. "That thing puts me to sleep every time."

The doctor turned. "Reviewing the birth plan is a good idea but let's keep it positive, Zelda."

Zelda gave her a salute.

The session concluded twenty minutes later after they'd all shared their top three things they looked forward to doing with their child when it was born.

Lana's group had a "boomerang-meeting," where they'd said goodbye to everyone, went inside to pee and came back out ten minutes later. This time it was four of them: Lana, Zelda, Erika, and Darcy.

"You're not mad?" asked Darcy.

Lana leaned over to pat her shoulder. "You recovered. We recovered together. We'll do better next time. Now, listen. I need you to work on Kiki. The last meeting with the deserters didn't go as well as planned. We need more mothers, more babies. I've got an assault group set with myself, Fleta and Nigel, Lavinia, and Roel. But they want to know any crusading they do for me will be supported by all of you."

"Roel is on your assault team?" Zelda laughed, brushing her messy, blonde bowl-cut out of her eyes to join the mullet in the back. "What's he gonna do, cough on them?"

Lana couldn't bring herself to smile as the memory of Roel's daughter taking her last rapid breaths by the snowy river on the dark side of Wyan spilled into her thoughts. He had fuel for his anger, his desire for revenge. He didn't need to know it wasn't the Wyans that killed her but the cave creature's poison while they fled the Night Chasers. All he needed was to be pointed in the right direction.

"We'll find use for him," said Lana. "If we can get our numbers up. So, Darcy…"

"Right." Darcy was doe-eyed again. "I just have to be careful around my dad."

"Yes. I don't have to explain what will happen if he finds out."

Darcy shook her head.

"Good." Lana turned to the other two. "Do either of you have a track on Monica?"

Zelda and Erika shook their heads in unison.

"I can work on her," said Zelda, but she doesn't want to have anything to do with me."

"I can try too," said Erika. "We talk hair sometimes. Something Z can't relate to."

She smirked as Zelda gave her the finger.

Lana stood. "I need your best efforts. Recruit some of the other deserters if you need to."

"Will do, Boss." Zelda pushed off her chair. "For now, I'm hitting the hay."

Lana watched them go, one by one back to their little apartments, hoping they'd dream of Wyan, though they didn't love it the way she did just yet. All they'd need was to see what it would look like under her rule, and in time, that's exactly what she would show them.

Chapter Eleven

Six weeks later, Zane stood at the barred window wishing the forest would come to life and swallow their prison whole. There was so much color in the trees. So much sprawling life, but though it was just beyond their door, it felt like he was viewing another planet. Like the window was a portal to a place they could never go. All the vibrant greens seemed gray from Zane's side of the bars, and when he turned, the inside was no better. Marlow lay on her back, her belly protruding as she slept on the mattress, arms splayed at her sides. Avani was tucked into her armpit as Marlow's breast was out a few inches from where she'd unlatched.

Zane softly padded over, pulling a blanket up to cover his girls. He lay on the floor next to Marlow, recalling the past few months. Avani was fifteen months old, walking when she was awake and trying to mimic random words. Marlow was about a month and a half away from her second birth. They only hoped it would produce favorable results. Something so good that all past grievances would be forgiven. It was an absolute pipe dream. They'd heard the murmurings on the trip back. The next plan was to impregnate Marlow with a Belter. And after that? Who knows? But likely another pregnancy. It sounded like Marlow's eggs were doing well in Tiffany and Layla. She'd told Zane they could have them all at that point. Just to take the burden away from her, but her genes were too important to them.

Zane felt like they were living for the second pregnancy to end. It would be like Marvin the duck dying all over again. The point where he'd ask himself the question again, if he didn't plan on eating, what did he plan on? But this time, they both agreed, if a few months passed and they were back in their prison, Marlow pregnant and Zane a universal surrogate, they'd find a way out. Only, it wouldn't be through the walls that time.

Marlow reminded him before she'd passed out that when Marvin died, everything changed. Maybe it would be the same when the baby was born.

He looked over his friend and their baby and felt nothing. Their existence was like being on a boat in the middle of the ocean. They would float until they couldn't stand it anymore, then they would fall in.

~ * ~

The day passed like the others, slowly and painfully. Avani wandered the bare house, trying to climb the couch, then making it onto the mattress, then back down. She went to the door as her parents laid around like drug addicts on a relapse. She knew sometimes people came through that way, and while it wasn't always pleasant, it offered a breath of the outside air, a taste of color. After banging on the door a few times with no change, she waddled over to the window. She was three feet short of the bars, craning her neck to see the tops of the trees through it. She lost her sense of balance and fell onto her butt with a flop. The view from further back was even better, so she stayed, spitting out words that made little sense to anyone but her.

Then there was movement at the door. The handle turned and Avani gave a big smile to a woman that was one of her first caretakers.

"Lana?" Zane jerked up.

Marlow stood, cautious, scooping up Avani, who reached her arms out for Lana.

"Hey." Lana wiggled her fingers at Avani, then stepped aside for Desi, who set their case of NutrientPanels down.

"Just delivering those," he said, "and it's just me. Okay?"

"It's what?" Zane looked confused.

Lana eyed them both. "What I'm about to say never leaves this room."

Marlow narrowed her eyes. "You're the reason we're still *in* this room. You're out there. You're one of the only ones who know we're still alive. You stopped Ice from saving us."

"She was going to kill my father."

Marlow scoffed. "She was going to break his arm, and she did." She smiled at that portion of the memory.

"I don't think she would've stopped there." Lana held up a hand to pause any retorts. "But it wasn't time yet anyway. That wasn't the time to make your break."

The Earthlings' faces changed, feeling hopeful. "And now is?" asked Zane. "Are we—"

"Not today." Lana looked around as if to confirm it was just her and Desi that came on the Rock-Hopper. Despite it being just the four of them and Avani, she lowered her voice, "Where would you have gone that day? To the shipyard? The government building? What do you think would've happened?"

Marlow shrugged. "Probably a civil war."

"And then what? What's your role here after a civil war? You going to work the NutrientPanel?"

Marlow's eyes lit up in anger. "I could do something. Something besides make more babies for them."

Lana rubbed her own bulging stomach. "I know. What do you think *I'm* doing? I'm just doing it on the outside because I'm laying low until the time is right."

"What time?" Marlow shifted Avani to her other arm. "What are you talking about?"

Lana took a quick look out the window, then turned. "You repeat this to anyone but who's in the room and we're all fucked. Any chance of ever getting out of here is gone. Do you understand?"

"Repeat what?" Marlow found herself yelling the last word.

"I've built a team of deserters. Acquaintances old and new. People who have had enough of the Belt rule. People who want a new beginning. We're planning a trip back to Wyan."

Marlow and Zane shared a look, then burst out laughing.

"You're going *back* there?" said Zane. "After how it went last time, you're going back?"

"Karath betrayed me," Lana pointed to them, "betrayed us. Without her making a deal with the Night Chasers, without Davis and

Peter taking off, we'd be ruling Wyan right now. The Belt would be begging us to allow them to immigrate. We were so close. Despite the way it all ended, we were so close. We took out the Night Chasers regardless of the circumstances. Now, we go back, and we set up our colony. We're taking as many as we can get the first go-round, but then they'll come. They'll have to follow our rules, and people like Robin Visser won't be welcome. I'm making that clear. What he's doing to you out here is not okay, but I've been powerless to stop it. You think I didn't want to tase my father that day instead of Ice? I did, but we weren't prepared to go then. I'm sorry I couldn't share that with you, but I needed to lay low until I could find a way back out here without causing suspicion."

Lana looked them both over, gears turning in their heads. "I know you think you can't trust me, but just understand, this is a big political move. The fact that I have even an ounce of freedom is only through my 'loyalty' to their process. That attack on Ice was to prove I was here to stay. You think I can get anything started with them suspecting? I had to do what I had to do, to consider the long term. You wanna know what I've been up to?" She rubbed her belly again. "Me and five other mothers—"

Marlow cut her off, "It's nine if you count all of us. I know that much. You six, me, Layla Ramirez, and Tiffany Visser. We're 'building the future,' according to Robin."

Lana smiled. "Yes, but we're taking that future elsewhere. There are four of us from the village, you, Tiffany…" She paused when she saw Marlow's face. "Oh, get over your past. She was in a very different position when you first met. You can strike that back up when we all get to Wyan if you want, but I think you'll be too happy running through those mountains again. Down the sand dunes. Into the lake. Do I need to go into more detail?"

"I remember it," said Marlow, "but who says we're going with?"

Lana took a step back. "Nobody says. This is your choice." She waited for Marlow, once again, to decide between imprisonment or some unknown entity. Only, Wyan wasn't unknown. She'd been there. They'd fought the Night Chasers and lived to tell the tale but was that really where they belonged? Back out there, fighting for their land? Without knowing Lana's full plans, Marlow already knew there was no plan for peaceful coexistence with the Wyans anymore. Still, as she looked around the room, she tried to consider what she *wouldn't* do to get out of there.

"Listen." Lana could sense Desi's growing nerves as he kept watch at the window. "I don't have time to sit out here and chat. I need an answer."

Zane eyed Marlow, hopeful and she held a hand up. "Okay, but answer me this first, what happened to the others?"

Lana narrowed her eyes and Marlow helped her out.

"You and I came back from the dark side with Arjen, Julie, Williams, and that alien guy Amun. Then I find out later, they'd already grabbed Zane and Ice. So, are they here somewhere? Are they dead? What happened?"

Lana sighed. "I'll tell you what I know. The deal with Visser and my dad was to come get you guys, me, Ice, and Arjen. The others weren't part of that deal. I think they could only handle the rebellious that were still useable or part of one of the families. Julie is barren and Williams is too old and hardheaded for Visser to trust. I assume they planned to get Admani, maybe Walters, Percy, Peter, and Davis, I don't know. But they offered Arjen and I the deal. I took it, he didn't."

"He stayed?" Marlow's eyes were wide.

Lana shrugged. "He didn't want to be controlled by his dad anymore. He wanted to make his own way but…" She looked around. "I guess that was to stay, or I don't know." Her face was dark for a second, then brightened. "But now we can go find out."

Marlow was shaking her head in disbelief.

Zane stepped up. "So, we go with you and what? We build the colony we missed out on last time? Bring a bunch of babies with us?"

Lana was nearing the door, feeling her message hit home. "In more words than that, yes, and I would like you…four, to be part of that. Visser's plan is after the deliveries, to give it at least two months before starting round two, or *three* for you. We're leaving before that. We're building up the 'Panel for travel since there will be all of us mothers staying awake this time, but the Iris is ready. My group is ready. All I need is for you to stay ready."

Desi opened the door, ushering her out.

Lana gave one last look to her captive audience. "Stay ready. I'll see you in two months."

Chapter Twelve

A few weeks passed on the Belt. Robin paid a visit to Dr. Ianesso to see her progress in real time. The recent additions of Tiffany and Layla helped move the conversation along, as well as having Wesley, now stumbling around the circle, visiting each chair before taking off back to his mother.

They discussed the friendships they'd built, how their group would continue after the delivery. Their support circle wasn't going anywhere, according to Dr. Ianesso, and that made Lana proud, proud that she was so ignorant to the fact she'd unknowingly forged the beginning of Lana's deserters. It was something Lana had no chance of doing on her own without being found out.

Robin sat with them as Monica tallied up their votes on who would pop first and last. Most votes were for Darcy, as she showed more than the others. Lana was considered the likeliest to go last.

After the laughing and speculation died down, Robin whispered to Dr. Ianesso who raised her hands.

"Everyone, if you could give Mr. Visser your attention for a second."

The ladies turned to him with his polished grin and wise eyes.

"Can I first say how proud I am of all of you? I know these months have not been easy. Feeling the weight of what's inside of you. It's more than a child. It's our future. But you all knew that stepping into this role, and for that, I think you deserve a round of applause." He started the clap, quickly joined by Dr. Ianesso and spreading through the ladies. "Now, I know you're not there yet, but I have all the confidence in our doctors to get you the rest of the way." He nodded toward Darcy, and she smiled back. "I didn't come here to admonish you with praise, though you deserve it. I come here because I love this village you have. What Dr.

Ianesso has reported about your progress as women and friends, I feel confident this all has been a good experiment, but I don't want to see this village empty in a couple months. The problem is, we're short on ladies to fill it back up. Not many volunteer for this kind of life. So, hear my next proposal. We expand the Motherhood Initiative, but we don't minimize it. I want you all here supporting each other through parenthood, but once you're ready, I want to start round two." He waited for a few reactions, but no audible comments came until Monica said,

"You want us to have another baby?"

"That's precisely it." Robin stood. "But you wouldn't be alone. You've all shown you can handle this. Like I said, I want to expand this village, but not without your input. I want you all to take ownership. I want you to decide what it's lacking." He raised his arms. "And it's *lacking*."

Giggles and laughs came from the group.

"But I need the commitment from you. For another round." He put his hands on his hips, feeling the awkward pause when Lana said,

"I'll stay."

She nodded to the others. One by one, her group also agreed. Soon, there was at least partial agreement from all. Robin shared a wide grin with Dr. Ianesso. They clasped hands. Their work was a success, at least in their minds.

When the group chat ended, Lana, Robin, and Dr. Ianesso took a walk out front.

"You really got them together," Robin said.

As Lana went to reply, Dr. Ianesso interrupted her.

"It was hard at first, but I got them talking." She smiled at Lana.

Lana's mouth closed and she swallowed her words. *Right, take the credit, bitch. You have no idea.*

After a little more ass kissing, Dr. Ianesso took a Rock-Hopper back home and the two were left alone.

"I know Maynard's not great at telling you how he feels," said Robin, "but he's proud of you." He put a hand on her shoulder. "You two have a sordid history that I don't fully understand, but the way he talks about you lately…I'm happy to see you could reconcile your differences."

Robin took a quick look around. "It started when you took out Isolde. I don't think he knew until then, but he's proud of the change you've shown."

Lana allowed her suppressed smile to show. He didn't need to know what it was really for. "It's been a long, strange ride for sure. I'm happy I can contribute." She saw Robin's approval but took it a step further. "Things just went wrong with our team on Wyan. I couldn't see it at the moment. I'm glad you guys came back for us."

Robin nodded, solemn. "I wish everyone saw it that way." He turned and climbed in a Rock-Hopper.

Lana watched him fly off, considering how he must feel to never see his last living son again. It surprised her that he'd choose the Belt's advancement over Arjen. But then again, knowing his story, the way his parents chose to send him off rather than to stay with them, it kind of made sense. For a moment she wanted to tell him her plan, to play the Arjen card as she had with Tiffany and Marlow. To promise to reunite families and friends, but Visser didn't speak that language. He only spoke Belt advancement, and she knew it would be his downfall.

~ * ~

The next meeting of the deserters was teeming with enthusiasm as time drew near. Fleta and Nigel were ready to pilot the Iris, ready for a real flight and not more rock hauling. Amelia and Shirley drew up plans for all to see, expansions on the huts the humans lived in on Wyan before. They passed around the designs. Lavinia claimed one on the edge of the village and when Lana marked her name on it, Lavinia had to give up her tough act for a second to thank her. Luis and Hudson added in details for the fields adjacent to the food processing building, making the process simpler for all involved. The mothers-to-be wanted close quarters like they had on New Pangaea for raising their children together in a new land. Even Tiffany agreed to that for the time being. Roel cared nothing of housing, where he'd be placed, only that he'd have a chance to avenge Admani. Lana promised him he'd have plenty of chances. She never brought up that Admani rarely spoke of his existence, and when she did it wasn't fondly.

"Where's the security kid?" Luis's straw hat was missing for the first time Lana could remember.

"Duty," Lana replied. "Didn't want to tip anyone off."

"You mean your dad?" Hudson barely came to her chin but dared to speak to her like that. *That will change,* thought Lana.

"That's a good thing to note." Lana spoke just loud enough for all to hear. "You're all leaving family behind. It doesn't matter if it's your dad or your third cousin. You've got to drop that from your mind. They won't be loyal to you. When and if they ever come to Wyan, they will be the second wave, and we all know the second wave gets what they get. They don't get to choose their housing or be part of the setup of laws. They will take what we give them. Is that clear?"

Hudson backed down next to Luis. "Right."

"Now, this will be our last meeting with most of us together. It's why I had Amelia and Shirley give us a mock-up of our housing. I wanted everyone to be clear, to have a say. Does everyone know their role over the next couple weeks?"

There were nods all around.

"When the last baby is born, assuming everything goes smoothly, we'll give time for a recovery week, the first few checkups and then I'll send word. If you need me, send a coded message and we will meet up. For now, buckle down. Don't let anything leak. I'll see you when it's time to fly."

Lana headed out of the forest, Zelda, Erika, and Darcy catching up to her. They stopped at the edge, members of the group leaving one or two at a time in different directions. It was Lana's turn to leave last. The other ladies of the village waited with her. Walking together wouldn't cause much suspicion. When the coast was clear, they started off, complaining about their backs, ankles, and anything else that ached when thirty-eight weeks into pregnancy.

Erika was going on about potential baby names. She was stuck between Martin and Steven.

"*Those* are what you're stuck on?" said Zelda. "Those plain-ass names? Why don't you just name him Dave and be done with it?"

Erika widened her eyes and shook her head.

"What?" Zelda went on. "I'm just saying—"

Erika bumped her with her hip, nodding toward Darcy.

"It's okay," Darcy said. "I know David isn't the most exciting name, but I want something to remember my father by. Since I probably won't ever see him again."

"No, hey…" said Zelda. "I…" But her foot was firmly in her mouth.

When they reached the apartments, Darcy was the first to branch off.

"See you all at the group meeting in the morning." She smiled at Zelda. "Don't forget your birth plan. Maybe we'll get to read through the whole thing."

She went in and Zelda sighed. "How was I supposed to know his first name was Dave? We all call him Dr. Crouch."

Erika laughed but Lana was eying a Rock-Hopper sitting out front. She walked to her apartment without saying goodbye. She tried the door, and it was unlocked. Maynard sat on her couch watching an eighties cop show.

"Oh, hey." He clicked it off. "Welcome home."

Lana stood just inside the door. "What's this about?"

"That's the kind of response I get? I came to visit my only girl."

"You broke into my apartment without warning. I have a data-pad. You could've sent me a message."

Maynard shrugged and patted the seat next to him on the couch. "Come on, sit down. I'm sure your legs are tired of carrying all that around." He pointed at her belly.

Lana sat, leaning forward, uncomfortable but not wanting to get too relaxed. "So, you were just in the neighborhood?"

"No, but listen. You know my security team is small. Since Peter took off with you and didn't come back, it's been me, Desi, and a couple volunteers when they're not working their other jobs. We don't really have crime to justify a bigger force, but with…situations going on, Visser approved to have one full time on each base around the clock. I'm already pegged to be the captain on Ceres, and I thought Desi would be my lead guy on New Pangaea, but he just doesn't seem up for it lately. His heart's elsewhere if you know what I mean."

Lana nodded. "Okay." But didn't expand on Desi's motivation.

"So, you've been back with us for a while. I was thinking after the baby, you take over as the security lead here. Since you already live here, it will be a simple setup. You're not doing any gathering being pregnant and caring for a child all the time, but you could handle disputes and things out here. I saw the way you took down Isolde. You really knew where to insert your authority when needed." He rubbed his arm, healed but forever reminding him of their battle. "Though, you could've been a few steps quicker."

Lana didn't know what to say. She obviously wasn't even considering the position. She wouldn't be there to worry about what goes on, on New Pangaea. But she couldn't tell him that.

"I…that could work for me." She faced him, giving a tired smile. "Can I decide after the birth? You never know how it goes."

Maynard pushed her arm playfully, then stood. "You'll be fine. I'll mark you down." He headed for the door. "Let me know when the baby gets here and let's hope it doesn't resemble the father."

As he left, Lana wondered if she should message Desi or try to meet up with him. Her dad sensed something. Had he offered Desi the job and he turned it down, or was it truly that he didn't seem ready for a promotion? Lana didn't care either way, only that he didn't crack over the next few weeks.

Chapter Thirteen

When Maynard landed at the government building, Gilbert stood up from his place in the grass and gave an attentive wave. The kids played freely inside the fence as their caretaker walked to meet his relief. Gilbert's job got even easier when they stripped him of the headcount and bringing them in for the night. All he had to do was break up fights and take the occasional nap against the government building's back wall.

"James had a rough day." Gilbert squinted out at the group. "Mandy, too. Had to separate them a coup—"

"I've got it." Maynard clutched two nutrient pouches. "You're free to go." He stood staring at Gilbert.

"Oh-okay." He hiked up his pants and trotted off toward a Rock-Hopper. There was no point in arguing with the head of security when he was in a mood. Just fly home to your apartment and keep your mouth shut. Gilbert would message Delia on the way home. They'd broken up months ago, but sometimes he found absence made the heart grow desperate, and he'd take what he could get.

Maynard watched him fly off then stepped up to the fence, banging on it with his taser. "I want no trouble out of any of you for the next five minutes." He clicked the button to shoot sparks out of the end for effect. "You hear me?" The feral children watched him with fright. Most had stopped moving and playing. "Good."

Maynard turned and headed in the back of the building. He had a special set of keys that only a few had to unlock the basement door. It added a burden onto those that possessed them but prevented the discovery of their prisoners.

Isolde and Kaia stood and approached the bars when he got to the bottom of the steps.

"Where are the children?" asked Kaia.

"Oh, they're just having an orgy up top." Maynard sneered. "Gilbert's watching 'em. I figured we could have a quick chat before I bring them down."

"Have you come to your senses?" Kaia asked. "Do we get our trial?"

Maynard's face scrunched up. "Well, here's the deal. In a couple weeks, we're going to know if Marlow's magical vagina can cure those kids, or at least future ones. At that point, you all," he pointed one of the nutrient pouches at them, "become expendable. The only reason you're still down here is because Visser has a little conscience left. Once he knows we don't need the Earth kids, well…it's only a matter of time for you two."

Kaia gripped the bars. "Send Robin down here. I demand our trial. It's not right to hold someone so long like this."

"Sorry. He's busy." He extended out the pouch. "At least he's still ordering you to be fed."

Kaia grunted. "Robin will see the truth." She reached for it. Isolde called out a second too late, "Mom." But he already gripped her wrist, pulling her arm toward him and her face into the bars. She hit them hard enough to be dazed. Maynard straightened out her arm, sizing it up, when Isolde reached through, chopping down to break his grasp on her mother, but he let go just before her hit came, catching her wrist next and forcing her arm in against the bars, bending it backward until Ice screamed out. When Maynard felt the pop, he shoved her chest, knocking her onto her back, holding her broken arm.

"How does that feel?" he screamed as Kaia rushed to her daughter's side. "Huh? Payback's a bitch." He turned, stepping on the nutrient pouch to spray its contents across the dirty floor, then headed for the stairs to bring the children in for the night. "There won't be a trial. You're gonna die here."

Part III

Chapter One

2052. 39 years ago.
Ceres Water Initiative

Helena Coates stood on the rocky shore watching the waves crash below. Her back was to Ahuna Mons as men connected giant pipes at her command. A boat sat a hundred yards out installing a pump deep below the surface as Robin Visser oversaw their progress. It was difficult work but a desperate need for the Belt as their first setup was full of flaws. The new one promised to last through a lifetime with minimal maintenance.

It took months to see the full project through, but when it was complete, a large celebration was held at Dr. Ramirez's house. It was a two-story, built on the first asteroid he'd gotten a TechBubble to take on. There was a lawn of neatly trimmed grass surrounding the house like a tree skirt. Beyond it, just a rocky path to the edge. Juan-Carlos Ramirez hit golf balls toward the end of his island with Petra Gammen and Wendell Coates and his daughter, Helena.

"I told you she was the woman for the job," Wendell said to Dr. Ramirez.

He cracked a ball off the end of the driver, losing it in the dark of the edge.

"I never doubted it."

Dr. Ramirez barely winged his ball. It rolled off the tee just a few feet ahead and he retrieved it, turning back toward them. "I'd like her overseeing more projects in the future."

"Why stop at projects?" Wendell leaned on his driver like a cane. "She could do bigger things than that." He raised his eyebrows.

Dr. Ramirez twisted his face in thought, his gaze shifting from them to a man standing out on the second-floor balcony with his son, Oscar. "I know what you're getting at, but I can't guarantee your position will just be passed down." He motioned between himself and Petra. "We have other thoughts in mind."

"But Oscar and Kaia are clearly on the path to succeed you two. Why shouldn't my daughter succeed me?"

Dr. Ramirez joined them at the tee box. "These are future conversations, my friend." He placed his ball back on the tee. "Let's just celebrate tonight."

"Yes," Wendell held up his hands, "you're right."

He turned to his daughter. "Helena, would you check if there's any of that swill this guy is serving left? I'm going to need a few more drinks if I'm to give him a chance to out drive me."

"Yes, sir." She started off, then found her father falling beside her, whispering. "If it wasn't clear, there aren't going to be any future conversations about you becoming a judge as long as Robin Visser is still around."

Helena stopped. "Yes, that was clear. You should've seen him at the sight today before you got there."

Wendell looked back as Petra said something to make Juan-Carlos Ramirez break into a belly laugh. "The kid is like a son to him. We knew it was an uphill battle, but…" He shook his head, looking up toward Robin and Oscar, talking and pushing each other as brothers do. "We've tried everything else. Are you ready to do what it takes?"

Helena stared at her father with strong set blue eyes. "Yes."

He gripped her shoulders one time. "Make me proud." As he let her go, he added, "And let your hair down."

She nodded and pulled her golden locks loose, tossing her head side to side as she entered the house.

From the upper balcony, Ceres engulfed the view like an oversized moon. When Helena stepped out the French doors, the young men turned. She wore a snug pair of red pants, white blouse, and held two drinks.

"Oh, Robin, they think I'm a lush." She held one of the drinks out.

"Can you help?"

Robin smiled and stepped up to grab a drink, then her hand to lead her to the balcony's edge.

"Where's mine?" asked Oscar.

Helena shrugged. "Probably with Marcie downstairs, but she's cornered by that Gilbert guy."

Oscar's head snapped back. "Gilbert? With the janitorial team? What's he doing here?"

"It's a free belt." Helena smiled. "Looks like he's having a good time."

Oscar stormed down the stairs and Helena turned, leaning on the railing, the light of Ceres making her hair glow like a golden veil over her.

Robin watched her. "We did well, hey?" He raised his drink.

Helena met it. "We did. I'm afraid it's not enough for me, though."

"What does that mean? Dr. Ramirez loves your work. He's told me."

"Yeah…"

Robin put a hand on her forearm. "Hey. You're going to do great things here. We all can see that."

His talk, she thought, *he already knows he'll be a judge. I'm not a threat to him.* Helena raised her glass again. "Well, to the future, then." Robin drank to her toast and when he lowered his cup, her face was a few inches closer. "We made a great team out there. Wouldn't you say?" Her voice was just above a sultry whisper.

Robin swallowed hard. "Uh, yeah. I'd say so."

She stuck a finger in the middle of his chest, gently. "Hopefully it's not the last time." Then left him on the balcony alone.

~ * ~

A year later, Wesley was born. Helena kept her plans to stay in politics. A judge's wife was better than a judge's reject. She took her son to every event, every project she worked on, but her second pregnancy changed her. It took her to her limits, and she spent weeks in recovery after many hours of hard laboring that finished with an emergency c-section.

As her recovery progressed, her help dwindled. Then she was alone with her two boys. Both were easy going, making parenting an overall joy. She found her desires for higher offices wane. Soon, the last thing she wanted was to return to governmental meetings. As Arjen began early school, she went back into the workforce to become the overseer of the water plant and all its entities. It only felt right to pick up where she'd started. Where she'd been most successful.

Her father was more than disappointed at her change of heart, but when he would come to see the boys and get into talks with Robin, she'd tell them to take the policy talk outside. It all came to a head when Wendell told Robin a few of the details from that night on Dr. Ramirez's island. A few more than he should've. Robin wanted to discuss it, but they only fought, both saying things they could never take back. As the boys grew, Wesley showed such promise in woodworking that Helena put all her energy into encouraging him to do it, much to spite his father. This only made Robin push harder on Arjen. Helena backed off, knowing her son better than he did. Arjen rebelled, joining the gathering program. Robin cursed her for ruining their legacy, reminding her their whole marriage was built on becoming a political power in the Belt, even if it was a lie in the first place. He became cold, staying together for hopes that one of his boys would come back around.

The boys grew and spent more and more time with the studies that came with their chosen professions. During this time, Helena took another lover, Martin, the man who performed the monthly service on their TechBubble. She moved out when Wesley was nineteen, working on his first house for him and his brother, feeling she was no longer needed. She stayed out of the Visser affairs from there, just keeping in touch with her boys who spent those years deep in their careers.

Martin had an island with a view of the other side of Ceres, showing more of a haunting glow she came to love. Martin could tweak the 'Bubble in any way he desired, much like the rooms on the Iris. Helena was content with her life with Martin, updating their island with varieties of plant life as they each served the Belt during the day and came home at night to serve each other.

Nineteen years later, they were one of the few solo islands left after New Pangaea was developed.

~ * ~

Current day

Helena heard sounds outside earlier than she planned. She had a pile of freshly cut flowers on the table that she meant to decorate the living room with. Martin enjoyed the colors, and she was excited to give him a show that night. Their bath was bubbling with scented oils and she was wearing a special outfit that wouldn't stay on long if she knew her husband.

She felt goosebumps raise up around the crimson lace as she stepped outside. They always kept their island a little cooler than the rest. It made the baths more enjoyable. "We have to stay close," Martin would say, "to keep each other warm." Helena was fine with his reasoning but that night, her pale legs felt exposed as she looked out at the island. Down past the flower garden, she saw movement, but there was no Rock-Hopper to signify Martin's return.

"Hello?" she called. "Who's there?"

A redheaded woman she didn't recognize waved a hand. She was carrying a bag with safety pins up one side. Helena squinted at her.

"Who are you? How did—" But she stopped when she saw him, her son back from the dead. Helena ran down the rocks to him, calling out, "Arjen!"

Chapter Two

Helena couldn't stop kissing the emaciated cheeks of her son. She held his face in her hands, seeing the scarred top where the hair grew only in sporadic patches. She hated when he left with Lana but understood all the same. He'd been in love with that girl since they first met. When Robin returned and announced his death, she broke down. As much as Arjen traveled in the past, just knowing he was out there with the girl he loved made her heart content, but thinking he'd died out there, so far from home…Helena couldn't handle it. But now he was here, sitting next to her on the couch, looking just a step ahead of death.

"You didn't see the ship at all?" Arjen asked. "Coming or going?"

"No. Nothing." Helena fidgeted with the hem of a blanket she'd wrapped around herself, concealing her evening wear. "What ship? The Mack?"

Arjen turned to Julie. "They weren't kidding. Their stealth mode is legitimate."

"Whose?" Helena asked. "Those Wyans you met?"

"No. Others. They aren't here anymore. We'll explain later." He took his mom's hands. "It doesn't matter right now. Where's Marlow and Zane?"

"I'm sorry, Arjen, they're de—" Helena caught herself as Arjen was shaking his head. "They're not dead?"

"Dad picked them up. We survived a battle on Wyan. We were all together, but Dad and Maynard stole them from us."

"Your father saw you? Alive?"

"Yes."

She slammed a hand on the arm of the couch. "He told me you were dead. That bastard lied to me about my only living son." Her eyes narrowed further. "Why didn't he take you back?"

"Long story." Arjen eyed the door. "Listen, you said Martin's going to be home soon. What's he going to make of this?"

"What I tell him to make of it. You're my boy, back from the dead."

Arjen gave her a quick smile. "Yes, but we can't have him spreading the news that I'm back. I need a few days to recover, then we need to find where he's keeping Marlow."

"Okay." Helena stood, wrapping the blanket around herself. "I'll keep an eye out for him and catch him before he gets inside. What can I get you two?"

"Food—a 'Panel. We had to revert a GammenVat into its original form. We were doing okay until it broke on us in the wormhole. It's been a long ride back."

"Of course." She started for the back of the house. "Martin always has us stocked a week ahead." Helena went to their tub and brushed off flower clippings, opening the slot for the 'Panel. She took one of Martin's from a little refrigerator nearby and loaded it. "Okay."

Arjen and Julie came back. He undressed and climbed in, feeling the flow of warm water and pure nutrients absorbing into his body. Julie and Helena cringed at his skeletal figure. The ride back hadn't been kind to them but more than once, Arjen passed the bigger portion of their rations to Julie. It was obvious as she looked at him, so she focused on other things.

"I love all the fresh flowers," Julie said to Helena.

"Thank you. They're all from the garden where you came up."

"Ah, I see." Julie started piecing it together. "So, the lingerie and the flowers…"

Helena blushed and put a hand to the side of her mouth to whisper, "It's our anniversary."

"Oh, my." Julie gave her a broad smile. "The tub then…"

Helena giggled, pulling her hair back, a mixture of gold and grey.

"What's that?" said Arjen. "I can't hear you over this way-too-quiet tub, that smells like lavender. Nope. Can't hear any of those details."

"Oh." Helena waved a hand at him. "Just be glad you didn't show up any later. You might have walked in on us."

As Julie's bath ended, Helena heard Martin, touching down after a day's work of TechBubble maintenance. The two refugees waited in the living room as Helena, now changed into comfortable pants and a shirt, went out to meet him.

~ * ~

Julie looked at Arjen. "Is it okay that I'm freaking out a little?"

Arjen put an arm around her shoulders. "Yeah, I am too, but it's probably because we just had some nourishment for the first time in a week. I'm jittery."

"Yeah but…we're back in the Belt, Arjen. I didn't think we'd make it this far. I planned to die on Wyan."

Arjen nodded, watching his mom from the window. "Well, you didn't, so now you're going to have to help me overthrow my father."

"Can we sleep first? On like a mattress instead of a pile of our clothes?"

"That can probably be arranged."

~ * ~

They shared stories long into the night. As Arjen and Julie learned of the death of Kaia and Isolde, Helena reminded them how close Robin and Oscar were. The Belt was run by a monopoly of adopted brothers. They had to focus on finding Marlow and Zane, keeping any details far from the ears of Robin Visser or anyone working with him. There were zero leads on the whereabouts of the Earthlings. Martin promised to do some digging at work the next day, as did Helena.

When they finished their tales from Wyan and their return home, Martin moved a spare mattress into the living room as he saw the utter weariness of the travelers. He and Helena laid out the sheets, then Martin sat right in the middle of it.

"You take our bed. It'll keep you away from the windows just in case anyone comes calling."

"You don't—" Arjen started but Julie grabbed his arm.

"Thank you." She started back toward the bedroom as Arjen hugged his mother and stepfather one more time.

"Thanks for taking us in," said Arjen.

"Oh, baby." Helena felt a few tears start down her cheeks that she rubbed away. "I'm just so happy you're alive."

"Alive, and a lot left to do."

Martin put a hand on Arjen's shoulder and met his eyes. "First, just rest tonight. We'll talk in the morning."

Arjen headed back to the bedroom and found Julie giggling at the side of the bed. She wore a long, nightshirt and borrowed underwear from Helena.

"What?" he asked, and she pulled up the shirt just enough to show the granny-pannies before letting it drop back down. Arjen shrugged. "At least she didn't give you that thing she was wearing earlier."

"Not just that." Julie motioned toward the bed. There were multicolored flower petals forming into a heart across the comforter.

Arjen rolled his eyes. "We really stepped into the middle of something."

"A night of passion." Julie smirked.

"Not anymore." He grabbed the comforter to pull it back, but Julie held it down.

"No. Don't shake them on the floor."

Arjen put his hands on his hips. "I'm dead tired."

"Just wait." Julie collected the petals in the palm of her hand and set them on the nightstand.

"We good now?"

"Mm hmm." They lay side by side as she clicked off the light. "Just try to keep your hands off me. I'm really tired tonight, okay?" She snorted out a laugh and Arjen pushed her through the blanket. Then he sniffed a couple times.

"God, you even smell like her. Did you use Mom's perfume?"

"Just a little. It's floral."

Arjen shook his head, resting on the pillow, his eyes no longer able to stay open. "Good night, Mo—I mean, Julie."

Julie sighed, and in a dreamy voice, said, "Good night, dear."

Chapter Three

The next morning, Martin landed at the Belt Forest. It was thinning from all the building being done on New Pangaea. He took his time on the TechBubble, checking every little detail, though it was in perfect condition and would soon be shut down when the last of the trees were used up. Then, they'd transition to New Pangaea like many others. When Martin saw Tyron coming out of his little office, he made haste.

"Morning." Martin waved and approached with purpose.

Tyron was tall and muscular, keeping his short beard edged to perfection. He took over when Wesley died and while he wasn't quite the same builder, he kept good order over the forest.

"Hey, Martin." Tyron's face looked concerned. "Everything check out or…?"

"It checked out, but if you have a minute for me…" He eyed the office as a pair of workers passed by with a stack of logs.

Tyron waved him to follow back into the office, a small room with a computer monitor at a desk, a bathroom attached, and not much else.

Martin checked back to see they weren't followed.

"Alright, what's going on?" Tyron asked. "Looks like something crawled into your trousers and died."

Martin let out a smile. "Quite the opposite." He took one last look then said, "I know you were close with Wesley."

"Yeah, you could say that alright."

"And I know neither of us are the biggest fans of his dad."

Tyron chuckled a little. "You more than me, mate."

"Right, and with Kaia gone…"

"Damn shame. For both of 'em." He rubbed his chin and stared off. "You know Ice and I used to date."

Martin crossed his arms. "I did not know that. It's just terrible what happened."

"Yeah, I even tried to chat her up a little when she got back. It sounded like she wouldn't be traveling much this go-round. That was always our issue, but things just weren't the same. She was different after that last trip. She'd seen things. She never seemed to get right again. Even at the end."

"I hear you. I think they all saw things out there. I think Visser saw things when they went back. Not trying to go all conspiracy on you, but half the time, I'm wondering if he's telling us the whole truth."

Tyron leaned in, whispering despite having the room to themselves. "Those are big accusations."

Martin stepped back, raising his hands. "I'm saying, the Belt was founded on democracy. Doesn't it worry you that we're hiding out here whispering about these things?"

Tyron considered it. "It does, but what do you want to do about it? Leave the politics to them. You worry about the 'Bubble, and I'll worry about keeping us housed and furnished."

"Speaking of that…"

Tyron shook his head. "I've really got to get out there."

"Last question, I swear."

Tyron lowered his eyes. "Let's hear it."

"You ever been part of building a place to hold people?"

"Like a jail?" Tyron paused in the doorway.

"Just anything fishy. Didn't sit right with you?"

After a long moment with his eyes narrowed, Tyron did a quick shake of his head. "Can't say that I have." He stepped outside. "Cheers."

~ * ~

Helena was distracted when she did her walkthrough of the main water plant on Ceres that morning.

"Ms. Coates?" said a woman standing beside a large intake valve. There was a clear drip coming from it, but Helena watched the few other employees with suspicion. Upon finding her dead son alive, she wanted to know what other things were going on on the Belt that she was unaware of.

"Sorry." Helena turned to the woman. "What were you trying to tell me?"

"That." The woman pointed at the drip.

"Oh, yes. Cut it back at seal thirteen. Check the connection. If it can be repaired, just take care of it. If not…"

Her attention drifted off to Oscar Ramirez, outside the facility talking with someone. *Did he know about Arjen?* She wondered. *How many did? What if everyone knew but her?*

The woman forced a smile and a polite laugh. "I'll message you if I run into anything big."

"Thank you."

Helena was already walking in the direction of Oscar. It wasn't a deliberate walk, but one equivalent to someone about to ask for directions, first seeing if their swaying walk would point them in the right direction before they had to ask.

By the time she got close, Oscar was off in another direction. She considered calling out to him, asking him to give her any details he knew of Robin's trip to Wyan, but she knew it would only go straight to Robin. She stopped outside the plant, wondering if they all already knew, just like they had with the judge position. This time she couldn't just flirt with Robin to find out. Or could she…?

~ * ~

Back at the house that evening, Arjen and Julie waited anxiously for any word. They couldn't risk using a data-pad and alerting someone that they were on the grid, so they watched the windows in pacing shifts. Finally, Julie gave up and laid on the couch, while Arjen made his way to the door for a peep, then back, plopping down next to her. She poked him with a sock-covered foot with a large purple cat on it.

"Mr. Mittens says, 'Sit down.'"

Arjen looked at her with determined eyes. "I am sitting."

"Good. Stay for a while. You can't will them to come home."

"No, but I can keep an eye out for anyone else."

Julie sat up, bringing her knees to her chest. Her Pearl Jam shirt was clean, and she was excited to wear it again. "Who's gonna show up? And more importantly, if they do, what are we gonna do? We can't run anywhere. We're on one of the smallest islands out here."

"I just want to be ready."

"Yeah but—"

She paused when they both heard a Rock-Hopper landing, then they were at the window together, keeping a curtain in front as Martin and Helena climbed out. Once they were sure it was just the two of them, they waited on the couch, as if they'd just been relaxing all day. Arjen kept his eyes on his mother and stepdad when they entered, hoping he wouldn't have to ask.

The couple shared a look, then Martin spoke first. "Not a lot of luck on my end. I have another lead I'm going to try tomorrow."

"Yes," Helena agreed. "About the same for me."

"Okay," said Julie.

"Tomorrow," said Arjen. "Who or what are the leads? Why can't you check them out now?"

Martin rubbed the back of his neck. "It's been a long day, Arjen. We were up late last night and—"

Arjen stood from the couch. "A girl's out there being used and tested on. Who knows what they're doing to Zane and Avani?" He pointed to Julie, then himself. "We're in no condition to fight right now. If we're seen, it could be the end for us. That's why we need you."

Helena came over, stopping just short of her son. "Surely you don't think it would be that way with your dad."

Arjen tilted his head. "Mom, do you still love Dad?"

"I…" She stumbled over her next words. "What we have is not the same as—I love what we created." She reached a hand up to rub his cheek.

"Good. That will make it easier for what I'm probably going to have to do."

Helena's eyes shifted to fearful concern. "What does that mean?"

"Never mind. We have to find Marlow and Zane first."

"Give us time tomorrow." Martin pushed his palms downward to try to ease the mood. "We'll do our best to help your friends, okay?"

Arjen sighed. "Okay, but we can't sit out here much longer without going crazy."

"Speak for yourself," said Julie. "I've hid out in worse."

Chapter Four

Zane watched the window to see familiar faces that gave him the creeps at the same time.

"They're here," he called back to Marlow. She was sitting in a pile of her few changes of clothes.

"I don't know what to bring. Last time…" She stopped herself, not wanting to even think about the end of her last pregnancy.

"You probably don't need much. I'm sure they have gowns and stuff."

Dr. Vell and Dr. Crouch showed up at the door with Desi behind.

"Marlow," Dr. Vell said, with her fake smile.

Marlow didn't return the greeting, only crammed an outfit into the bag and slung it over her shoulder. She stopped at Zane who was holding Avani.

"Warm up the pouches with your hands. She doesn't take them cold."

"I know," said Zane. "We'll be okay." He leaned his head onto hers and Avani giggled at their family circle. "You're going to come out of this fine," he whispered. "No worries. They want you alive. Just cooperate."

Marlow hugged him, then Avani, kissing each corner of her face. There would be so much to tell her in the future. So much guilt for the trauma she'd already endured, but Marlow could truly say she'd always done whatever it takes. She headed off with the doctors as her little family watched from the window.

~ * ~

Shortly after they arrived at the medical facility and entered through the back door, Martin landed just down the way at the water processing plant on New Pangaea. He could've just as easily sent Helena to try this lead, but it was his conversation to have. Who knew better how to get you to talk than your own dad?

Zelda met him outside on a bench flanked by two budding cherry blossoms. Her belly was stretched tight, and she had visible sweat stains under her armpits.

Martin sat next to her with a grunt. "You hear my back? I hope you've got someone inside that can help us both off of this bench or we're sleeping here."

Zelda smiled and gave him a side hug. "What's going on? Did Hela tell you about my recent performance review?"

He winced. "You know she hates when you call her that."

"Well, I don't call her that to her face. At least not during my review." Zelda waved at a passerby. "It's a joke anyway. What are they gonna do? Replace me with the next generation?"

Martin put a hand on his developing grandchild. "Not for a few years, I'd say." He shifted to face her better. "I had a question for you. You know Lana Royal pretty well now, don't you?"

"Well?" Zelda scratched at her neck. "Not like, well, well, but we live in the same place over there. Group meetings and all. I'm not like *interested* in her if that's what you're asking."

"No, no. I'm just saying, you may have heard some stories from her about her time," he pointed off into space, "out there."

"I mean, she's talked about it but, I think it's a sore subject for her. I don't know."

"I just…" Martin lowered his voice. "You know Helena's son Arjen was out there. She hasn't heard much about him since. All we've heard was that Visser got there, and he was dead. But think about that as a mother. You get word that your baby died on another planet but nothing else? Wouldn't you want to know more?"

Zelda shrugged. "I mean, sure, *I* would, but I'm not sure there's more to say."

"Yeah, it's just, Helena has these nightmares, and it would just be nice to give her something. A little story about him. You know what I mean? You ever hear anything from Lana about him, or maybe the others out there? How they lived? What happened to them all before she left?"

Zelda's pit stains were growing. "Like I said, it might be a little sore of a subject for her, and with the baby coming, she doesn't need any extra stress. Maybe down the road we could get something out of her." She pushed off the bench. "I've gotta get back inside. Only got a few days left before they'll be without me."

"Right." Martin stood and hugged Zelda.

"Love ya, Dad."

"Love you."

~ * ~

After the group meeting, Lana sat in the chairs with Zelda. The other ladies went in to rest early. As the light framed Lana's face through an opening in the trees, Zelda saw what they called 'the pregnancy glow.' She knew she didn't have it. The mirror was very clear about that each morning, afternoon, and pretty much any other time she stepped in front of it, but Lana was something. Zelda realized what she'd told her dad was now a lie. She was interested in Lana. She may have been all along and just hadn't thought about it because she was starstruck. Lana was polarizing. Half the Belt hated her for daring to leave without government approval. Others thought her a hero. Zelda saw how Lana used her celebrity to influence others to join her for another quest. Zelda wanted badly to be out on some gorgeous planet, working with Lana day in and day out. That's why it hurt her so bad to say it.

"What do you mean you can't go?" asked Lana. "We're just weeks away. We—" Lana held back a grunt of frustration.

"I know, I know. I'm so sorry." Zelda sat facing her, as close as she dared. "But after talking to my dad, I just want him to have a chance at being a grandfather. I think he'd be great at it and Helena too. They're good people, unlike my mom. I just…I didn't think he'd want to be involved. It all felt like a science experiment to me until now. It's obvious that it's something real for him. For me too, now that I think about it."

"It's not…" Lana regrouped, bringing her voice back even. "You will get to keep your baby when we go to Wyan. I know what they've told you here but there's no guarantee. It *is* a science experiment to them. If there's something about your baby that they need to further study, they will take him away." Lana leaned forward and grabbed one of Zelda's hands. "And it's not like your father can't come. He's just more of a wave-two kind of person. We need the fighters and the mothers, then everyone else that wants to join us."

"I know. I just…what if I hung back with him? Then if I can convince him and Helena, I could come later. Might be tough with her though, leaving here to see where her son died. I don't know."

Lana stared off, pulling thoughts from the sky, then said, "What if I had a guaranteed way to get them to come on the second wave. Would you come on the first?"

Zelda furrowed her brow. "What? Like what?"

Lana whispered the next part, and Zelda's eyes widened with each word.

~ * ~

As they settled in for the night, a Rock-Hopper landed just outside the garden. Helena came down the steps with a basket and shears, hustling more than needed on a quiet evening.

"Oh, hello, Zelda." Helena stopped just in front of her as she touched the ground. "We haven't seen you out here in quite a while. You're looking so beautiful with that baby on the way."

"I don't know about that. I feel like a bit of an asteroid myself. Oh, and congrats on the anniversary. You two do anything special?"

Helena felt a smile creep across her face. "Just a quiet night at home together."

"Well, you know I hate flying but when the baby gets here, I promise to visit more often."

"Oh, nonsense. We can come to you, too."

As they exchanged their pleasantries, Martin came down to meet them.

"Hey. Long time." He smirked at her.

"Yeah. I uh…got some more details you might like to hear." She looked around the dim rock. "Mind if I come in? It's a little chilly out here."

Helena exchanged a look with Martin who nodded.

"Yes, sure," he said, taking her hand, slowly leading her to the house, while Helena power walked ahead.

They sat her on the couch, Martin next to her and Helena standing, keeping an eye on the hall back to their bedroom.

"So, tell me," said Martin, "what did Lana say?"

"I…" Zelda glanced at Helena. "I'm not gonna beat around the bush. She said Arjen's still alive out there."

"Oh." Helena was too caught off guard by a fact she already knew to give it the proper response. "Oh, my. H-how do you know this is true?"

Zelda turned to face her. "When she left, she said Visser and Arjen had a fight. That Visser left him out there alive with others."

Martin was shaking his head. "When were they planning to tell anyone? That's her son we're talking about. Shouldn't she have a right to know that he's still alive?"

Zelda held up her hands. "I can't speak for Visser. He may have his reasons, but Lana hasn't told anyone because she's actually planning to do something about it. You can't repeat this to anyone, okay?" Zelda waited for agreement, then continued, "Lana's leading a group back out there, to live on Wyan. To start her colony for good this time, and she wants to invite you to come."

~ * ~

As Zelda flew off, Arjen and Julie were in the hall, Arjen holding a wall for support.

"She's going back?" he said to no one in particular. "She's got another mutiny going already." He was half smiling in disbelief. "I've gotta talk to her. You gotta get Lana out here."

Chapter Five

The room was painfully similar to the last. The smell of antiseptic. The cold walls. The beep of machines. Only, she was awake this time. Marlow's belly was like a small hill, blocking the view of her feet before they raised a sheet in front of it. Her hands were already strapped down as Dr. Crouch came around and fit a mask over her mouth and nose. "Just breathe normally," he said, but Marlow felt a hitch in each inhale. The second birth wasn't going to be a beautiful experience either. She'd heard their plans. She went first because they had a line of mothers almost ready to pop and only so many doctors to help deliver. She wished Zane was there for support but was stuck with two doctors who moved with such proficiency that she was certain they'd performed the last delivery. Maybe she'd ask them about it later, but she saw the tray of tools Dr. Vell rolled next to her and felt a dizzy spell come over her.

"Can you feel that, Marlow?" Dr. Vell asked.

"Feel what?" Marlow tried to keep the fear out of her voice but failed.

Dr. Vell smiled and nodded at Dr. Crouch. "I'd say we're ready."

The next few minutes were awful. Marlow was loopy from the anesthesia but could still register the jarring movements below her chest. When they emerged with the child, there was no delightful revealing, only another figure, Mateo, who showed up and rushed away with her baby. Marlow barely caught a glimpse of dark hair, her neck straining to see the stolen child.

When she was sewn shut, they left her in the room. She had time to consider her position, once again, at the mercy of the Belt, or Lana's calculated proposal of another chance at Wyan living.

She was too tingly to rest, too scared to accept her only real choice to run off again. Marlow didn't feel strong. She assumed leaving meant leaving the second child. She wasn't attached to it the way she was with Avani. Maybe the Belt would use it for what they needed and leave her alone to quietly slip away. She hadn't prepared any names and didn't know if she'd need to.

Marlow cried alone.

~ * ~

Her eyes opened, feeling crusty from dried tears. There were voices outside the door. Marlow wanted to straighten up but was still strapped and uncomfortable. The door came open and Robin Visser stood, his head tilted and eyes full of artificial compassion.

"How are you feeling?"

"Like I've been cut open and abandoned." Marlow swallowed, trying to loosen up her dry throat. "But now I see I've gone to hell and the devil is here to greet me."

Visser's face was unphased. "You've once again done the Belt a great service. Mateo is confident with all the samples we've been able to take this time, we'll be able to set ourselves up for the future. He's confident we can replicate the genes you pass." He gave a slight bow. "But I should let you rest. On to phase two."

Marlow watched him leave. *Phase two.* She knew what that was—impregnating regular belt couples and implanting the missing genes to see if they could pull off what they did with baby Wesley. Marlow felt her veins go cold. She looked down at the I.V. in her arm, knowing it wasn't medication, knowing that they *had* pulled it off with Tiffany's baby, even during the exodus of their test subjects. If Mateo was confident they could replicate the gene, what would they need with Marlow? She hadn't liked Visser's smile. Maybe last time, if she'd kept quiet, she could've slipped back into Belt life. Now she was worried. There was no place left for her in their society. Not with all she knew. The only real place for her was somewhere else, before they decided to turn the lie they'd been telling into truth. She tried a weak tug at her restraints, then let her head fall back.

~ * ~

Lana crammed a dress into her bag. Her c-section appointment was about ten hours away. What better way to lead by example than to be the first cut open? *Second*, if you counted Marlow, and Lana did. They needed her on Wyan, not just for the babies, but because Marlow could do her own thing. You didn't always have to tell her, unlike others. Some needed a reminder to take a few breaths so they wouldn't suffocate.

Lana had little fear about the birth. It wasn't about the child. She was able to separate that. It was about getting it over with and getting the recovery out of the way so she could move on to planning their last weeks in the Belt.

There was a tap at her back door. She swore if Dr. Ianesso showed up to ask her to describe her feelings with a few words, she would explode on her. Lana looked over to see Zelda bloated with her own child. She insisted on still wearing pants and baggy shirts that looked to be stretched uncomfortably. Lana waved her in, and she slid the glass door open.

"You ready to get sliced?"

Lana let out an inadvertent laugh. "Not when you put it that way." She stood up, putting a hand on the couch for support as a little dizzy spell hit her. "Promise me you won't say it that way to Darcy."

Zelda waved a hand. "No, never. She's freaking out enough. Think she's a hypochondriac." Her face twisted up. "You think that's common for doctor's kids?"

Lana shrugged. "Could be."

Zelda stopped at the other end of the couch. "So, I spoke with my father. Gave him the deal and all…"

"Yes, you told me. Have they made their decision?"

"Well…he messaged me today but said this." Zelda raised her data-pad and read, "'Hey, Z. You should really bring Lana out here to see the flowers. I think it would really make Helena happy to talk about them.'" She frowned at Lana. "You think…?"

Lana thought for a second. "They may need a little more convincing and they want to hear it straight from me. Makes sense. I appreciate that they're keeping it coded."

"Oh yeah. Dad would never spill it. I mean, no one on that island is a fan of Visser."

Lana checked the time. "I should really get out there before the pregnancy. I know the recovery might slow me for a bit. I don't want them asking around or anything in my absence."

"You up for it?"

Lana put her hands out. "I'm pregnant, not crippled."

"Alright. I'll let him know we're ready to talk flowers, then call a 'Hopper?"

Lana nodded and Zelda stepped out.

When Lana made it to the front of the apartments, she saw her father walking and talking with a friend of his from the clothing factory. Zelda waited by a Rock-Hopper nearby and Lana signaled her to hold for a minute, approaching Maynard and the man whose name she should remember but couldn't.

"There she is," said Maynard. "We were just talking about the baby."

"Yes," said the nameless man. "I think Royal will look great on the back of a onesie. Already got the design ready."

Maynard patted him hard on the back. "That was gonna be a surprise."

"Oh, sorry about that."

"I'll try to forget it," Lana said with a smile.

"Thanks."

Lana turned. "Dad, if you have a minute…"

The man took his cue and left them alone.

"I've been thinking about the job." Lana squinted up at him. "I think it will be a great fit for me. The sooner, the better."

A proud smile crossed Maynard's face. "Alright. Any idea how soon that's going to be?"

"The doctors say a week with the 'Panel doing its thing, but we can talk details as soon as you're ready."

~ * ~

The Rock-Hopper passed around Ceres; Lana ignored the view to discuss their game plan.

"Remember, you're going to Wyan. His grandchild is going to Wyan. We want him to see both of you, but the way he does that is by coming with. He has no leverage otherwise."

"Just sounds harsh." Zelda stared off.

"Sometimes it has to be. If it was easy, he'd already have punched his ticket and I wouldn't have to be coming out here."

Zelda turned. "Sorry, I—"

"No. It's not your fault. Parents complicate things. We're about to find that out for ourselves."

"Thinking about the baby?"

"A bit."

"You picked out a name yet?"

"No."

Lana saw the flower beds coming into view as they descended on Martin and Helena's island.

Zelda shrugged. "It's not here yet. You got time."

Lana sighed but didn't reply.

They landed as Zelda got a call on her data-pad. Lana stepped out to a greeting from Helena. Arjen's mother. She wondered how she'd handled the news of her son. Lana couldn't sense any animosity in her right off the bat. Only an eager curiosity. Her movements, her words, all calculated. Lana looked up at the house to see Martin in the doorway, but he wasn't alone. There were shadows at the windows. She wondered if it was some kind of ambush. But who? If Visser knew her plans, he would've waited a day for the baby to be born, then he'd take action. He would've never called her out there to confront her.

"Having a party?" Lana motioned to the house, letting Helena know, if there was a double cross, she was already aware.

Though, she wished Zelda would get out of the 'Hopper and provide the only pathetic backup she had.

Helena glanced up, then smiled back. "Oh, just friends of ours."

Lana waited, looked at the unmoving figures in the house, then back to Zelda who finally emerged from the ship. Her face was going pale where it wasn't flushed.

"We've gotta…" Zelda looked between the two women, then back to the 'Hopper.

"What is it?" asked Lana.

"Darcy's gone into early labor, but something went wrong. They're not sure if she's going to make it."

"Shit." Lana pulled back toward the ship. "Is she at the medical facility?"

"Yeah. They had trouble getting her there but…oh, god." Zelda held her head in her hands. Helena was at her side.

"Is this one of your friends there?"

"Yes." Zelda gave her a quick hug. "Sorry, tell Dad we have to go. It's an emergency."

Zelda made it into the Rock-Hopper first, then Lana behind. Looking back at the house as the glass closed around her. Her eyes narrowed at the windows, feeling like they may have just dodged a bullet, but not knowing the extent of it all.

They flew off back toward New Pangaea as Arjen and Julie stood watching.

Chapter Six

The waiting area at the medical facility was full of pregnant ladies. Lana and Zelda were greeted at the door by Erika, who couldn't take the pacing of Monica anymore. They sat, legs twitching with nerves, not just for their close friend and neighbor, but for themselves. It was a reminder that no matter the plan and medical technology, sometimes bodies just couldn't take the strain. Lana knew the stress had been getting to Darcy. There was the baby, but so much more. Leaving her father, family, and friends. It was a lot for her to deal with. Lana had hoped she'd just tough it out until the move, then they'd figure it out in their new colony. Instead, she sat, wondering if all the pressure and borderline manipulation drove her to an early, dangerous labor.

Finally, Dr. Vell came down the hall. She observed the ladies for a minute before saying, "She's stable, but I can't have all of you in the room with her."

The ladies looked between each other, then Zelda turned. "Lana should go; she's our leader."

"Well…" Lana started.

"Then come." Dr. Vell crossed her arms. "You'll only have a minute. She needs her rest."

Lana stood as the others sent their love with her.

The room was silent. Dr. Crouch sat in the corner, head in his hands as Darcy lay, pale, in the bed. There was a weak turn of her head and half smile as she saw Lana.

"Hey." Darcy sounded as frail as she looked.

Lana took her hand, strapped with tape over an I.V. "My girl, you had us scared."

"It just hit so fast. I panicked."

"It looks like they took care of you and…" Lana paused, knowing the lump under her covers was smaller than it should be. *Did they lose the baby?*

Dr. Vell read her mind and said, "The child is with Mateo. Now, our patient needs to rest."

Lana stroked Darcy's head. "Everyone sends their love. We're around if you need us."

The soon-to-be mothers chatted in the lobby for a few minutes after Lana returned, then dispersed back to their apartments. As Zelda stepped ahead of her, Lana excused herself back inside the medical facility, lying about needing to ask Dr. Vell a question about her upcoming c-section.

The lobby was empty. Lana took off down the opposite hall from Darcy's room. She padded quietly, listening for crying or sounds of any kind. She stopped at the last door before the emergency exit. The exit was propped open and a Rock-Hopper waiting. She heard shuffling feet. Before she could find a place to hide, Robbin Visser stepped out, closing the door tightly behind him.

"Lana? What are you doing down here?" He stayed in front of the door like a bouncer.

"I was visiting Darcy."

"Oh." He broke into a smile. "She's down the other hall."

"I know." Lana crossed her arms. "When are you going to tell her, the baby didn't make it?" It was a guess but a good one, as Visser's face drooped.

"She's in recovery. We wanted to give her time. She's a bit fragile, you know."

"I know. I live with her." Lana craned her neck to see the door over his shoulder. "You get what you need?"

Robin sighed. "Let's not simplify it like that. This is a tragedy."

Lana put her hands up. "Not saying it's not." She turned. "Gotta get going. I'm next in line. Hopefully it goes better for me."

~ * ~

Lana managed a short nap on the couch before she woke to kicks coming from inside her. She stared at the wall, feeling like her belly might tip her off the edge. She knew what losing Darcy's baby meant. Her usefulness just dropped. Not only would she be coming alone, but she may be afraid to try again, and Lana couldn't have that. She could find someone else to work in clothing. Hell, she could hit up that friend of her dad's if she could remember his name. Visser was right though, Darcy would need time, but she couldn't give her much. She'd have to break the news soon.

Darcy wouldn't be coming to Wyan after all.

~ * ~

Avani waddled, giggling in nothing but a diaper between her parents. She made it a foot from Zane, and he smashed her in the face with a pillow. She squealed in delight, then tottered off to Marlow, catching a pillow to her side. This time she went down into a roll. Marlow cringed for a second until she popped back up, pushing off the floor into an awkward stance, smiled big, then headed back toward Zane.

"You sure you don't want to talk names?" asked Zane. "I have some good ones."

"No, and I doubt you have good ones."

Zane bashed their offspring once again, then raised his finger, taking a deep breath when Marlow said,

"Stop. You can suggest names, but nothing nostalgic like Jason or Marvin."

"You think I want to name our boy after a dead duck or dead lover?"

"I just want to cut it off before you even think about it. Also, don't get stuck on a boy name. I heard them say, 'him,' but it could've been a general comment. Not necessarily—"

"Okay. I get it." They paused their conversation as Avani grabbed Marlow's half-hearted hit with the pillow and took off, dragging it by the case to the couch. Her parents laughed, then Zane turned.

"Karamo."

"Karamo?" Marlow made a face.

"Bobby."

"No."

"Jonath—"

"No."

"Tan?"

"Tan? Like, we need a tan because we've been stuck inside like prisoners? No."

"Okay, what about Antoni?"

Marlow shrugged. "I don't hate it, but where are you pulling these names from?"

"I don't know. I heard them somewhere once. Can't remember."

Marlow nodded, then motioned toward the couch. "Don't look now but somebody's playing hide and seek."

Avani lay on the couch with the pillow pulled over her head, her bare back and diapered butt sticking out as she stayed as silent as she could.

Zane smiled. "Someone should go *find* her."

Marlow leaned back. "You? I need to rest my incision."

Zane crawled on all fours, making as much noise as he could. "Where's 'Vani?"

Her chubby thighs clenched together as she squeaked in excitement.

~ * ~

Lana was led to the surgical unit after she arrived. The operating table was waiting for her. Dr. Crouch and Dr. Vell moved around the room setting up supplies. Dr. Vell presented her with a gown, then they stepped out to give her time to change. It was an almost humorous protocol to give privacy as your patient changes clothes before cutting them open and rearranging their organs.

While she was in the middle of that thought and just getting her gown over her head, the door opened, and Dr. Crouch pulled it shut behind him. She turned, tugging at the gown to make sure she was covered. He'd stopped just inside the door. Before Lana could get out more than a surprised, "Hey," he held up a hand to quiet her.

"Thank you for visiting my Darcy yesterday. She really looks up to you, you know."

Lana felt her cheeks flushing. "You're welcome. Where's Dr. Vell?"

He waved a hand at the door. "She always needs a bathroom break before surgery. We've got a few." He stepped forward a few feet. "Do you know what Visser said when she was brought in?"

"I don't—"

"Save the baby." Dr. Crouch's face crunched up like he meant to growl or cry. Lana couldn't tell which. "Save the goddamned baby. That was his concern. Well, you may have already deduced this, but we did the opposite. I'm sure he isn't pleased, but I haven't heard from him since." He went around the table and patted it. "Jump up for me."

Lana narrowed her eyes. "Are we starting?"

"Once Dr. Vell gets here, but we can get you prepped." He waited and Lana climbed up.

"I'm sorry about…" She considered how much she dared to say. "Just everything with Darcy."

"Yes." Dr. Crouch snapped on a pair of gloves. "He'll regret it." He leaned closer. "Darcy told me about the plan." He watched Lana's eyes, searching to see if she understood what he knew, then smiled. "Don't worry. Your secret is safe, but it sounds like you could use a doctor out there." He pushed her shoulders to lay her back, then attached an oxygen sensor to her finger. "I'm here to offer my services." Running a hand along her belly. "After we get this baby out of you, of course."

Chapter Seven

Tyron left the Belt Forest with a sick feeling in his gut. When the head of security asks for a load of timber meant for building, you hand it over, no questions. Especially when the order is signed by Robin Visser, but something came back to him in the form of Martin's words. "You ever been part of building a place to hold people?" *He* hadn't. As far as he knew, the Belt had no jails. Sure, they kept the kids somewhere, but he didn't need to know about it. He just prepared the wood and usually helped with the contracting, only he wasn't asked about this job. He hadn't even known about it until he checked past records. He considered interrogating Philip, the one who'd signed off on the order, but after just a couple questions, he could tell he wasn't going to get anywhere. Sometimes it was a lucky day if Philip remembered what color pants he was wearing without having to look down.

Tyron's Rock-Hopper landed out front of the government building. The front doors were locked. It took him by surprise as he knew the doors *could* lock but rarely were anywhere he went. Around the back he found Gilbert, standing at attention as if he were some kind of inspector.

"Oh." Gilbert's shoulders relaxed. "Thought you were someone else."

"Just me." Tyron raised a hand. "You seen any of the big wigs around?"

"Nope. Just me and the kids today. I think they're off attending one of the births for that initiative."

"Right. Well, I shipped off an order with Maynard and I needed to double check it to make sure it was the right stuff."

Gilbert scratched his head. "An order?"

"Timber, mate. Trees. A project for him and Visser. I'm afraid he's got the wrong stack."

"Sorry." Gilbert waved his hands. "I've seen it go in but haven't seen it since."

Tyron stepped to the back door. "In here? Mind if I take a quick look?"

Gilbert came over. "Oh, I'm not supposed to let anyone else in."

"You serious? I just want to double check their order."

"We could call them." Gilbert raised his data-pad but made no effort to push any buttons.

"You really wanna do that? Listen," he spoke low, "you ever screwed the pooch so bad you're afraid to even look at the person you gotta own up to?"

Gilbert had. More than once. He shook his head.

"Well, good on you," Tyron frowned, "but I have, and I don't know what they're building with that wood, but it could be a new daycare for all those babies. You want the roof to cave in on them?"

"Could that happen?"

Tyron shrugged, then lied, "Fifty-fifty chance I'd say."

"Well, hell." Gilbert considered the request. "One quick look."

"That's a sport."

Gilbert unlocked the back door, and they went in together. With the lights off, it was like a haunted museum. Pictures of the founders hung in the main room. The offices were empty and as usual, there was one door they couldn't open.

"Kid's room." Gilbert stood next to it.

"Aren't they outside?" Tyron looked out the door they'd come in.

"Well, yeah, but we keep it locked up just in case."

Tyron put his arms out and twisted at the waist. "We haven't seen my timber up here. It's gotta be down there. Just a quick peek then I'll be out of your hair."

Gilbert saw the pleading in Tyron's eyes. He thought back to Oscar and Robin going to town on him over his negligence on the clothing island TechBubble. He wouldn't wish that wrath on anyone, though he'd never talk about it again, and surely wasn't going to mention it here.

"I just gotta grab the key." Gilbert started off. "They don't know

I know where the spare one is hidden."

Tyron nodded and swallowed hard. He didn't know what he was getting himself into, only that the knot in his stomach just tightened a little more. He willed the man to hurry.

~ * ~

Lana sat in the bed in the recovery room she'd been sent to after her delivery. It was more of a removal than a delivery. They took the baby out and disappeared, all while she tried to stay focused, reminding herself these were necessary steps to her end goal. Steps that took her a little closer to leaving. First, she would have a few dull days of recovery. She'd already been visited by her father and Robin. She realized how much she missed the final comradery they had on Wyan. Just before the end when all seemed right. Zane and Isolde had their bird farm. Percy played them the occasional song. Even her and Arjen were in a good place, then it all went to hell, and she was left to rebuild. It would take time, but she'd always think back to those moments around the fire when they ate and talked about anything but the impending war. Her heart ached for Arjen, still lost on Wyan. She knew their ending was less than ideal, but she hoped he'd welcome her back, join her new group, and maybe even pick up where they left off the last night before total darkness. There was something to be said about knowing someone out there loved you, despite your flaws, that wanted to be with you regardless of the path you took to get to where you are. There was something to be said for it, but Lana wasn't certain she'd ever feel that way about someone.

Two quick taps at her door broke her from her thoughts, then it opened.

"Oh," said Lisa, the other gathering leader. "I'm glad you're awake."

"Hey," Lana replied. "What, were you planning to smother me if I was asleep?"

Lisa forced a smile. "I think our past can be water under the bridge. I didn't understand why you'd leave the Belt. Why you'd take some of our people. Then I got to come out there and see Wyan and…wow. I mean, it was glorious," She looked back at the door, "but those bastards made me stay on the ship. I went all that way, and you know, as a gatherer, you want to be the first to hit the soil, the first to test it out. Instead, I'm stuck watching, but then…" She stepped closer, her dirty blonde hair swinging down too close to Lana's face. "I heard you're going back."

Lana felt her nostrils flare inadvertently. *What did her people not understand about keeping it a secret?* Her face gave her away and Lisa continued,

"I know Roel. He used to be on my crew. We'd dig sites together years ago. Anyway, he told me about the opportunity, and I want to come."

Damn Roel, Lana thought. She threw him a bone because she watched his daughter die. He was one of the early people when she was just trying to get others onboard with her. Now she regretted it. If Lisa knew about her plans, the secret wouldn't stay a secret long. But what was she supposed to say? No? Lisa was spiteful if she was anything.

"Okay," said Lana. "I just really need this to stay silent or it all falls apart. You can't tell anyone. Are we clear?"

Lisa straightened up. "Of course, but one question, when do we leave?"

Lana thought, *Sooner than I planned because of you and your mouth.* Then said, "About two weeks. I'll let you know after all the pregnancies."

Lisa saluted her, turned, and walked out, so proud of herself for getting her way, for knowing a secret. Lana shot daggers into her back. *Just give me time to recover.*

~ * ~

Martin waited as the flowers in their garden swayed in the breeze of the landing Rock-Hopper. Tyron got out and stayed with one hand on his transportation. His eyes were set on Martin, gathering his words.

"What did you find out?" asked Martin. "Surely something or you would've said it over the message."

"I got the children's watchman to let me into the government building when nobody was around. It's like a ghost town, but they keep one of the doors locked."

"For the children's room. Yes, I've heard."

"But the kids were outside in that play area they have for them. You seen it?"

"Yes."

"That door inside leads to the basement where they keep their cages. I think most prefer to never see a sight like that. We do what we must for them but it's not pretty." Tyron pursed his lips. "It was the other thing I saw down there I can't quite understand."

"What was it, Tyron? You can tell me."

Tyron shook his head. "I should've stayed out of this. Now I can't help but wonder." He pointed a finger at Martin. "You never saw me. We never had this conversation. This just became more than I want to think about. They had the rogue shipment of my timber down there. Normally those type of orders go through me. We handle the building and everything at the forest, but for some reason, they gathered the supplies to build them down there."

Martin frowned. "To build what?"

Tryon shook his head. "Coffins."

~ * ~

"It's for them." Arjen paced the living room. "It has to be. Tyron is right, any coffin building is done right at the forest, then they're sent off when needed. We don't have a lot of deaths, so there's not a big backstock. They're almost built on demand, but if you wanted to put someone in one without anyone knowing, you'd have to build your own. Otherwise, the forest workers would know someone died, and with such a small community, questions would be raised. Wes always knew before the rest of us. Sometimes before Dad."

"But why a coffin?" asked Julie. "We're talking the whole space, send-off burial, right? Why go through all that? Why not just toss them in the ocean?"

Helena looked solemn. "Because it's someone important. Someone even your rotten father couldn't just sweep away."

"Marlow?" asked Julie. "No offense, but she wasn't even born here."

"Maybe it's not Marlow," said Arjen.

"Kaia," said Helena. "They said she died but…"

"He'd kill a fellow judge?" Martin asked.

Helena nodded. "If she threatens life on the Belt."

Martin slammed a hand down on the back of a chair. "This is preposterous. We need to go to Ceres and have a talk with all of them. Make it big and public. They can't stop us all. It's not the Belt way."

"It's not," said Arjen, "but it sounds like it's becoming it. We don't know who all is involved. We've got to get Lana out here."

Martin shook his head. "Zelda told me she had her baby. She's recovering. We can't drag her out here like before."

"Then we go to her." Arjen stood. "What do you have that I can use as a disguise?"

"Oh, fun," said Julie. "I'm totally helping."

Chapter Eight

Zelda waddled to the door and was met with a bouquet bigger than her head.

"For me? You shouldn't have."

"Actually," Martin peeked around the bright blooms, "I was hoping to drop them for the new mother."

"You've got the right place." She stepped back and ushered him in.

Lana sat on the couch, her feet propped up, rocking a bassinet next to her. "Oh wow," she said. "That's a lot of flowers."

Martin smiled and set them across from her. "We grow a solid crop." He bent over to see her baby sleeping sound. "Look at that. What a beauty."

"Thanks."

Lana's droopy eyes said it all. It was a trying experience for her.

"So." Martin coughed. "I was hoping to pick up on the conversation we were unable to have the other night."

"Dad," said Zelda. "Right now? She's obviously—"

Lana cut her off. "It's fine. Word's been getting out further than I'd wished, and I need to know where we stand with everyone."

"Right." Martin scratched his arm, bumping a few buttons on his data-pad as he did. "Z, do you mind if we do it alone?"

"What?" Zelda put her hands on her hips. "Anything you have to say to her, you can say to me. Especially if it's about me."

Martin put a hand on her shoulder. "Please? Just a few minutes. Helena had some questions I wanted to make sure I cleared up, but they're a little personal if you know what I mean."

Zelda tilted her head and frowned. "I don't, but maybe I don't want to." Then turned to Lana. "Are you okay for a few?"

Lana waved her off. "I'm fine. I'll call if I need you later. You gotta get ready for your own date."

Zelda sighed. "Yeah…okay. I'll be next door if you need me."

As she left, Martin tried to fill the space. He had many questions, but none were relevant to what his host was likely thinking.

"So," He wandered toward the back door, checking the latch, then turning. "We heard about your little venture from Z. I think it's a very brave thing to try again."

Lana lazily raised her eyebrows at him. "I hope you don't plan to try and talk me out of it."

Martin shook his head. "Not exact—" He cut his word short when the slider opened behind him. Arjen tucked in, covered in a hooded robe and enough makeup to give question to his gender.

"What is…?" Lana tried to sit up and groaned in pain.

Arjen stepped in front of his stepfather. "Lana."

Her initial confusion changed to recognition. "Ar—you…how did you…?"

"Long story." He sat next to her, pulling back his hood. His blushed cheeks and cherry lipstick stood out the most, but the burnt off hair up top and shaved sides didn't complete the look as he would've liked.

A smile crept across Lana's face as she leaned forward to hug him. "I was coming back for you. I swear. Ask Martin here."

"I heard," said Arjen, "but I couldn't stay out there anymore. What my father's done; I can't just let happen anymore. It's my responsibility. The Earthlings…everything."

"It's not. You were trying to help them. We just had a bad turn there at the end. We couldn't have known how all that would go down."

Arjen leaned away. "You seemed to be pretty on point with Dad's plans."

She held up her hands in defense. "I was just rolling with it. At that point, what did we have left to salvage? We had to regroup. The Belt was the best place to do that. To get more manpower. To go back out there knowing our place."

"You want to go *back*? Like, to stay?"

"Of course. I told you I was playing the long game. What did you think that meant?"

Arjen rubbed some of the makeup from his cheek accidentally, then wiped it on his robe. "I don't know. I thought it meant you had plans to take over the Belt, or at least this new object."

"No. That was all temporary. I was just biding time 'til I could build back up the ranks. There are mothers now. A whole group of them. There are others too, ready to get out there and do better than we did before."

"What about Marlow, Zane, Avani?"

"They're coming with."

Arjen let out a breath. "So, they're alive?"

"Of course. Marlow just had her second child."

"Oh, Jesus."

"It's okay. It's just more for Wyan. More future. More of the colony we'll build."

Arjen shook his head. "This is just…I know you think this is all lining up, but something worse is going on."

She put a hand on his arm. "I know it's not good. Our dads and Oscar…the Belt is over. It's time to leave for good."

"What about Ice and Kaia. Have you seen them?"

"Well…"

Arjen frowned. "Well, what?"

"They were locked up. They know too much about what's going on. Ice just can't play it cool."

Arjen grabbed her shoulders, resisting the urge to shake her. "They're locked up? Where? Tell me."

"Arjen, please. I have a plan. If you go *rescuing* people now, it's going to fuck it all up."

Arjen raised his voice more than he meant to. "Everyone thinks I'm dead. I go out there," He pointed at the front door, "and it *will* fuck it up. But I've got to find them first. If Dad will leave me on another planet, he'll lock me up too. I can't be found out. I have to find Ice."

"Just wait. I'm telling you; my plan will work. Give it—"

"We don't have time. They're building coffins in the government building."

Lana frowned. "What?"

"Yes. Some secret order of timber and they've got coffins built. For who? Who do you think they're saving a proper send-off for?"

"Fuck."

"Yes."

~ * ~

The sun was a distant glowing orb peeking over Ahuna Mons. A pair of coffins made from the finest cherry wood the Belt had to offer, waited beside each other on a plateau. A special Rock-Hopper was parked, waiting to lead a final voyage.

Robin Visser stood beside the 'Hopper while Maynard Royal carried a body over his shoulder with braids swinging as they went. She was loaded in the first coffin as he went back for the second. Robin worked on securing her arms.

As Maynard lowered the second body, she gave a groggy grunt.

"Hurry," whispered Robin.

They secured the arms together, then the legs. Isolde thrashed against the restraints, her eyes working their way open, fighting off the drugs in her system.

"You fucks."

Kaia started coming around. "This is...have you gone insane, Robin? What are you doing?"

Robin pursed his lips. "I'm sorry. None of this went the way any of us would've wanted."

Kaia turned her head, fully grasping the situation. "No. You can't. We're the last of a founding family. You can't just kill us."

"It's time for some new families to rule." Maynard's shadow hung over her.

"Hey, tough guy," said Isolde. "How about you let me out and you can kill me like a man? Or are you too afraid?"

Maynard scoffed. "I've already had my way with you. Time to say goodbye."

"No," Kaia yelled. "Listen, Robin, just tell me what it would take. Anything is better than this."

Robin stood over her coffin shaking his head. "Don't embarrass yourself, Kaia. You're part of the founding families. You do have a right to some last words if you want. It can be your legacy to echo off these mountains."

Kaia pursed her lips, so many thoughts of her family's legacy passing through. "Why waste words on those who will not hear?"

"Your choice." Maynard grabbed the lid to her coffin and set it over top her. Kaia's screams were muffled as he snapped the latches tight. He moved to one end and grabbed ahold, giving Robin a look.

Robin saw Ice watching him. "Shouldn't we…?"

Maynard waved a hand. "Let her watch. Grab the other end, would you?"

Robin was hesitant, hearing the curses of Isolde, knowing his old partner was behind the wooden cover. She didn't deserve this kind of end, but he knew her too well. There was nothing he could do if she was let free again. It would be the end for all of them. Maynard slapped Kaia's coffin to bring him out of it. "Let's go."

The men carried Kaia to the back of the Rock-Hopper and loaded the casket on. They stepped away, Maynard clicking on his data-pad. The engines ignited and it started the trip off Ceres. Isolde screamed from the coffin, watching her mother be sent off to die alone in space. The ship grew smaller and smaller in their view, then it was out of sight. Ice broke down to a heavy whimper as Maynard stepped over.

"Your turn." He raised the lid as Isolde screamed every obscenity she knew at him. Soon she was quiet as the sound of the 'Hopper returning could be heard. It landed where it took off from initially and the men grabbed the ends of Isolde's coffin. As they loaded her, Robin tilted his ear toward the engine nearest him.

"Thought I…" He looked to the sky and felt his guts jump into his throat. Another Rock-Hopper came onto sight and began its descent.

"Come on." Maynard smacked Robin's arm. "Let's get her loaded. It's sealed. If we send it off, they're not going to know who's inside."

"No. That'll look suspicious. Let me talk to them. Send them on their way." Robin approached the Rock-Hopper, keeping himself between it and the coffin Maynard struggled to lock into place on his own.

The cab opened and Robin almost fell over. His son stepped out, wearing a black robe and the remains of a violet blush on his cheeks. Next to him was the failed experiment, Julie, then came Lana with the help of his ex-wife, Helena, and her husband, Martin. Every diplomatic word Robin had, flew out of his head as he took in what he was seeing.

"Son…you…"

Arjen pointed past him. "Where's Ice? Where's Kaia?"

"Just wait a minute." Robin held up his hands as Arjen approached. "Tell me what happened. How did you get here?"

"I found a way. No thanks to you." He pushed past his father. "Who's in that coffin?"

Robin caught him by an arm. "No one. What are you getting at? We're just testing the ship's calibration."

"Then open it up, Visser," called Martin.

The rest of the group flanked Robin as he backpedaled toward Maynard. There was a loud *ka-chunk*, and Maynard brushed his hands off.

"Everyone hold it." Maynard held up his arm, showing his data-pad with a finger near the screen. "Another step and I launch it."

Robin shook his head in dismay as the onlookers became outraged.

"Who's in there?" Arjen yelled. "Is it Ice? What did you do to her?" He took a step but quickly stopped as Maynard inched his finger closer.

"Huh uh." Maynard shook his head. "I need you all to back up."

"Dad?" Lana gaped at her father. "What are you doing?"

"Stay out of this, Lana."

Robin raised his hands. "Everyone needs to take a breath. We all need to talk this out."

"No." Arjen shoved his father until he stumbled out of the way. "We tried talking." He reached in the robe and came out with the pistol he'd found on the Mack, aiming it at Maynard's head.

"Whoa." Maynard squinted at the deadly relic. "Where'd you get that?"

"Doesn't matter. All that matters is that it still works. Now open that coffin."

"You think you're going to shoot me?" Maynard laughed.

"Put it down, Arjen." Robin stayed a few feet away with a hand out toward his son.

"Open the coffin." Arjen's teeth were gritted together.

"How about this," said Maynard. "You hand over the gun and I'll give you the coffin."

Arjen didn't have to think long about the danger of giving Maynard Royal a weapon like that. "No."

Maynard shrugged. "Fine then." And hit a button on his data-pad. The engines fired to life on the Rock-Hopper.

"Hey." Arjen came forward but by the time he reached the ship, the heat and force threw him back. The 'Hopper lifted off the ground. Arjen felt his whole body go tight, wanting to turn and put a bullet into Maynard's skull, but it wouldn't do him any good in stopping the ship. Instead, he braced himself, aimed and fired into the thrusters. There was the sound of metal ricocheting as it continued up. Arjen fired again and again until the pistol came up clicking on the empty clip. Smoke trailed from the barrel and the gun slumped to his side. Everyone watched as it grew smaller.

"Call it off," Lana yelled.

"Too late." Maynard shook his head. "It's—" He paused to blink at his data-pad, then the sky.

The others saw it as well, a small gray cloud forming around the ship. It took an arcing path over the mountain, losing altitude with smoke trailing it in an ashy tail, then it disappeared.

"Let's hope it pulled off an emergency landing." Arjen finished his sentence and turned just in time to see Martin fall to the ground in convulsions.

Maynard held out the taser, backing toward the ship as Julie, Helena, and Lana kept their distance. Robin was already climbing into a seat as Maynard joined him.

"Shoulda shot me." Maynard sneered as the glass closed around them.

The Rock-Hopper took off, leaving the others stranded. It didn't follow the path of the other 'Hopper and the coffin, but went west, alongside the river.

"Where are they going?" Helena stomped a foot on the rock floor.

Lana pursed her lips. "To get Marlow and Zane. It's their best bet."

Arjen stood, torn between the path to the smoking ship, and his father. "How far are they?"

"A couple miles." Lana looked down the path, feeling sick at the memory of tasing Isolde after she broke Maynard's arm. It had all gone so wrong. "We can call a 'Hopper…or two. We can—" She stopped when she saw Martin shaking his head, sitting up on the ground, still coming around from the shock.

"What does this mean?" He raised his data-pad.

Emergency Protocol was all it said.

"Goddamn it." Helena held her head. "Robin's downed the data-pads."

"What?" Martin asked.

"It's in the case of a security threat. It prevents control of Rock-Hoppers and communications. At this point, only he or Oscar could initiate it."

"I'll go it on foot then." Arjen started off in the direction of the smoking ship.

"I'm coming with," said Julie.

"Arjen." Lana watched him as he turned back. "We have to find help."

"I know, but…" Arjen looked over the group. "Mom, Martin, help Lana get down to the shipyard. Find help and hope they're on the right side of all this."

"Okay." Helena watched her son take off down the side of Ahuna Mons with Julie behind. She turned to the others. "It's a long way back.

We'll be careful, but we've got to get moving."

Lana held her incision. The stitches felt hot but were holding for the moment as she followed the older couple down the other side of the mountain.

Chapter Nine

The game of pillow ping pong only grew old when a toddler was too tired to hold her body up. Marlow played from the edge of the mattress, giving half-hearted swings each time Avani would come near. After Zane sent her back toward her mother, Avani was staggering. Drool ran down her chin as her head lopped to one side then the other, threatening to take down the entire ship. Marlow swung the pillow behind her, letting the mattress take her out at the shins, she went down, and Marlow pulled her into a hug. Avani smiled up a sporadic, toothy grin, but her eyelids drooped. Marlow shushed her, petting her head, then her back as she gave in to the nap. Zane raised a thumb in the air, slinking over to the couch to rest himself. The anxious monotony of waiting around to hear if they'd ever get to meet their second child wore on them. Avani kept them going, but they knew she'd eventually have to go out and make friends with other kids, to be incorporated into society. The problem was her parents couldn't come with and they knew it. At some point, they'd have to be separated before they could tell her the truth about the Belt. Before she could repeat it. That time wasn't far off.

Just as the girls drifted off, Zane heard the gate outside. It clanged like someone was in a hurry. He jumped up; afraid the time was now.

There was no knock, just Maynard at the door, still holding the handle.

"Get up. It's time to go."

"Go?" Zane sat up to the edge of the couch. "Go where?"

"I didn't say it was time for twenty questions. Get your asses up."

Zane looked confused. "All of us? At the same time?"

"Yes, goddamn it. Now get up."

Maynard looked out the door.

As Zane took a few hesitant steps, he saw Visser, fearfully looking into the woods.

"What's going on?" Marlow tried to hold Avani who was now crying and kicking. She landed one in Marlow's stomach, and she doubled over in pain as Avani rolled off the mattress. Avani was surprised by the six-inch fall and turned her cry into a wail. Zane came over to scoop her up, then lowered a hand to help Marlow.

"Where are we going?" Zane asked as they huddled together.

Maynard's face was flushed. "I said—"

Zane yelled back, "We need to know what we need for the baby. Good god just tell us something here. You've never let us leave this place."

He paused, wondering how soon the taser would come out, but Maynard seemed to actually consider his remark.

"Grab an overnight bag for all of you but make it fast."

The Earthlings shared a look, then started gathering anything they might need. Overnight was better than dead, they figured. You didn't pack for funerals.

~ * ~

Arjen and Julie hit an impasse. The cliff they were on came to a ledge. There was a huge drop between, landing them in a rocky body of water below. The next peak was smaller, across the crevasse, and had a small stream of smoke rising behind it.

"No way." Julie hugged herself. She looked down the divide, then turned back before her head could get too loopy.

Arjen turned one way, then the other, shaking his head. "There's not another connection for miles. Then we'd have to double back."

"We don't know for sure there's even anyone in that box."

"They commandeered the wood, built the coffin, and went to the Belt's funeral launching point. There's someone in there and we don't know what shape they're in."

"Better shape than us if we miss that jump."

"We won't." Arjen put a hand out. "We fought off the Night Chasers and whatever the hell those things were on Melinger. We survived the flight back here despite running out of food. I think we can handle this jump."

Julie squinted, shaking her short red hair. "Damn you and your inspirational speeches." She took his hand. "We jump together then? On seven?"

"Seven?"

"Fine, four."

"That's going to totally throw off our pacing." He raised his fingers. "Three. We jump on three."

"Whatever."

They backed up to give themselves a runway. Arjen looked over and nodded. Julie made the sign of the cross and Arjen looked confused.

"What does that mean?"

"No idea." She smiled. "They did it on all those shows in the nineties before troublesome situations."

"Well, let's hope your hundred-year-old magic helps us."

They ran together, pushing off the last of the ledge and soaring through the air. The water and rocks below went by in a blur as they landed, stumbling then sliding onto the next cliff. Julie called out, "Righteous," as she lay on her back.

Arjen was over her, once again putting out a hand. His forearm was streaked with blood and dirt.

She took it and stood. "You alright there, macho man?"

He raised his elbow, then wiped it on his shirt. "Let's go."

They skirted the edge of the next cliff, not having to climb the highest part but coming around the side, following the trail of smoke the best they could.

The next hill led them in a moderate slope down. The Rock-Hopper was wedged where the next cliff rose. The coffin on the back was intact still, though there were skid marks where the ship tried to land and continued until the rocks broke its fall.

Arjen ran as fast as he dared, sliding the last of the gap to the back of the 'Hopper. He detached the clamps that held the coffin in place, then started tugging to pull it free. Julie caught up and pushed from the other end. It finally got moving and almost landed on Arjen as it came off the back. They worked the lid together, popping it off and tossing it away.

Isolde blinked at the brightness. Blood ran across her ear from a gash in the side of her head. She smiled her bright, perfect teeth and said, "Jesus, what happened to you?"

"Ice. You're alive. Is…?" Arjen looked around, knowing there wasn't another coffin.

Isolde shook her head, her mouth tightening. "They sent her first. She's up there."

"Damnit. I'm so sorry. I didn't know what they were planning until it was too late." He reached to undo her ties. "Shit, your arm."

Ice craned her neck. "Oh that? It's fine. It's been broken."

Arjen had a concerned look but went at the ties until she was free. Julie helped him pull her out of the coffin. Ice wiped the blood off the side of her head with her arm.

"How was the landing?" asked Julie.

Ice shrugged. "Better than a successful flight would've been."

"I'm sorry about your mom."

"I am, too. I just don't have it in me to mourn right now."

"Right." Arjen stared back the way they'd come. "Dad and Maynard are out there. I think they're after Marlow and Zane."

"They had a 'Hopper though," said Julie. "I don't think we're going to be able to catch them." She turned and kicked the crashed 'Hopper. "This one's not going anywhere either."

Ice looked at the sky, then followed it to the horizon. "They're off in no-man's land, too. We'd be better off heading for the shipyard."

"That's where Lana, Mom, and Martin are headed. Hopefully we can meet up with them at the bottom."

"Lana?" Ice crossed her arms. "If I see her, she's dead."

"Ice…"

"No, Arjen. You don't know what she did while you were off playing dead. She—I don't even know where to start." Her face changed at her next question. "Tell me it was all lies. Tell me Admani's still alive somewhere."

Arjen slowly shook his head. "I buried her myself. That's the truth. I'm sorry. I couldn't save her."

Isolde's face scrunched up. She balled up her fists and raised them like she planned to pummel him into pieces. "You said you'd bring her back. You said you'd go to the dark side, find our friends, and bring her back. Now look at this." She motioned to the smoking ship. "I'm the only one left."

"It should've been me," said Julie. "I was so scared, but Admani found a way through her fear. She helped us pull off the escape."

Arjen nodded in agreement. "She only wanted to make you two proud. That was her dying wish, but I didn't get to tell Kaia."

Ice shook her head. "I'd rather she wussed out and came back alive." She started down the mountain, wiping at the blood trickling down her head.

~ * ~

The side of the mountain led down to a small river. Helena, Martin, and Lana followed it, knowing eventually they'd end up behind the shipyard. The path was treacherous at first, but most of that was behind them. Lana could see spots of blood blossoming on the bottom of her shirt. She didn't have time to think about the damage she was doing to herself. If they could figure things out, she could find Dr. Crouch. She only hoped he'd still be on her side.

"Lana," started Helena, "since you're a mother now, I feel like I can ask this."

"Oh boy," Martin muttered.

"Shush." Helena kept walking. "You knew my son was alive all that time and you didn't once think to tell me?"

Lana raised her eyebrows in surprise. "It's way more complicated than that."

"Is it?" Helena pointed to the path ahead. "Do tell, we have time."

"Okay. If that's what you want." Lana cleared her throat. "Your son chose to stay. Robin offered him a ride back. He stayed. I didn't tell you because I didn't think he wanted you to know."

"Now that's—" Helena started, but Martin put his hands up between them.

"Listen, we all have our disagreements on how this went down, but we need to focus on the task at hand. We get down there, get it straightened out and you two can talk all you want. I'll even supply the bottle, but let's get down first."

Their conversation stopped as a Rock-Hopper flew overhead. Lana waved and yelled at it, but it kept flying.

"What are you doing?" asked Helena. "That could be them."

Lana pulled back. "It could be one of my group. That's our best bet at this point."

They continued alongside the river.

~ * ~

Arjen, Isolde, and Julie were less than fifty feet from the downed 'Hopper, when another came swooping in. Ice bent to arm herself with a rock as it landed on the side of the path they'd just come down. A woman jumped out, looking up the hill at the dwindling smoke of the crashed 'Hopper, then down.

"Hey. Everyone alright?"

Arjen raised a thumb as they waited on her to catch up to them.

Lavinia stopped ten feet back from them. "Your 'Hopper looks like it's seen better days. I can try to repair it, but I'll give ya'll a ride back first. You sure everyone's okay?" Her head tilted, dark freckles narrowing in as she squinted. "Hold on. Aren't you supposed to be dead?"

"Who?" asked Arjen.

"*All* of you."

"Guess not. Can we still have a ride to town?"

She crossed her bare arms. "Well, I knew *you* weren't dead." She pointed at Arjen. "Lana said you were still out there."

Ice huffed. "Some bad stuff is going on. Visser just killed my mother, Kaia Gammen. He's probably going to kill more. We need to get back to civilization before shit gets worse."

"Okay, whoa." Lavinia looked back up the mountain. "How about you follow me to my 'Hopper and we can talk more in the air."

As the cabin was sealing, Lavinia looked back at Arjen. "Did Lana tell you the plan? Were you in on this the whole time?"

"Sad to say, she left me out of most of the details."

Lavinia got an alert on her data-pad, looked down, then spoke calmly, "Damn, change of plans." She leveled her eyes at the group. "Looks like you all are fugitives. I'm going to have to take you in."

The Rock-Hopper launched before they could refute the claim, then they were off.

Chapter Ten

The old Ramirez property was still supported by a TechBubble but hadn't been lived in for over a year. Oscar wasn't ready to let his father's house go, so he kept it on the maintenance rounds, though that didn't include the lawn. The two-story with the perfect view of Ceres contained a lot of good memories. It was the first lavish thing his father built, becoming a symbol to all that they were going to be okay in the Belt. It meant resources were becoming easier to gather. Ingredients for the NutrientPanel grew and could be harvested. Wood and other materials could be grown and manufactured without struggle.

The Belt was going to work. The people would thrive, and they could forget the Earth. They could recreate the nice things they had out there. Slowly but surely, it would all be okay.

Oscar stood looking at the grand, family dwelling with the overgrown putting green staring off at Ceres and infinite space. He found himself laughing at the absurdity of it all. This had to be a joke, his whole life some cosmic tale of folly. He sat on the steps to the front porch and sighed until his lungs were empty. A Rock-Hopper approached in the distance and he decided then, that this would be the last wild scheme he would help his adopted brother with. If this failed, he would give up the burden of leadership placed on him by his father. They'd have a new vote, and give someone else a chance to lead them to their impending doom.

Robin and Maynard stepped to the porch with the refugees from Earth between them.

"Upstairs?" Robin asked.

"Room should be ready." Oscar pushed himself up and led them inside. The master bedroom had a king-size platform bed, made from the finest polished wood the Belt had to offer. There was a rocking chair in one corner by the window and an attached bathroom with a shower. Zane and Marlow shared a look. They hadn't seen a shower since they left Earth. At least not in that capacity with stone tiled flooring and a waterfall showerhead.

Marlow looked back at the bed, raised at least a foot and a half off the floor with a monitor overhead. "Well, this seems safe."

She held Avani, who was all too eager to go bouncing off the edge of the bed to the hardwood floors. The door closed them in.

The men met at the top of the stairwell just down the hall.

"The message is out." Oscar watched the balcony as he spoke, remembering the old parties. He had to turn away to finish his thoughts. "I don't know how the people are receiving it yet since we downed outward communications."

"We're already ahead of it." Robin tapped on his data-pad. "We need them to know they have no leverage. Without travel or communication, they're at a disadvantage. They should be met by an angry mob if they make it down that mountain."

"What if they believe your son's story?" Oscar rubbed at his chin.

"Arjen sold himself out for the girl in that room." Robin pointed down the hall. "As long as we have her, we have the advantage."

~ * ~

Lavinia flew them over the mountains, trying to piece together all they'd said in such a short time.

"So, you're saying there's a secret hideout they're keeping the Earthlings in, and you ain't never seen it, but we've got to go there and try to save them?"

"I can get us close," said Ice. "Can't you control this thing?"

"I can do anything with a Rock-Hopper."

"Then go that way." Ice pointed down toward the place she broke Maynard's arm. "Follow the water out."

Lavinia took it slow until they reached the misfit forest. Soon it was too thick to see the ground, then came the shore and the ocean.

"You sure it's—"

"There." Julie's face was against the glass looking behind them.

The others followed, seeing the clear marks where a 'Hopper had landed just at the edge of the forest. Then there was the unnatural blocky object built under the canopy.

They landed and sprinted around the side. Arjen found the gate first. It was hanging open, as well as the door to the cabin. Inside, they all took a corner of the room. There was the couch, the mattress, and other signs it was lived in recently.

Arjen slammed a hand on the wall after finding the bathroom empty. "This is where they've been all along."

"Yes." Isolde stared out the barred window. "I wish I could've told someone. Anyone."

"There's nothing you could do."

Julie grabbed a baby blanket she remembered from Wyan. They must have taken it when they abducted her from the alien planet. She tucked it into her bag. "So, where to now? Any idea where your dad would hide?"

Arjen nodded. "I have a few ideas, but I think we should go find Lana, Mom, and Martin. They're probably getting to the shipyard by now, maybe Lana will know something."

Lavinia stood in the doorway. "So, back to it then." She tapped her data-pad. "Looks like communications are still down. That means 'Hoppers too. She can't have made it too far. We'll scan the cliffs if we have to. You're lucky you're riding with the master."

They left the Earthlings' prison and took to the skies.

~ * ~

Lana held her stomach, feeling like it was on fire as she had a distinct, spotted red line across her shirt. Helena ducked under the branch of a banyan. The back of the shipyard building was spread across their path. As Helena stepped in the open, a man came wandering toward them. He waved a hand, then looked away. Helena approached him.

"Hello? We need help. We were stranded on the mountain."

The man looked back, recognizing Lana, and giving her a wide-eyed stare. "What are you doing out here?"

"It's a bit of a story, Captain Miller." Lana walked over gingerly. "Are your communications working? We need to get a message out."

He shook his head, blinking frequently as he did. "Nope, but Lisa's working the old radio inside. You can check with her." He turned away, then snapped his head back. "There're fugitives out there." He shook his head again, then walked off.

Helena gave a blank stare to her husband. Martin shrugged as Lana pushed on toward a back door.

The inside opened to a large hanger with Rock-Hoppers in various stages of repair, and a Rock-Hauler with huge drills on the front of it. There were a couple offices on the left side. When the door slammed shut behind Martin, a head poked out.

"Lana?" Lisa had corded headphones over her ears that she pulled down and tossed on a table with a *bang*. She came over almost at a jog. "What happened to you?"

"Something…" Lana looked around, making sure they were clear. "Something we need to talk to the group about. We may need to push up the date." She started toward the office. "Can we get through to anyone from there?"

Lisa caught her shoulder. "Already taken care of. I've set up a meeting. I was just trying to find you." She took a quick look at Martin and Helena. "Should we…?"

"They're okay." Lana eyed Helena. "I hope with what they've seen, they won't give us away."

Helena crossed her arms. "The whole Belt needs to get back together and work some things out. It's more than your little *mission*."

Lana pursed her lips. "Then you do that." She turned to Lisa. "So, the meeting…?"

"Got a 'Hopper already set up." Lisa waved her to follow, and they left Helena and Martin where they stood. "Lavinia showed me how to jailbreak these in cases like this. Comes in handy."

Lana climbed in the front with a groan. Lisa sat next to her, nodding while looking at the blood on her shirt.

"Hopefully Dr. Crouch can look at that when we get there." She pulled open the screen and typed in a number sequence. The Rock-Hopper responded, and they flew out of the hangar. A scattering of people lined the path from the shipyard to the government building.

"Daddy put the word out," said Lisa. "Surprised he turned on his own son."

"Yeah," Lana spoke absentmindedly as she watched the path the 'Hopper took. "Aren't we going to New Pangaea?"

Lisa shook her head as they exited Ceres. "Too hot. We found a better spot where nobody will see us."

"Okay, but with the ships down, how is everyone going to get there?"

Lisa looked forward. "Lavinia will take them, no problem."

As they left Ceres' 'Bubble, Lavinia loaded up Arjen, Julie, and Isolde to head to the shipyard.

~ * ~

Helena and Martin reached the government building, hoping to find some answers and instead came upon the frantic caretaker of the feral children.

Gilbert was slapping his data-pad and cursing at the point they approached.

"Hey, Gil, you okay?" asked Martin.

He looked up and a wave of relief washed over his face. "Martin, hey man. I'm in some trouble here. Usually someone shows up to help get the kids in for the night, but no one has. Communications are down and I'm not sure who I can trust." He held up his data-pad, the screen gone blank from the abuse he gave it. "You hear about the vigilantes?"

"I have, but Gil, no worries. We can help you get the kids in."

"Really? That would..." Gilbert's expression twisted. "Would Visser be okay with that? I mean, sorry to ask this, but you're not one of *them,* are you?"

Martin waved his hands in denial. "No, no way. We actually just came from a meeting with Robin. He's a bit tied up right now, so we thought we could help."

"Oh, okay. Well, let me get the key." He turned back before he made it to the door. "Don't mention this part, okay?"

The three of them worked together to coax the children back to the basement. Martin took a slight detour when Gilbert wasn't watching, then, when they were finished, Martin and Helena walked out with another key.

They headed for the communications building just down the road.

~ * ~

Club Earth was abandoned at the point the decision was made on New Pangaea. They couldn't justify supporting an entire island built just for down time with the crisis at hand. Any workers were relocated to more useful, albeit, less fun jobs. The TechBubble was buggy toward the end and Martin recommended a complete overhaul if they were keeping it. That was when it was voted unnecessary.

Lisa touched them down on pavement meant to look like actual parking spaces. She took a deep breath and opened the top, feeling the colder air rush in.

Lana gave her a look. "Are we sure this is safe?"

Lisa got out with a look of confidence. "Oh yeah. Luis vouches for it. He's the one that suggested it, and judging by the last time we talked, he probably beat us here."

Lana was hesitant to join her. "Where's the 'Hopper?"

Lisa turned back, her ponytail swinging with a bright smile like she was about to lead a cheer for their non-existent football team. "Lavinia, remember? She probably went back out for the others. If the damn data-pads were working…" She huffed and started for the door to Club Earth, resisting the urge to hug herself against the cold.

Lana was slow but followed.

Lisa held the door open for a second, ten feet ahead. She called inside, "Yes, she's with me." She stepped in, letting the door swing shut as she said, "Oh, Zelda, you brought the baby."

Lana felt her heart tug to see her baby. It had only been a few days. The fact that she'd already left him with Zelda and disappeared was not a good start into motherhood. She picked up her pace, then stopped.

Nothing felt right about the island. It was clearly abandoned. They always met in the forest of New Pangaea. They had other backup meeting points available, but Club Earth was never one of them. Yes, Luis could've gone rogue at the turn of events and thrown something together, but it didn't track.

Lana rubbed her arms. The temperature had to be forty degrees lower than other islands. The building might be a bit better, but she resisted the urge to see. After ten seconds, her feelings were confirmed. Why hadn't Zelda come out with her baby? Why would Zelda even bring a two-day-old baby to a place like this? Another fifteen seconds passed, and Lana wished she saw what Lisa did to trick the 'Hopper into flying without a data-pad telling it to do so. After a look back, she heard the door. It banged against the barstool Lisa gripped like a two-handed baseball bat. She walked in a fury.

"You couldn't have just made this easy, could you?"

Lana held up her hands, backing away. "What are you doing?" She knew she was in no condition to defend herself. She barely dared to move as she was.

"They've had their chance to follow you." Lisa frowned. "And look where it got them? Dead. I think it's my turn for a real adventure."

"What the fuck, Lisa? We trained together. We were going to go conquer another planet together. You think I agreed you should come with us lightly? I need someone with your skills. With your gathering knowledge. You could lead your own damn village out there, but not without me. I translated the language they speak. I was planning to teach you on the way. Seriously."

Lisa let the barstool dip just slightly, then tightened her fists and cocked it back. "I'm not that dumb, Lana, but I'm also not a killer. Give me your data-pad, go inside and I'll be on my way."

"Inside?" Lana looked at the gloomy abandoned club. "You're going to strand me here?"

Lisa shrugged. "Or I could clock you with this barstool. Your choice."

Lana shook her head, seeing no alternative that didn't leave her bleeding from the head and still stranded. She removed her data-pad, tossed it on the ground and started walking.

Lisa watched her, then up at the, mostly, invisible bubble around them as it fought to keep the vacuum of space from killing every living thing on the asteroid. When Lana was near the door, Lisa bent and tossed her data-pad inside the 'Hopper, then got in and kept the barstool raised. "Inside," she yelled.

"Come over and make me," Lana yelled back.

Lisa huffed and worked the panel with one hand, while keeping the barstool ready. As the top began to close, Lana took off in a sprint. Her muscles screamed at her for the attempt. Her lungs burned with the cold air. Lisa tossed the barstool out in her general path. When she was five feet back, the seal began and the fear on Lisa's face subsided. Lana slammed her fists on the side of the 'Hopper, unable to scream as she was catching her breath. She pushed back, falling to the ground, and covering her head as the engines kicked in.

Lisa flew off and Lana was left to struggle back inside the old building as shivers overtook her.

Chapter Eleven

The communications building was blocky and dull with a lone door at the front that Helena stood knocking at. She grew impatient as she waited, but the handle wouldn't turn when she tried it. There had to be people inside considering what was going on.

Finally, a woman poked her head out looking annoyed. Before Helena could speak, the woman said, "I'm going to tell you the same as I've told everyone. Oscar's ordered a lockdown until this threat is over."

Helena put a hand up to stop her from closing the door. She didn't want it to be personal but the 'threat' the woman was talking about was her son whether she knew it or not.

"Listen to me. I'm the head of the water processing plants and I'm telling you, the only threat to the Belt is Oscar and his illegitimate brother. We need the communications back on before we have a real problem."

"Oh yeah?" The woman cocked a hip out. "And what's that? You can't call a Rock-Hopper when you want to?"

Helena took a deep breath. She'd never been one to punch people in the nose, but she considered it for a moment. "No. We need to call a 'Bubble Tech to fix the damages and we can't."

The woman had a flash of concern that quickly slipped behind a frown. "Damages?"

Helena shrugged. "Don't ask me what. I'm not a tech, but if we don't get one out here soon, things are going to get bad."

The woman rolled her eyes. "I'm sure they are." And slammed the door in Helena's face. She could hear the lock turn on the other side. She crossed her arms, waiting. The timing hadn't worked out as perfect as she'd hoped but she trusted Martin knew what he was doing.

A few minutes later, Ceres fell into a twilight type darkness, the temperature dropping a few degrees as it did. Helena had to repress her smile as the woman returned to the door, relieved to see her still there.

"We're rebooting the system right now." The woman tapped on a tablet in her hands. "Then we can call someone." She met Helena's eyes, quizzical. "How did you know?"

Helena checked to see her data-pad reconnecting with the network. "My husband knows a thing or two about it. I'll call him now." She walked off to meet Martin.

~ * ~

Lisa couldn't believe her luck as she saw the data-pads coming back online. Everything was lining up perfectly. She grabbed Lana's from the seat next to her and sent out a message to their expedition group, then flew to the shipyard and landed next to the Iris. By the time she got out, others were already joining her. Amelia and Shirley, the builders, were the first there. Hudson came shortly after with a 'Hopper and trailer loaded up. Luis walked out of the hangar; his clothes permanently stained with dirt from the fields. He was talking with Lavinia as they met up with the others.

"What's going on?" Luis asked. "Where's Lana?"

"You saw the message." Hudson pointed a stubby finger at the Iris. "She wants us to load up and be ready to go. Now, someone help me with the 'Panel."

Amelia and Shirley loaded cases of NutrientPanel they'd prepared for their journey while Luis stood with Lisa and Lavinia.

"A bit strange, isn't it?" He crossed his arms. "We get an alert about vigilantes, then the network is down. The lights go down, then come back up. Next thing we know, it's time to go. Think Visser and them found us out?"

Lisa shrugged. "Could be, or she just wants to use the distraction."

"No." Lavinia looked back towards the hanger, then to Luis. "There's something bigger going on. I uh…" She waved. "Come on. I've gotta show you something."

Before Lisa could protest, Luis followed as they went back into the hangar.

Lisa scrambled, seeing Fleta, one of the Rock-Haulers joining.

"Hey. You ready to fly?"

Fleta nodded. "Just waiting on my co-pilot."

"Great. Can you help get everyone aboard? I've gotta take care of one thing for Lana, then we should be ready."

"Okay." Fleta looked around as only half their group was present. "Shouldn't we—?" She was unable to finish as Lisa jogged to catch up with Lavinia.

Luis waited outside one of the offices inside the hanger as Lavinia opened the door. Lisa caught up just in time to see Arjen, Julie, and Isolde chugging down nutrient pouches. She put her hands to her face.

"Wait." Luis had his arms akimbo. "You're here? And Isolde, I thought you died."

Ice swallowed a gulp from the pouch, wiped her mouth and said, "Can't say they didn't try."

"Is Lana out there?" asked Arjen. "I've got to talk to her. She can't be trying to leave in the middle of all this."

Luis shook his head. "She got us rallied, but I haven't seen her yet. I have so many questions right now."

Arjen exchanged a look with Lavinia.

"We all looked," she said. "There isn't tree cover over there. We would've seen her if she was still out there."

"What about my mom and Martin? They should've been together."

Lisa quickly shook her head but didn't reply. Luis confirmed. "No. I know Helena pretty well. I haven't seen her around."

"Shit." Lavinia eyed her 'Hopper. "I can head out and look again."

"Good idea," said Lisa.

Arjen scoped out the Iris through the hangar bay. "We'd better stay here and make sure she doesn't show up."

"Okay. I'll keep you updated." Lavinia ran off.

Lisa wrung her hands. "This office is a good place to wait. Until we find out more, that is."

"No." Arjen waved Julie and Isolde to follow him. "I'm done with hiding. Plus, I got my bodyguard back." He threw a thumb over his shoulder at Ice.

"Guard yourself," she said, with a smirk.

Lisa forced a smile as they walked away and spoke to herself, "Okay. We'll figure this out."

Luis gave her an odd look. "I'm going to go check on the others."

More 'Hoppers filled the shipyard. Dr. Crouch, Darcy, Zelda, and Erika got out. The latter two, still pregnant having just missed their planned c-sections due to the events of the last day.

Darcy held Lana's baby as Arjen, Julie, and Ice met them.

"Arjen and…Isolde?" Zelda stood, confused. "We were coming to see you," she motioned at Arjen, "but *you*…you're supposed to be dead."

"I knew it," said Dr. Crouch. "Visser's been hiding something." He pulled Isolde into a hug, then Arjen.

"He has Marlow and Zane," Arjen agreed. "Any idea where they could be?"

Dr. Crouch looked sheepish. "They've been locked up in a cabin, but it was just temporary. We planned to take them with, I swear."

"We've been to the cabin. They're not there."

"Hey."

A call came from a group marching to the shipyard. They were ten strong and angry. A woman of Asian descent led them, stopping to point a finger in Arjen's face. He remembered her from music lessons growing up. She was always better than him and made him want to quit all together.

Her face was scrunched up as she said, "We won't let you do this."

"Seiko, hold on." Arjen put up his hands, hoping to deter the rest of the group from trying to perform a citizen's arrest. "This is not me." He pointed at the movements of Lana's team. "This is Lana's doing. I just got back from her last colonization, and I barely survived it."

"It sure looks like you." Seiko crossed her arms. "You've been gone over a year, pronounced dead, and now you're back with a new group loading up a ship. Where are you going now?"

"Not me. I don't know what they're doing. I just want to talk to Lana."

"Let's hear it from her, then."

Arjen nodded. "Great. Once we find her, you can ask."

Seiko signaled two guys behind her, and they dispersed onto the Iris. Once they moved, the rest circled him.

Ice gritted her teeth. "Back up. This isn't Arjen's stupid idea for once."

"For once?"

Arjen meant to further his retort when he saw Helena and Martin coming up the path. They ran to him.

"Hold on, everyone." Helena waved her hands. "That message was sent by Robin Visser. He's trying to distract you all from the real evil that's taking place."

Another group came from the other side of the Iris. One of the men called, "We've got a bunch of deserters."

"Wait."

Martin stepped in front of Arjen as they poured in. The shipyard was quickly becoming a mosh pit.

"Oh, hell." Luis held his head and muttered to Lisa, "So much for seizing the opportunity."

A couple men came down the ramp of the Iris, dragging Hudson between them. They brought him over to Seiko.

"We caught this guy loading up enough 'Panel for an army."

Hudson hung his head as Luis came over, raising his hands and projecting as loud as he could, "Everyone listen for a minute. We're all reasonable. Let's talk this out." He turned to see Lisa struggling with a crate while the attention was off the Iris. "Lisa, put it down." She stopped dead in her tracks, lowering the crate and stepping away from the ramp.

Luis gave one more look around at the growing mob. He took his straw hat off and fanned himself as Admani's father, Roel, came up and joined him.

"This all started when Lana returned," Luis spoke, looking for Lana, wishing she'd take over and get some of the heat. "She had a plan for the new mothers to join a group of invaders to colonize this planet. She began all this on the last trip. It was a damn good plan. We had all the right people and once we finished the initial settlement, we'd send for everyone else that wanted a change in *scenery*." He stared at the direction of the government building as he said the last word, hoping most got his meaning.

"You can't just abandon the Belt," came a call from the crowd, followed by chants of agreement.

"We've tried changes and they've haven't worked. How long will this next experiment last? One generation? Then what?"

Arjen tilted his head at Luis' words. He was parroting Lana's speech that got him to go to Wyan the first time. She'd obviously recycled it on these people.

There was a commotion at the back of the crowd as people parted in a hurry. Maynard Royal came pushing through with his taser snapping at anyone who took too long to move. Robin and Oscar appeared from behind him, stepping to the front. Luis shrunk back as Arjen moved forward.

"Any deserters need to be taken to trial," Robin called out.

"You heard him." Maynard pointed to the Iris. "Anyone who was planning to board that ship, front and center."

"What about your daughter?" came Dr. Crouch's voice. "She was the ringleader of all this. Bring her to trial."

Others yelled for the same.

Maynard and Robin shared a look.

"Now, I'm sure that's not true." Robin looked around for Lana. "She was the first volunteer for the new motherhood initiative."

"Then let's bring you to trial." Isolde stepped forward. "You killed my mother and tried to kill me."

The crowd grew into an uproar, seeing the woman believed to be dead eight months prior.

"That's right." Arjen waved his mother, Martin, and Julie to join them. "We all witnessed it."

"Now, hold on." Robin raised his hands to quiet the crowd. "This is a sick power play by those that wish to steal my title." He swept a finger across Helena, Arjen, and Ice. "She married me for that reason alone. The other two think they're entitled to it just by being born into the families."

"You're a lying bastard," Ice screamed. "My mother—"

"I am not the one who abandoned the Belt." Robin appealed to the onlookers. "I've been here with all of you, trying to solve our problems." He stuck a finger toward his son. "He's the one who left. Now he's come back to take more from us, and you'd believe anything he says?"

"Lana was there," Julie yelled. "She was in Wyan with us, and she's been here. Let's ask her what she saw."

The majority agreed but no one could locate Lana. Arjen looked to his mother.

Helena shrugged. "She came down the mountain with us. She met up with the other gathering lady and they flew off together somewhere."

"Lisa," said Arjen.

Luis looked over his shoulder and Lisa was gone. "She was just—"

"Call Lavinia." Arjen looked toward the mountains. "She was out searching for Lana. See if she's seen either of them."

Luis started typing into his data-pad.

Maynard stepped up to Arjen. "You can call all the witnesses you want, but this isn't court. You're coming with—" Before he could tase Arjen, a foot came out of the air and caught his shoulder, turning him as he stumbled back.

"Damn." Ice was in her fighting stance but obviously not pleased with her performance.

Maynard raised his taser, but Robin caught his shoulder, seeing the eyes of the crowd.

Oscar tried to calm the mob. "We'll have a fair trial for all. Just give us time to figure all this out. For now, I motion we shut down the Iris and the Knox. Nobody leaves until we work this out."

"We have the right to leave," called out Fleta, now joined by her co-pilot, Nigel. "You can't force us all to stay. This isn't working."

"We will discuss all options, but this is not how the Belt operates. Anyone opposed to reasonable actions must be detained."

The crowd moved in, unorganized and hesitant. Lana's crew began to disperse. Some took to the Rock-Hoppers they'd come in on. Others just ran. Arjen felt his mother link arms with him. He looked down, then tapped Julie. Soon, they formed a circular, human chain with Isolde and Martin as well. A pair of scientists approached and just missed another kick from Ice. They backed off and were followed by Seiko.

She came face to face with Arjen. "Look what you've done here. You think the Belt's ever going to recover from something like this?"

Arjen gave a quick shake of his head. "No."

She groaned in anger, turned on a heel and went towards the Iris.

After inciting the madness, Robin, Oscar, and Maynard slipped back, though they found the Rock-Hoppers grew scarce with the retreating rogues. Ice broke the chain first, trotting up to them as they made their way further toward the line of trees before the government building.

"You killed my mother," she screamed. "You don't get to walk away so we can *talk about this later.*"

Arjen and the others joined behind her.

"That's right," said Arjen. "You should be tried for murder right here."

Robin confirmed who was within earshot, then said, "Who's going to try us? You and Isolde? The deserters? You have no legs to stand on."

Arjen eyed them, remembering his stare down with Biral on Wyan. The nerves were there but the fear was not the same. "You're not going anywhere." As he spoke, blinding lights spotlighted the two groups. A high-pitched whining cut the air before a droning noise overtook it.

"Get back." Isolde grabbed Arjen, and their group moved just as a Rock-Hauler came crashing in front of them. The huge drills spun, just missing tearing them to pieces. The lights blinded everything.

Voices called from the rear loading area. The unmistakable nasal tone of Lisa. There was little time to process as she crammed the judges into the back. Isolde and Arjen came around to find her and Maynard guarding the door as it closed.

The 'Hauler took off and left Arjen's group in its wake.

~ * ~

From the cockpit, Captain Miller was wide-eyed and confused.

"Sorry about that. Bit of a rocky landing."

Robin strapped into one of the seats behind him. "Good timing, I'd say." Then turned to Lisa. "What in the hell is going on here?"

Lisa buckled herself and cocked her head. "You're welcome for the rescue."

Oscar narrowed his eyes at her. "Whose side are you on?"

Her reply was quick. "Yours. *And* I found out something else you don't know." She held up Lana's data-pad with a message displayed from Desi.

Is it time? I need to know. I've got the Earthlings, but I need transport. The hopper request lines are blowing up. Don't leave without me.

"There's your real traitor."

Maynard growled, slamming a fist against the wall. "I should've never trusted him with this. The sympathizing little bitch."

Oscar lowered his hands to calm the room. "He's without transport. Let's get there before that changes."

Captain Miller took them up towards orbit. "Just tell me where."

Chapter Twelve

The chaos in the shipyard began to calm as Seiko set up sentries at each of the gathering ships to prevent another attempted exodus.

Dr. Crouch, Darcy, and Erika stood in disarray with bags packed for a long journey sitting at their feet. Arjen's group met up with Zelda, Luis, and Lavinia near the hanger entrance.

Martin hugged his daughter and they each shed a few tears, starting and stopping sentences that couldn't quite describe what they were all feeling.

Lavinia spoke first, "Are we...?" She gave a confused look between Luis and Arjen. "I'm not sure what's going on anymore. Are you with us?"

Arjen pursed his lips. "We have a lot to discuss about all that." He waved a hand toward the Iris, flanked by two men trying to look intimidating, but really looking like valet parking attendants on a planet without cars. "It looks like no one's going anywhere for now. Can we all agree we need to find Lana, Marlow, and Zane, then go from there?"

Luis nodded.

"I can probably help." Lavinia turned to Helena and Martin. "Arjen said you were with Lana when you came down the mountain, right?"

"Yes," Helena replied, "and she took off with that Lisa."

"In a Rock-Hopper?"

"Yes."

Lavinia had a slight smile cross her face, then waved them to follow her back to the communications office Lisa was using earlier. She sat at a computer terminal and started clicking around. Soon, sequences of numbers appeared across the screen. Lavinia turned the monitor. "These are the flight paths of all the Rock-Hoppers. I keep track of them for errors and issues, like the one yours had up in the mountains. Now, you can see, we've had a ton of flights in the last half-hour or so, but if we scale back the time…"

"She took off from right over there." Martin pointed at a bare place in the hanger. "Does that help?"

Lavinia nodded, narrowing further. "I've got three flights from before all this started. One went to the apartments, one went to New Pangaea, and one went to…" She paused as the others read the screen with her.

Club Earth.

~ * ~

The Rock-Hauler touched down on the Ramirez property. Maynard was the first off, trudging toward the house. Desi was on the porch to greet him.

"Hey, Boss. Everything go okay on Ceres?"

"Sure as hell didn't." Maynard kept an eye on his surroundings. "Where are the kids?"

"Up in the room." Desi fell in line as Maynard started up the couple stairs to the front door. "Hey, I wanted to show you something with the lock up there anyway." Maynard opened the door as Desi reached for his taser. "I think it's broken or some—" Before Desi could finish his sentence, Maynard turned and jammed his taser in Desi's belly. Desi's body flailed and he fell to his side, his weapon bouncing away.

"Fucking traitor." Maynard kicked him in the ribs, causing him to roll and convulse down the steps into the grass.

Robin, Oscar, and Lisa stopped next to the fallen guard as Maynard turned just in time to raise his forearm and block a swinging golf club. The shaft bent on his arm as Marlow pulled it back. Maynard rushed her when a second club hit him in the side of the knee. This blow took him down. Marlow backed just out of reach as he landed on all fours. Her second swing hit the back of his head, driving him into the floor.

The Earthlings stood, assessing their situation as Lisa, Oscar, and Robin blocked their way to the transport. Captain Miller stood next to the

Rock-Hauler. Their only support with a data-pad for calling transport lay twitching on the ground. The transport available wasn't a 'Hopper; it needed a pilot. Avani cried from upstairs, reminding them that even if they made it through the current group, they'd have to find a way to go back for her. Marlow poked out the golf club like a sword at the others. Maynard's big body lay in the doorway and as much as she wanted to slam the door on him, she waved to Zane. They retreated up the stairs and closed themselves in the master bedroom.

~ * ~

When they landed at Club Earth, Martin made them all sit in Lavinia's 'Hopper. The cold air and the waning haze the 'Bubble was giving off was a clear sign to everyone, but he pulled up diagnostics on his data-pad.

"Can't tell from here." Martin looked across the ten-foot gap to the door. "Probably just a bad wire, but we weren't going to waste parts on this old place." He shook his head. "They should've just shut it down. Lisa must have had to override like we did just to get in here."

"How's the oxygen?" asked Arjen.

Martin held up the readings. "O2 is low but…okay, but that can change in an instant if it shuts down completely. All I can do from here is reboot it, but that would kill everyone on the island."

"You have that power?" asked Julie.

Martin nodded. "Only a few of us."

"We should've stopped for some suits." Helena peered out the window. "If those goons weren't guarding the ships."

"Let me just go." Arjen patted Lavinia's shoulder.

"You're exposing us all," said Martin. "If something goes wrong…"

"If something goes wrong, shut the top."

"Arjen…" Helena started.

"You're not going to stop him." Isolde could see the look on her long-time partner's face.

Arjen raised his voice, "Let's go."

Lavinia groaned and hit to open the 'Hopper. Eight-degree air shot through the seams. Everyone gasped and wrapped themselves up as Arjen gripped the side of the ship, ready to throw himself out as soon as he could fit through.

"I can't—" Helena looked at Martin. "Is there enough air?"

He pursed his lips and nodded.

"Can't we just honk the horn?" asked Julie.

As soon as the gap was wide enough, Arjen jumped out. He ran for the door, feeling the thin air barely filling his lungs. Inside the club was strange and dark, with a few dim lights still pulling from the weak TechBubble.

"Lana." He looked for movement. The tables were still, the dance floor empty. Behind the bar was no better. Most of the glasses were gone. The liquor rack was bare. He pushed open the swinging door to the back room and found her. Lana lay on her side on a stack of bar towels with a few pulled over her like a sad blanket. When he turned her over, her arms splayed out in a way that made his stomach sink. Her lips were blue. Her face tinted as well. She felt too cold. Arjen tried mouth to mouth but felt himself going lightheaded. He needed all the air he could suck in to be able to lift her.

~ * ~

The occupants of the Rock-Hopper shivered together, watching the door. Finally, it swung open, and Arjen stumbled out holding Lana. He was heaving breaths as he handed her into the ship. Isolde lowered her onto a row of seats as Julie and Helena helped Arjen in. Lavinia closed the roof, sealing out the cold and keeping a solid flow of oxygen. Julie tried mouth to mouth next, crying between breaths as she felt the cold skin beneath her.

She pulled away after a few minutes, shaking her head and weeping. Arjen wept with her, knowing he and Lana would never have the chance to reconcile their past. The cabin was silent otherwise.

Lavinia turned in her seat after a minute and spoke softly, "This may not be a great time, but Fleta from our group just sent me a message.

She tracked the Rock-Hauler that Visser and them took. She's asking if I think she should take Nigel and go retrieve it."

Arjen looked up; his attention broken from Lana. "No. Tell her we're going to go get it."

Lavinia sighed. "I was afraid of that." She typed her reply, then looked back. "Should we do something with…?"

Arjen shook his head. "We've gotta go help the Earthlings first, before my father does something else crazy."

Chapter Thirteen

Captain Miller got back into the cockpit after watching the scuffle on the porch. He popped a couple pain pills he'd stolen from the Iris. He'd known something was going on with Lana's team. He assumed it was another retreat of sorts but didn't care as long as he knew where their secret supply stashes were stored. After seeing Desi get tased and Maynard clubbed, he knew he'd need his head to be straight. Miller shook the bottle to hear the last two pills rattling around. He considered them as a message came through from Robin Visser.

Get over here. We need all hands on deck.

Miller frowned, then looked up to see Visser staring at him from thirty feet away. He ducked into the back of the 'Hauler, popped the two pills, dry swallowed them and tucked the empty bottle away. He leaned on the back exit door for a minute, staring at the motors for the drills absentmindedly. What if he just flew off without them? What would they do? There were plenty of people in more trouble than himself that they'd be seeing in court.

Outside were more sounds. Miller tucked next to the door.

Lavinia landed the Rock-Hopper next to the 'Hauler.

Arjen assessed their surroundings as everyone deplaned. He nodded to Lavinia. "Can you fly one of those?"

She shrugged, looking up and down the 'Hauler. "If we need, but I don't want any part of all that." She motioned toward the house.

"That's fine." Arjen counted their group. "If we add on Marlow and Zane, our group's not going to fit in one 'Hopper. See if you can get this thing ready for all of us."

Lavinia went to the front entrance by the cockpit.

Martin tapped on his data-pad. "I've got a connection."

"Meaning?" asked Arjen.

"I'm locking down entry and exit. The 'Bubble will reject anyone who tries until I say so."

"Okay." Arjen saw Oscar and Robin help up Maynard, who was holding his head. Lisa led them inside and the door closed behind them, leaving Desi handcuffed to a post. "We've gotta get over there. Ice?"

She bared her teeth and started toward the house. Helena followed.

"Hold on," said Arjen. "Mom, this might not be the safest situation."

"Don't." She fell in line with Ice, not looking back.

Arjen huffed, his hands on his hips.

Julie was next to him. "Tell me what you need." She gave a hesitant look toward the house.

"Can you help Martin load Lana into the 'Hauler? Then be ready in case we need backup."

"Will do."

He jogged off to catch up with Isolde and Helena. When they reached the porch, Desi gave them a desperate look. He hung off one of the posts on the porch with handcuffs behind his back like a ship's figurehead.

"I'm not with them." Desi motioned with his head towards the door. "I swear."

"We know." Ice lined up the post and sent a kick just above his shoulders, cracking it loose. She grabbed it before he fell and helped slide him free. Desi wiggled his hands.

"Can't help with that," Ice said.

"Just wait here for now." Arjen tried the door, but it was locked.

Isolde cracked off the rest of the post, holding it up next to her like a six-foot battering ram. Arjen got the idea and they lined it up together. It only took them two hits before the door gave way. They took a hesitant look inside.

"Dad?" Arjen called. "Let's end this."

Over at the Rock-Hauler, Martin and Julie went through the painstaking process of moving a corpse out of two seats she lay across. They walked off the 'Hopper and crossed the grass, Martin going backwards with his arms under her shoulders. He leaned against the side of the 'Hauler as Julie set down Lana's feet and opened the back entrance, then they were back at it. Martin stepped up, adjusting to the darkness when he saw the wide-eyed look of Captain Miller over his shoulder. The man approached him like he meant to hug him from behind, maybe even help with the body, then the rock chisel he wielded jammed through Martin's back and jutted out his midsection.

"Huh," was all Martin managed before he fell back, dropping Lana's weight at his feet like human dominoes. Julie screamed as Miller looked around for another weapon.

"Get off my ship," Miller yelled, then was hit from the side by Lavinia's shoulder. He fell against a drill motor, bashing his head against steel before he joined Martin and Lana on the floor.

"What the fuck?" Lavinia was breathing heavily as Julie joined her inside. They moved Lana off Martin to see the chisel protruding just below his ribs. Blood soaked his shirt as he gasped and coughed.

"Shit, shit, shit." Julie tried to find any good position to put him in.

"I didn't see him." Lavinia was nearing hysterics. "I was up front checking out the controls. I would've—"

"Just shut up and help me."

Back inside the house, Arjen called for the Earthlings. "Marlow. Zane. It's me." His voice echoed off the halls as Lisa came from the left side and Maynard from the right, holding his head. They both kept tasers raised as Robin and Oscar waited at the staircase.

"Let's talk," said Robin.

"Yes, let's," Arjen agreed, "but no bullshit. Everyone here knows what really went down. You killed Kaia. You've held these kids hostage ever since they left Earth. No more."

"Listen to you." Robin dared a step closer. "What I said out at the shipyard *was* true. You are a deserter. Now you've returned to take more Belt resources, a ship, and abandon us once again. I won't have it."

"That has nothing to do with them. They aren't your property. Let them out and we can let the Belt decide all of our fates from there."

"Let them out." Robin scoffed. "So, what, you and Lana can take off with them? I know about your plans. I know what she whispered to you out there. I—"

"Lana's dead." Arjen let the words hang, then took in the reactions of confusion and shock, even from Lisa.

"You're lying," said Lisa.

"You would know. You're the one who left her out at Club Earth." Arjen turned to Maynard. "She forgot to mention that?"

"It's more of your lies." Robin put a hand up to calm Maynard. "He's trying to divide us."

Helena spoke up, "It's true, Robin. Lisa found us when we came down the mountain. She took Lana for some secret meeting."

"And you're in on it." Robin shook his head.

"Her body's out there. Go see," Helena yelled at him. "Get it through your thick head. You're on the wrong side of all of this."

Oscar stepped out. "None of that matters right now. The Belt is divided. My father's dream is dying before all our eyes. We're dying. We're killing each other. This is never what he intended; what Petra intended. We've lost our way."

"Got that right." Ice stayed in her fighting stance, keeping an eye on Maynard. "So, give us the kids and let's be done with this."

Robin shook his head. "You know that's not going to work. If we fall," he motioned to Oscar, "our whole society falls."

"I'd like to test that theory," said Arjen.

"Not today." Robin tapped his data-pad. "Our allies are on their way."

"You sure they're on your side this time?" Ice winked at him.

"They're not getting in anyway," said Helena. "Martin's got it locked down."

Robin's face turned beet red in anger, but Oscar said, "That's okay. Now I know who to call."

"Won't matter who you call. Martin's connected inside. They can't break that."

Robin frowned at her. "I don't know about that."

"I think I'd know. I'm married to him and we actually talk about things."

Robin crossed his arms. "It helps when you have no ambition."

Arjen hated listening to his parents trade jabs but realized she was just causing a distraction. Zane snuck down the stairs during the conversation. When he hit the landing at the halfway point, Lisa spotted him.

"Look out."

Zane swung a bent golf club at Robin, who jumped forward. Arjen took the opportunity and shoved him in Lisa's direction, then grabbed his mother's hand. They went up the broad staircase, pushing past Oscar. Ice grabbed the founder's son on her way, using him as a human shield against Maynard's advance. She pushed off as she hit the bottom stair, darting up as Maynard and Lisa followed.

Upstairs, Zane ushered them in, closed the door, and locked it.

Arjen's face lit up. "You guys, okay?"

Marlow wielded a damaged golf club in one hand and a toddler in the other. "More or less."

"There's enough of us." Isolde faced the door in a fighting stance. "Let's take them."

"No." Arjen blocked her way. "They're wounded. Desperate. There's nothing my father wouldn't do at this point. Let's not give him the chance."

"So, what then?" Zane paced the room. "Out the window? It's a little high. They put us up here on purpose."

"I can fix that." Helena went to work on her data-pad.

Arjen pointed at her. "My mom, by the way."

"Whoa." Marlow raised her eyebrows. "Does she keep a ladder up her sleeve or something?"

Helena didn't raise her head. "Better."

A thumping could be heard outside the door, then a loud slam, pushing the door inward. The wood split, but the door held. Zane carried over a nightstand, tossing it in the way as Ice evened it out. The next hit came, busting a hole through and the faces of Maynard and Lisa appeared.

"To the window," called Helena.

In the back of the Rock-Hauler, Julie and Lavinia were accompanied by two dead bodies and a third barely conscious that they had tied to one of the motors.

"Not your ship," Captain Miller muttered.

Julie saw the message come through on Martin's data-pad. It sounded like there was action inside as well. She didn't have the time, or the heart, to tell Helena her husband was dead. She just replied, *Tell me when.*

"Is he tight?" Julie examined Miller's wrists as Lavinia knotted them one more time.

"Yeah. I think so."

"Come on, then. We're going to need to see this."

They took to the grass leading to the house. Desi was backing away from Robin and Oscar as Lavinia ran to help him. Julie strapped on Martin's data-pad as if it were her own, holding her finger to the screen.

The message from Helena came, *Now.*

Julie replied, *Go.*

Helena was the first to jump, followed by Zane, then Marlow and Avani. Soon the whole group was floating slowly toward the ground. As they touched down, one after the other, Julie increased the 'Bubble's gravity a little more. Ice was last, hitting with the most force as she tucked into a roll, then ran behind the others. As Julie saw Lisa reach the window, she upped the gravity a little further than even a normal level. She fell from the window like a rock, landing in the grass with a scream and rolling onto her back. Maynard stuck in the window, halfway out, then turned back.

Julie met the others as Lavinia and Desi joined. Robin looked as if he meant to give chase but realized how large their group was and slowed. Julie grabbed Helena by the arm as they retreated to the 'Hauler.

"Listen. Martin was attacked. He died. I'm so sorry. I—" Helena pulled away before she could finish and ran to the 'Hauler in disbelief. Julie called after her, "I'm sorry."

Arjen's face was blank as he passed her. More death. More suffering caused by his father. Lavinia loaded up in the cockpit, joined by Desi. Helena wept from the back. Arjen, Isolde, Marlow, Zane, and Julie stood just outside their ride off the Ramirez homestead. Oscar and Robin waited twenty feet back.

"So, this is it?" Robin called. "After everything, you're going to end the Belt like this?"

"It's not up to me anymore," said Arjen. "I'm done deciding for others." He patted Marlow on the shoulder.

"You don't own me anymore," Marlow yelled, covering Avani's ear while holding the other to her chest as she did. "You don't own any of us."

"You could've been our savior." Robin let his hands fall at his sides. "You could've…" He waved a dismissive hand. "We'll see you at the trial."

Zane raised his middle fingers as they boarded the 'Hauler. Julie stayed behind, meeting the eyes of the two men who'd kept her in the clinical trials to try to produce the baby to save the Belt. The two men who'd destroyed her young life and kept it hidden. She looked past them to Maynard on the porch. The man who'd done countless evil deeds. Beyond him was Lisa, limping in front of the house. The woman who'd killed Lana, the one person who gave her a chance after Oscar and Robin ruined her life. Julie's face welled up with tears when she felt Arjen's hand on her shoulder.

"Come on. We're done with them."

Julie wiped her face and followed. As they sealed the door to the 'Hauler, Lavinia engaged the drills, just to keep the others at bay. Julie stood behind her and Lavinia asked, "Did you open the exit?"

Julie clicked on Martin's data-pad. "Okay. We're good to go."

Arjen laughed and pointed at the clear skies. Robin's allies hadn't shown or didn't exist.

Lavinia typed a command into her data-pad with a smirk. "Watch this." The Rock-Hopper they'd flown in on, still parked next to them, sealed its hatch, and started its takeoff sequence without any passengers.

Desi laughed from the seat next to her; the others were more somber in the back with Martin and Lana's bodies. Julie strapped into a seat next to Marlow and Avani.

"I'm sorry about what they did to you," Julie said.

"And you." Marlow put a hand on her arm, recalling late night talks back on Wyan. "I hope we're done with them."

"Yeah." Julie turned away, fighting back sobs. As the ship began its takeoff, she bent Martin's data-pad right under her nose. She clicked a few buttons until the screen turned red with an alert. Once they left the 'Bubble of the Ramirez Island, Julie wiped away the alert and confirmed the command she entered. She rested her elbows on her thighs and took deep breaths for the first time since she could remember.

Chapter Fourteen

The Belt mourned the loss of its judges and founding families over the next week. As each detail emerged about Robin, Oscar, Maynard, and Lisa's actions, the Belt's people decided a total reconstruction of government was in order, though most were unwilling to be the spearhead for that. Arjen and Isolde were in line by birth to become the next judges, but they quickly refused the positions.

No one from the Rock-Hauler group spoke of the report that the TechBubble failed around Ramirez Island. It was a question most would never need an answer to.

Life had to go on, with a group of mothers still needing to deliver their babies. Darcy continued to care for Lana's son after losing her own. It was a natural fit for all parties.

A week after the deaths of so many, Arjen called a meeting at Helena's property where he and Julie were staying.

They circled the flower garden, Isolde, Marlow, Zane, Avani, and their son, Enzo. Helena passed out drinks to those who weren't breastfeeding, and Arjen stood with Julie in the walkway that went through the middle of the garden. Isolde wore Admani's jacket that Arjen returned to her from Wyan. She remembered how Admani would always wear it when she'd go out digging for samples in the ocean on Ceres and how she'd zip it up, struggling to fit all her hair under the hood when it was raining on Wyan. She tucked her hands in the pockets and sighed.

Arjen cleared his throat, so all eyes were on him. "You've all seen Wyan. It's pretty, but it's not home. Most of you have met Amun, the Pelosin and you wouldn't believe how many favors I owe him for getting Julie and me back here. So, I told you how there were others on the next planet over, Melinger. Well, they were set on living on Wyan as well, until they took some more readings of the star out there. Don't ask me to explain it further, but they think Wyan has a couple hundred years at best. Yeah, we'll all be long gone by then, but they want to preserve their species. Before we left, they took some of the tech we salvaged from the Mack. Their scientists, if you want to call them that, are way ahead of ours, but they got the concepts for what we were doing to keep breathable air and atmosphere." He turned and motioned to Julie. "We haven't spoken of this yet because we had a lot of unfinished business to take care of here. Before we got back to the Belt, Julie and I spent the last six months on Earth." Arjen waited as eyes widened.

"You what?" asked Marlow.

Arjen's smile was broad. "The Pelosins needed a home. The only way I could get them to leave Wyan was to promise a better option. Between their tech, mixed with ours, and the time that's passed on Earth, we were able to set up a colony. Your geography may be better than mine, but we located a place near Auckland, New Zealand. There was a rainforest we found to be rebounding. There were houses, likely built during the resurgence you guys told us about. I'm talking electrical grid, generator system, water plant. They were set. Before the Final War, I'm sure they were thriving. The Pelosins and us were able to get most of it back online, and the way they work, it's probably *all* back online by now."

Zane tilted his head, holding Avani on his hip as she picked bright pink petals off a flower. "Are you saying we can go back to Earth?"

"Exactly. Back where we belong."

Isolde's mouth hung open. "You waited all this time without telling us?" She faked a swing at him.

Arjen ducked away. "We had to take care of shit here first. I didn't know how it was all going to play out. If some still wanted to go to Wyan, I wanted to leave that up to them."

"To hell with Wyan," said Ice.

"What about the air?" asked Marlow. "Remember when you found us?"

Julie jumped in, "They're using our TechBubble, but it's powered and focused differently. The more the forest around our village grows, the less we'll need it. Eventually, we'll be able to expand, maybe even travel one day."

Marlow could see the excitement in Julie's face, remembering the license plates and all the other memorabilia when they were roommates on another planet.

"What about everyone here?" asked Marlow. "Would they just stay, or…?"

Arjen put his hands out, palms up. "I'm giving a speech before we leave. Before everyone decides on the new government setup here, I figure we'll give them a chance. Oh." Arjen dug in his back pocket and handed off Honey, the stuffed duck to Marlow. "I almost forgot. Also, Barchek wanted me to tell you…" He checked his data-pad. "'Now there's no looking forward, now there's no turning back.' Any idea what that means?"

Marlow's face broke into a sad smile. "Yeah." But she didn't expand for Arjen. She turned and hugged Zane. "We're going home. We're really going home."

~ * ~

A few weeks later, the Iris set off for Earth. Arjen, Isolde, Marlow, and Zane strapped in much like they had for the three-week journey through a wormhole when they'd first come to the Belt. So many things had changed, and yet, they still had each other, as well as others.

The Iris left the Belt and a few of its passengers took a moment to say goodbye to the only place they'd ever called home in search of a new adventure.

Epilogue

June 2093, eight months later
Former Auckland, New Zealand rainforest
Marlow dodged Avani as she sped down the path from her house toward Julie's on a tricycle they'd found when they moved in. She'd promised to behave for Aunt Julie, but what good was the word of someone still under three? Enzo was already over at Zelda and Darcy's for a playdate and Zane was tending to their garden with Asiv who turned out to have the greenest thumb of them all despite its chalky coloring.

Isolde trotted up to her and raised her eyebrows. "Ready?"

Marlow saw Julie as she opened the door for Avani to pedal in. She flipped up her Ray Bans and gave Marlow a thumbs up.

"Let's go." Marlow took off, ahead of Ice.

They jogged along the trees to a path lush with greenery. A rocky ledge looked over a lagoon, but the payoff was the waterfall. Ice made it to the top first and jumped over the flowing stream. When Marlow landed, they sat for a second, overlooking the cove below.

"It gets bigger every time we come." Ice dangled her feet. "Soon we won't be able to jump it."

Marlow pointed. "Look. Was that a fish?"

"I think it was. I'll tell the boys when we get back. They'll be excited to know."

They jogged down the other side of the waterfall to the village that spread more each month, between the humans and Pelosin's housing. As they hit every important milestone, they inched closer to the next request, a library with physical books and a movie theater. It wouldn't be long before construction started.

When Marlow made it back home, she could see the Pelosin ship was back in its dock. Arjen and Amun must have returned from their latest gathering trip from nearby towns. She was certain of it when she got inside and saw a physical copy of *The Talisman* sitting on her coffee table.

"He found it," she said aloud.

Zane poked his head out from the kitchen. "Cool, right? What are you thinking for dinner?"

Marlow turned the old book over in her hands. "Surprise me."

"You asked for it." Zane disappeared back in.

Marlow had some reading to do later, but first, she found the perfect place for her new book on a shelf, high up where Avani and Enzo couldn't quite reach yet. Marlow also had trouble reaching and had to get a stool to make sure her books were organized. After she tucked it next to her other favorites, she saw the edge of some blue fabric. She reached on top of the shelf and came down with Honey the stuffed duck. She smiled, remembering how Avani couldn't have it out of sight when they were on Wyan, but didn't care much for it when Arjen returned it. Enzo got bored with it once they got to Earth and found so many other toys to entertain him with. She took one good look at it, made from the fabric of her first jumpsuit, then tore its head off.

Inside was one shining, black feather from the real Honey. Marlow stroked it, wishing she'd been able to return to Earth with them, and had to settle for the piece that remained.

Acknowledgments

I have to start by thanking all of you for taking this journey with me. Especially Rogue Phoenix Press for wanting to publish Interstellar Islands which gave me the inspiration to keep this story going. This was my first trilogy and a lot to keep in my head for the 3-4 years it rolled around in there. It's nice to get it all out. I hope you enjoyed it. Unless you're some weirdo who reads the acknowledgments first and haven't read the actual book yet. In your case, be sure to start with the epilogue and work your way back for the best experience. Thanks to Stef with an F for the awesome artwork throughout this entire series. The Night Chasers' artwork even won an award. Many thanks to Jennifer "Barchek," Aunt Sharon, all the Erins I know, including the one who gave birth to Enzo, and the one who gave birth to the Iris and the Knox. Thanks for doing the initial readthrough of this novel to telling me why the orgy at the end just didn't work. Now, if you are reading this backwards, I bet you're really wondering what happened, aren't you? Hint: There's no orgy. Thanks to Amy for reading ALL my works in progress and giving thoughts. They will be better when they are published someday. Thanks to Charlie for getting me into the secret club (The Brandy Bar) to read bits of my works. It's been hard times staying safe and promoting books in the middle of all this. Thanks to the faithful watchers of Storytime with Scott Boss on my YouTube channel. It's been fun reading for you each week.

If you just finished this series, you know and I know there are future stories in the Cosmic Ark universe that could be written, but they may be too far down a wormhole for me to see right now.

Also, Anders, why didn't you check your messages, man? #justiceforHoney

Also by the Author
at
Rogue Phoenix Press

Interstellar Islands

The world finally had its third and then final war. Two remaining teenagers, Marlow and Zane are left surviving in a church bunker with nothing but a couple ducks. They've watched everyone they love, pass on from the toxic conditions and know they aren't far behind them. When they are found by a team scavenging for supplies, the teenagers don't believe the claims that they are from the asteroid belt, the last settlement of humans that made it off Earth just before it all went to hell. They don't believe they live out there on Interstellar Islands with artificial atmospheres. They don't believe but they don't have much choice but to board their ship and see where it takes them. Whatever the people from the belt have in store for them can't be worse than what's left on Earth. Can it?

Part I

Prelude

A cold, gray breeze dragged across the barren land once known as Inland Florida. Metal fencing surrounded the backlot of Bride of Christ Pentecostal Church, though no one knew the name, as the sign had been repurposed many years ago. Two ducks were inside the fencing. One, Marvin, lay on its side taking its last breaths and the other, Honey, was dipping its bill into a bowl of water.

Zane watched them from the roof of the church, shaking his head, causing his dark hair to swing in front of his small brown eyes, shielding his view for a few seconds. He was perched like a bird, looking out as far as he could through the unnatural fog. The wind cut through him and he wrapped his coat tighter, letting out a long crackling sigh as desolate tears welled up in his eyes.

Honey looked up when the back door to the church opened with a creak.

"Zane? Will you come down from there?" Marlow called up. She had a blanket over her shoulders, trailing in the dirt as Honey approached, looking for food.

"What's the point?" he called back, not looking away from the ominous gray. "What's the point of any of this? Look at Marvin."

Marlow whipped her head, a long braid of hair swinging with her, and hurried over to the dying duck.

"Why didn't you tell me?" she asked through intermittent coughs. "I coulda..." She trailed off, holding the fragile duck head in her palm. "Oh, Marvin."

Zane laughed a bitter laugh. "What? You gonna resuscitate him, again?"

She looked up towards him. "It's a she. Marvin is a she."

He laughed again, more lighthearted this time. "True." His reply was lost in the wind.

"Would you come down here?" Marlow called.

He sighed again, wiped the tears from his eyes and climbed down.

The chapel was filled with plants, mother-in-law tongue, ferns and dwarf pines, among others. Most of the leaves were browning up and falling off. Marlow stood near the back, holding a steel trapdoor open with one arm and Marvin tucked under the other.

"Come on," she said. "You really shoulda been wearing your mask."

Zane grunted, shrugged and followed, catching the door from her as they descended into the underground bunker.

The bunker had been built by a preacher with a zeal for Armageddon, Pastor Jerry Hill, who warned his congregation time after time that the end was near. Though it hadn't been exactly as described in the Bible, he wasn't far off. It had started with the threat of a nuke by

Pakistan, then an actual one launched by the US. Soon, North Korea, Russia and other countries joined in and World War III was well under way. This was forty-five years ago, in 2045. Three quarters of the population was lost during the war and the aftermath, but humans are remarkably resilient. The Earth had a resurgence about twenty years back. People went back to smaller communities, farming and taking care of each other. Power grids were restored for some areas. Nations were re-established, but many years of lawlessness couldn't just be undone. Countries once strong. were now weak and recovering. Others took advantage of that.

The Final War had happened two years ago. Zane, Marlow and their families took shelter at the church bunker during it. "Built for times such as these," Pastor Hill said, but the air was saturated with death. He, and most people with more than a few decades of using their lungs, passed on first, along with children.

It was five degrees the day Marvin the duck died, and it started a string of events Zane and Marlow couldn't have dreamed of.

Chapter One

Marlow set Marvin on a card table, sliding a couple plants with her elbow to make room. Marvin had stopped breathing, and Marlow was bending down to perform duck CPR when Zane grabbed her shoulder.

"Just...don't," he said. "She's dead."

"But maybe I can..."

Zane shook his head.

She sighed and took a step back, still focused on the duck in the dark room. "Then we butcher her and eat her tonight."

Zane threw his hands up. "What's the point? We're down to one fucking duck." His slight Indian accent normally made her laugh when he cursed, but not now.

"We'll go out. We'll—" She tried to continue, but a coughing fit overtook her.

Zane put an arm around her shoulders when she stopped. He wanted to tell her that her cough was getting worse, that it was probably lung cancer or whatever it was that took their families but what good would it do? He was afraid he wasn't far behind, as his own chest felt tight most nights. They hugged for what could've been five solid minutes, both parties recalling memories of their families finding each other as they sought shelter. Finally, they broke away and Marlow looked up at him, wiping tears as she did.

"Let's eat this fucking duck."

Zane wanted to protest but couldn't. *Let her have a last meal,* he figured.

Marlow butchered Marvin, apologizing to her that things had turned out the way they had. They built up their fire pit within the fence and Honey watched as they turned Marvin on a spit. Thankfully, she didn't seem to recognize her and quickly lost interest, scratching in the dirt for long-gone bugs or other edibles.

They sat down inside the church sanctuary, sharing a pew with a plate of duck meat between them. Honey had finally cornered a cockroach and was stomping it into submission as she pecked at it. It was the most entertainment they'd gotten lately.

"Do you think we're the last two people?" asked Zane, staring forward at the window frames taped over with plastic sheeting.

Marlow loosened a chunk of meat from the bone and chewed greedily. "Probably not."

"What if we are?"

"I'm sure there are others. Just not in this wasteland that used to be Florida."

"Do you think they'll ever make Earth *right* again?"

"Maybe, if there's anyone left to do that."

"You just said—"

"I know, Zane. I'm just saying, I'm sure there are people, I just don't know if they *can* make Earth right again."

Zane set a half-finished piece of duck on the plate. "So, why are we even bothering then?"

She looked at him, grease staining her lips and chin. "Because, we have to try, we promised our parents we would."

Zane slapped the pew in front of them. "That was all fine and good when they were alive, but now? No one's here to hold us to that. No one's here at all."

"Then do it for me, Zane. Survive a little longer for me."

He huffed. "Fine." And picked the duck back up.

~ * ~

After Marlow settled in the bunker for the night, Zane took one more trip to the roof of the church. It was his place to think. Eighteen months ago, his dad would do it, looking for a rescue helicopter or some sign of peace. His hope was always in vain. No one ever came for them and eventually, his father didn't have the strength to climb the ladder anymore. He'd died just over a year ago, followed a month later by Marlow's mom, then finally, their last companion, Jason. He was closer to their age, eighteen and vibrant, as much as he could be, given the conditions. Zane could still remember the choking wheeze of his last few breaths. The sound scraped up and down the walls of the bunker, as he lay clutching Marlow's hand while Zane paced behind them. In some ways, he blamed himself for Jason's death, deferring to him to take scouting duty more often and Jason had never complained. He'd just go out, looking for anything useful to keep them alive a little longer and his reward was death. Zane's reward for hiding in the bunker was to watch all his friends and family die out before him. He had half a mind to throw himself from the freezing shingles of the church roof, but he'd promised Marlow he'd stick around. Once she went—and it wouldn't be long—all bets were off.

Zane hugged his coat tighter. The temperature had dropped to the negatives, just a normal July night in Florida. The cold air kept his mind awake. He could almost hear his dad saying, "Once the politicians come out of hiding, they are going to need us to help rebuild. You are young and strong, you can help, have a normal life and maybe a family one day." Zane shook his head at the thought and how wrong it had been. He couldn't blame the guy for having hope but he knew better now.

His teeth were chattering when he headed for the ladder. He caught the first rung and almost slipped when he heard a whooshing sound in the distance. What used to be a norm during the Final War was now odd, to hear sounds of any kind in the distance. Zane craned his neck, trying to catch a glimpse of something, anything else, but the sound was gone. He finished the climb and went back into the bunker, locking the door as he did.

Also by the Author
at Rogue Phoenix Press

The Night Chasers

Stolen by a group of rebels, the spaceship Mack is hurtling towards a Goldilocks planet that offers a chance to start over, to build a new Utopian society. When they arrive, the Belters, along with the earthlings, find the planet a paradise, with fertile farmland, stunning beaches, and lush forests.

But something more menacing lurks over the planet's terminator line. Every four years, Wyan's orbit plunges the planet into total darkness and the peaceful settlers are massacred by shadowy creatures that prowl the dark side of the planet.

Now, led by Lana, Marlow and the other humans must prepare to survive the darkness, save the Wyan people, and end the cycle of terror. They must fight...the Night Chasers.

FOR THE FULL INVENTORY
OF QUALITY BOOKS:
http://www.roguephoenixpress.com

Rogue Phoenix Press
Representing Excellence in Publishing

Quality trade paperbacks and downloads
in multiple formats,
in genres ranging from historical to contemporary romance, mystery
and science fiction.
Visit the website then bookmark it.
We add new titles each month!